PRAISE FOR
SLOW SLIDE INTO THE TRUTH

"In *Slow Slide into the Truth*, Kim St. Clair deftly captures the complexity of personal identity and shifting family bonds in the brave new world of easily accessible DNA testing. Readers will find themselves rooting for Beth Linn—the smart, compassionate heroine of this thoughtful debut novel—whose attempts to unravel long-held family secrets make for a twisty, enticing read."

—**Michelle Richmond,** *New York Times* best-selling author of
six novels and two story collections, including *The Marriage Pact*

SLOW SLIDE INTO THE TRUTH

A THERAPIST'S TALE

KIM ST. CLAIR

RIVER GROVE
BOOKS

Published by River Grove Books
Austin, TX
www.rivergrovebooks.com

Distributed by River Grove Books

Design and composition by Greenleaf Book Group
Cover design by Greenleaf Book Group

Publisher's Cataloging-in-Publication data is available.

Print ISBN: 978-1-63299-853-8

eBook ISBN: 978-1-63299-854-5

First Edition

For Ron, my favorite person, who somehow saw me at seventeen and has never broken eye contact.

And for Courtney and Jessica, the lovely orbs of light who joined us on this wild ride, and who continue to bring the sparkle.

CONTENTS

1 - Beth 1

2 - The Couple 11

3 - Beth 15

4 - The Dancer 20

5 - Beth 31

6 - The Couple 38

7 - Beth 41

8 - Celeste 49

9 - Beth 54

10 - Celeste 67

11 - Ben 69

12 - Michael 72

13 - Beth 78

14 - The Couple 85

15 - Beth 89

16 - The Dancer 92

17 - The Queen 96

18 - Beth 101

19 - Celeste 106

20 - The Dancer 108

21 - Beth 112

22 - Beth 122

23 - Celeste 125

24 - Michael 129

25 - Beth 135

26 - The Dancer 142

27 - Beth 146

28 - Celeste 150

29 - Beth 154

30 - The Dancer 160

31 - The Couple 163

32 - Beth 165

33 - Beth 171

34 - Celeste 179

35 - Beth 186

36 - Beth 194

37 - Beth 200

38 - The Dancer 204

39 - Ben 207

40 - Celeste 212

41 - Beth 214

42 - Ben 223

43 - Celeste 225

44 - Beth 227

45 - Celeste 231

46 - Beth 234

47 - Beth 239

Acknowledgments 243

About the Author 244

1

BETH

Her hand shook as she gripped the vial and watched the foam from her saliva bubble precariously close to the rim like champagne in a flute. As she lifted it up to the light to ensure that the liquid had reached the full line, she wondered if she would regret this moment forever. Once the sample was mailed there was no longer an escape from the truth it would reveal.

You have no choice, she told herself, as she closed the lid and watched the liquid in the cap mix with her DNA. She shook it gently, exactly as instructed, and placed it in the bag marked SAMPLE, careful to firmly adhere the seal and confirm that the ID number matched what she had just entered online. The blank space designated for the user name remained empty as she wrestled with how to proceed. The truth was not an option. Her father would never forgive her for a betrayal of this magnitude, so she needed to choose either a fake name or initials. Initials screamed *This is a secret!* but a fictitious surname would mislead fellow identity seekers and that felt wrong. *What did you do?* she asked the specter of her father's angry face that loomed between her and the screen.

When her old friend Ben had handed her the kit she had accepted it with the thought that she could still refuse, but a sleepless night of dissecting the what-ifs had made her realize that was not an option. She needed the truth. *It's the only path,* she thought as she rechecked the number on the kit for the third time to make sure it matched the number she had entered on the registration page. She typed in her favorite author's initials and pressed send.

Aware that her courage might fade, she quickly placed the sample in the shipping box and sealed the lid. She considered the lab technician who would receive her sample and wondered if they realized the power in the secrets they daily uncovered.

Let's just get to the post office, she thought, as she put on her coat and slipped out of her office unnoticed. Once in the parking lot she darted down a back street and hoped for continued anonymity. She scanned the busy sidewalk for anyone she recognized before she crossed the street and briefly considered the outside mailbox. *Not to be trusted*, she thought, as she felt in her bag for the evidence of her deceit. She momentarily reconsidered and then reminded herself that each trip up the decision tree had led to the same conclusion. Time would not allow her to stand in front of the post office to run through it all again. She had clients. She had to get back to work.

As her foot made contact with the first step she felt the foundation of her life begin to shift toward an abyss she had sensed but never identified.

Don't do it, a young part of her pleaded while a logical part compelled her to move forward quickly. She had just identified these parts of herself in therapy and knew she had to get them to compromise. Logic had its arms crossed while Fear, who appeared to be a six-year-old child, glared in silence. She decided to work with the young part that was afraid.

I want you to trust me that this is the right decision, she said to the young part, who did not seem impressed. *It's a quest we must accomplish for the good of the entire kingdom. Will you help me?* The young part looked up with some interest.

If we accomplish our goal there will be a prize but it will take courage. Can you be bold for baklava? The young part smiled and nodded her head.

OK, there are three magical doors we must enter to complete our quest. We just need to open them without anyone stopping us and drop this little box into the belly of the last one. Think we can do it? The young part nodded and Beth quickly pulled open the first door before she changed her mind. The choice to act sent positive vibrations through her body and the young part began to relax.

I have to find the truth for myself, Beth thought as she turned to the right and opened the second door. "Almost there," she whispered, identifying the third door on the front of the mailbox. The royal blue vessel was snuggled comfortably between a supply kiosk and a self-service postage machine whose neon green WELCOME sign blinked brightly. *This is it*, she thought as she grabbed the cold metal handle. *No turning back.* She looked around the empty lobby again before she pulled the handle, creating a screech so loud she startled and released the handle. "Get a grip, Beth," she whispered, quickly pulling the door back open and placing her parcel on the flat surface. She paused, aware that the young version of herself was ready to dive into the mailbox to retrieve the package if she let it drop into the box. *I really need to call my therapist*, she thought. But right now, she told her young part, *I need you to be still while I let go of this handle. I promise it's OK.* The young part stepped back from the edge and Beth released the handle, the closing screech just as jarring as the opening one.

It's gone. There's no way to change it now, she thought as she quickly pivoted and walked back through the magic doors and into the fresh air.

Relieved the task was done, her logical part focused on a nearby trash bin where she could dispose of the evidence, but an image of her father's angry face floated in front of it in an attempt to reengage her fear. "Not today, Dad," Beth whispered as she dropped the shredded papers and packing material on top of discarded coffee cups and sandwich wrappers. The smell made her nauseous, so she quickly let the hinge close even though her young part wanted to be sure to cover everything up. *There's no need to bury the trash*, she reassured her younger part as she turned away from her father's torment.

At least my bag is empty, she thought as she walked to her favorite deli to order lunch. Aware that people in her hometown recognized her by her family's trademark curly auburn hair, even if they weren't entirely sure which wealthy Linn daughter she was, she made sure she maintained a calm demeanor to avoid attention. As she opened the door the comforting smell of the vintage oak booths and freshly ground coffee greeted her. Magical threes danced brightly across the menu board in bold chalk script. Three-cheese hoagie in baby blue. Three-bean salad in orange. Then the perfect number-three combo jumped off of the board in a rainbow of colors. Tuna salad sandwich with chips and dessert. She could get the promised baklava reward, enjoy a nice lunch, and encourage her young, fearful part to see it as a sign she was safe, since it was also number three on the list and their quest was all about the threes.

Be normal, she told herself. The adrenaline-fueled commands that pulsated through her mind consumed her. *Order the number three. Pay. Go back to work. Walk slowly so nobody will suspect. When you arrive and open the office door you'll know it's not magical. It's reality. You're fine.*

Beth's inner dialogue was a helpful companion as she made her way across the square to return to work. It comforted her that she knew every crack in the sidewalk she had traveled on since childhood. The green in the center of the square held memories of family picnics and hanging out with friends. She reminded herself that her sleepy town was safe as she held her breath and walked into the office.

"Good morning," she said, in her most normal voice.

Eleanor, the office manager and business mind behind Serenity, peered up at her over the top of the tortoiseshell reading glasses balanced delicately on the tip of her nose.

"I thought you were in your office," she replied. "Your client was early so I sent her upstairs."

"I ran out to grab lunch," Beth said, holding up her bag as proof.

Eleanor stood up with a look of concern. "I'll put it in the refrigerator. You OK? You look flushed."

"I'm fine," Beth responded without making eye contact. She passed the bag across the desk. "Is Dr. Ellis in yet?"

"I don't think so, but I thought you were here. Apparently everyone comes and goes as they please these days," she responded as she walked toward the refrigerator humming quietly beside the filing cabinet.

"I'm sorry I didn't tell you," Beth said, turning to navigate a path through the crowded downstairs lobby already full of clients waiting to see their therapists. Beth was grateful for an upstairs office away from the chaos at the front desk.

Her morning mission did not detract from her awareness of the austere presence of her client, a beautiful and well-appointed woman who waited in the smaller, less crowded lobby at the top of the stairwell. Beth said hello and let her know she needed a moment. The client's piercing dark eyes followed her as she shut the door briefly while she cleared her mind. She tapped her cheekbones to the rhythm of her breath to ground herself in reality. Before she reopened the door, she glanced at herself in the mirror hanging directly across from the picture window, which gave her a sneak view outside when she needed it. *You're fine*, she told herself. *Of course you're fine. You're always fine.* She opened the door with that mantra on repeat.

"Come on back." She waited for her client to enter the room and for the door to close before she spoke. "How are you?"

"Awful. You won't believe what he did this week," her client said as she caught a glimpse of herself in the mirror and appeared to admire her own reflection. Beth thought of this client as "the queen," partially because of the way she carried herself but also because of how she spoke with unquestionable authority.

"Probably not. What happened?" Beth asked. She slipped into a low-back leather chair, knowing that her client preferred the couch directly across from it and in front of the window.

"He shoved me into a wall and held me there with his hand around my neck!" On cue, she sank into the sofa while somehow maintaining perfect posture.

"For how long?"

"Long enough."

"What started it this time?"

"He was on a rant about land The Chapel recently acquired that had been earmarked for commercial development. When I gave my opinion, he called me a fucking idiot. Our son was in the room, so I addressed his inappropriate language. He lost it and called me a religious fanatic."

"He got that angry over your opinion? That seems extreme."

"The land was the original topic, but his anger erupted because I challenged him. He wouldn't let me go until I apologized. He thinks I'm

brainwashing our son so he has to counteract me. I'd find him humorous if
he wasn't so violent," she said as she tucked her hair behind her ear.

"Did he hurt you?"

"He always hurts me." There: Beth heard it, that lilt in her voice.

She felt a chill go down her spine. Something about this client's energy
felt off. Her stories were dark, yet her body language did not match the narra-
tive. Week after week Beth listened to her report the details of her husband's
outbursts, each account worse than the last, but Beth was distracted by the
qualities of her speech. It was lyrical, with a resonance you would use to
describe puppies or a gorgeous sunset, not abuse, and it triggered a familiar
fear in Beth. Her jaw tensed and her heart rate increased with each word that
flowed silkily from her client's mouth like a siren's song. The dissonance was
so minor that only a trained ear would hear it, but thanks to her father's loose
relationship with the truth, Beth had a lifetime of training in the detection of
subtle distortions. In the past, she had tried to downplay her intuition, but
experience had taught her that her father's historical rewrites were too dangerous to ignore. This client was too similar to her father to trust. This was
not the time to ignore her intuition.

"Did you call the police?"

"Why can't you accept the fact that I'm not involving the police? I've
told you repeatedly it's not worth it to ruin his professional reputation. Why
would I lower my alimony? Do you not understand that I just need to be free
of him?" The queen's eyes narrowed more with each question, challenging
Beth to change her response.

"He assaulted you. If he were under arrest you'd be free."

"Free and poor." She tilted her head to the left and looked Beth directly
in the eyes.

"His money won't matter if he kills you."

The queen smoothed the surface of the pillow to her right with long
deliberate strokes before she reestablished eye contact. "He won't kill me.
He'll berate me. He'll threaten me. He'll intimidate me. He won't kill me
unless I push back too hard. That's why I'm here. I need a safe place to vent
so I don't push too hard before I find a way out."

"Of course. Please, continue. I'll stop bringing up the police," Beth said, fixated on her client's hand as it caressed the pillow.

The story took a similar dark turn to those in prior weeks, and it reminded Beth of family car trips during her childhood listening to FM radio. One moment a station would come through clearly and then suddenly another song would break in and take over the frequency. Beth wished she could figure out if the message that broke through her client's monologue was real or a projection of her own unsettled thoughts. She tried to ignore the static, but her whole body felt hypersensitive to its crackle. The session ended with the queen calm and smiling.

Unsettled, Beth watched her walk across the green back to her office at the private school where she reigned as dean. The queen fascinated Beth. The queen said she required perfect punctuality and had no patience for wasted time or emotion. Beth imagined the queen wanting her staff to bow to her. When they started their sessions she'd made it clear to Beth that she had no desire for vulnerability; she just needed help to power through until she could divorce her husband. Her message stayed consistent: her husband was a sociopath and she expected Beth to get her free without any negative impact, which was why Beth now stood glued to the window in search of clues to who her client actually was.

What do I hope to see? she wondered as she watched the queen stop to speak to a student. It was a normal thing to do on a normal day, but Beth felt unsettled by her stance and the tilt of her head. *Stop making things up*, she said to herself, trying to shake the feeling of dread washing over her. *You've got to control your imagination*, she thought, pulling her gaze off the scene. *Good luck with that*, she heard her father say from the recesses of her mind.

The smell of pork chops cooking on a grill wafted up through the floor vents. Every Tuesday at noon, Eleanor grilled pork chops on an indoor grill behind her desk in the reception area just as Beth began a session with a client who referred to himself as "whine and dine." Eleanor decided it was fine to cook her pork chops behind the front desk when the kitchen was repurposed to create an office for Dani, the art therapist, since obviously there was nowhere else to cook them.

Whine and dine was a clever man with a dry sense of humor who had been her regular Tuesday at twelve o'clock for the past year. He coined the phrase "whine and dine" to describe his weekly therapy session experience. He said the aroma of the pork chops cooking one floor below stimulated his already rumbling hunger, which triggered his whine. He told her he imagined the owner of Serenity and her office manager dining elegantly a floor below while he and Beth tried to untangle his complex psyche. Each week, he found twisted ways to embellish his description of the meal prep happening downstairs, which he found amusing, but Beth was embarrassed by the unprofessional lunch ritual in an otherwise professional setting.

The grilling of lunch behind the reception desk was just one aspect of an office culture Beth found difficult to explain. Usually, she tried not to discuss it at all. Run by Dr. Carol Meadows and her colleague Eleanor DiAntonio in a historic house in the center of town, Serenity was always one step away from serene. The unique blend of therapists generally worked well, but occasionally their individual quirks created tension. The most recent incident involved Amelia, who secretly brought her Saint Bernard, Tiny, to work as a therapeutic support animal when she knew that Allen, who had the office beside her, had a severe dog allergy. On Tiny's first day of work, he happily explored the new space, which caused immediate constriction in Allen's lungs while he was in a session. Fearing an asthma attack, Allen grabbed his rescue inhaler and flew out of his door straight into the dog. Tiny yelped and tucked his tail while Amelia shrugged innocently. After that Tiny had to stay home, but articles about the benefits of therapy dogs began to appear around the office until Allen took a job in an OCD treatment center and Tiny was welcomed back to Serenity.

Of course no one called them Allen or Amelia because Dr. Meadows insisted that proper titles be used. It infuriated Beth that she had to be Dr. Linn when she interacted with clients or staff while pork chops grilled directly behind the reception desk for all to smell and see. The absurdity seemed lost on everyone but her. Not that she minded being called Dr. Linn; she'd worked hard for the title, but she hated being forced to use it. She also thought a Maltese might be a more appropriate therapy dog, but nobody asked her opinion about that either.

It was impossible for her to explain to her regular Tuesday client why pork chops were cooked behind the front desk at twelve o'clock because Dr. Meadows refused to discuss it. Raw meat on an indoor grill sizzling beside the filing cabinet seemed outlandish, and yet every Tuesday, without fail, meat got slapped onto that grill. And onions. There were always onions cooked with the pork chops.

So Beth smiled at his joke when he lamented that he should have eaten on the drive over because now his stomach was growling with hunger. Eleanor and Dr. Meadows dined, and he whined, and Beth settled into the comfortable rhythm of their session.

Hour by hour clients filled the room with their heartaches and victories, and Beth put her personal thoughts aside except for a moment when she envisioned a postal worker placing her package in a truck headed for the lab. She saw herself at the scene trying to decide if she should grab the package and run or explain to the worker that she had made a mistake and needed it back. She fought to focus on her four o'clock client as the alternative version of herself watched the postal truck drive away with her package.

Get it together, she urged the parts of her system that were distracted. *Focus is your superpower. Your client deserves your attention. Do not let her down.*

Beth had known she wanted to be a psychologist since she was nine years old and Miss Rachel helped her to find the voice she'd lost the morning her grandmother died. Prior to that day in therapy, she had disappeared into the books she and her grandmother always read together. As the youngest of four, it had been easy for her to slip into solitude unnoticed. Her grandmother died a few days before Christmas, and somewhere in the bustle of activity Beth had disappeared. When she returned to school after the winter break, still disengaged, her teacher contacted her parents in the hope of bringing back the inquisitive child who was lost in sorrow. Her mother realized that her mourning had caused her to miss the shadows of grief in her child. She immediately made an appointment for Beth with Miss Rachel, and they met every week until she returned to her body and herself.

It's hard to say what Miss Rachel did with the toys and tappers in her office, and it was impossible for Beth to know where her mind went for the weeks after her grandmother's death. All she remembered was feeling numb. That morning when she saw her grandmother crumpled at the foot of the stairs, so still, it took all of her air away. She wanted to remember the night before, when they had stayed awake laughing and singing silly songs until her mom insisted Beth needed to sleep. She had tried her best to be quiet, but when her grandma looked at her with mock terror her giggles grew into snorts and they both dissolved into hysterical laughter.

After the funeral she had tried to remember the fun times with her grandma, but all she could see was her lifeless body. Miss Rachel eventually helped her to release the image and when she let it go all of the happy memories mysteriously returned.

It was then that Beth knew she wanted to do that for other people: she wanted to give them back their happy.

2

THE COUPLE

*W*e don't need couples' therapy. He needs to stop being an asshole, she thought as she fought to stay seated. An ugly statue caught her eye and she decided to redirect her anger toward it rather than scream at her husband. *What the hell is it?* she wondered, disgusted by Dr. Linn's lack of taste. Her hatred of the space grew in direct correlation to her husband's insincerity, so currently nothing in the room was safe. The silver framed mirror was next in line for critique, until she realized she could view the activity outside of the window behind her in its reflection. *That's cruel*, she thought, *I don't need to be reminded that I'm trapped here.* She moved around to try to get comfortable, but her legs wanted to bolt out of the room not sit idly. She tried to direct her body to stay seated. Cross. Uncross. No, cross. At least the commands in her mind muted her husband's words. *Stop moving. Make eye contact. Fine, don't make eye contact. Scream. That's what I want to do. I want to scream. I hate this! I hate you both! What would they do if I screamed at them? Look at Dr. Linn, all buttoned up and in control.*

She wondered what Dr. Linn really thought of them. *Does she worry about me when I walk out the door with my wounds torn open, or is she just disappointed she's not clever enough to stop the hemorrhage? Does she judge us? Pity us? Forget us at seven o'clock when the lights go off? Oh crap, what did she just ask me? I need to pull it together.*

"Can you repeat the question?" She forced herself to listen.

"Of course," Dr. Linn said smoothly. "I asked if you could describe how you felt when you did the homework this week."

"I felt invisible," she said, glaring at her husband.

"Go on."

"I tried to explain how the hurt won't go away, but he doesn't hear me. He just repeats that I don't understand why he needed an outlet and blames me because I've never cared about his work."

"I never said it's because you don't care about my work," her husband responded, head in his hands. "That's not what I said."

"You're a liar. You said it started again because of stress at work and I don't care that you needed an outlet."

He sat back up. "See! She twists my words, which is why I don't want to answer her questions."

"Can you share that with her?" Dr. Linn asked with a glance in her direction.

"You twist my words. You aren't safe," he said, eyes closed in frustration.

She crossed her arms and waited until the awkward silence forced her to speak.

"Seriously? I'm not safe? All you do is lie and I'm not safe."

"My guess is that neither of you feel safe right now," Dr. Linn said. "So let's take a step back. Is it your intention to twist his words?"

"No."

"Do you want to make her feel invisible?"

"No."

She wanted to challenge him on his response, but at some level feared the truth more than his lies.

"OK. Let's try this again so it's more natural at home. We want to strengthen your connection until you can feel each other's emotions, which means you have to fully experience it before you respond. Does that make sense?" Dr. Linn held out the wooden owl they used to determine whose turn it was to talk.

"I will, but he won't do it!" She reached for the owl.

"I do it every time! I listen to your singular message that I'm the jerk who ruined your life. I get it. I know how mad you are. I've apologized. What else can I do?"

"You lie to get out of trouble. You're not sorry."

"See? It doesn't matter what I say. She doesn't believe me."

"Can you explain why you don't believe him?"

"You apologize to get me to shut up and move on. If you understood that you continue to hurt me, you'd stop."

"Stop what?"

"Stop asking for forgiveness." She paused when she saw his eyes begin to glaze over. "You make me feel like I don't matter when you brush off my pain and expect me to believe you're sorry after you've lied for years."

He attempted to respond, but a cloud of despair had already enveloped her that nothing could penetrate.

"Did I repeat what you said?" he asked when she remained silent.

"You repeated the words but you don't *get* it!"

"How do you know I don't get it?"

"It's in your eyes. You don't get it."

He sat back and shook his head. "What am I supposed to do now, Dr. Linn?"

Dr. Linn turned to her. "Can you tell him what it means for you to hear him repeat your words while it appears he doesn't understand your pain?"

"You want me to tell him what it means to me? It means that even though he can parrot what I've said a million times, he'll never *feel it!* This marriage is dead!"

"What do you want me to feel?" he asked.

"How you shattered my spirit and ripped away my dignity. You blame me and it's not fair. Do you think I'm always happy? I'm not. But I respect you. Can you imagine how it felt to find the receipt from that swinger's club and to hear you go there to watch? I want you to feel that humiliation. That rage. And I want you to know how it feels to be blamed for it all."

"I don't blame you, but we have problems to work out if we're going to stay together."

"'If we're going to stay together?' Why drag me to this office if you plan to leave?"

"I want to stay together, but things have to change," he said with his forehead back in his hands. The room went silent until she began to feel uncomfortable.

"You both want things to change. Can we agree on that point?" Dr. Linn asked.

"Definitely," they answered in unison.

"Good. You agree on the most important thing. Let's start with a different homework assignment. I want you to read something." Dr. Linn stood up and walked to her bookshelf. For a moment that stretched out a little too long, Dr. Linn looked out the window intently before reaching for a book on the shelf. "Ahhhh, here it is." She walked back to her chair and began to describe the research in the text.

That was weird. I think she just forgot we were here. She'd stared out the window like she saw a ghost and then snapped right into talking about relationship trauma. *What's wrong with her? What's wrong with me? Why do I want to stay with an addict who won't face his addiction? I can't listen to one more word. Do they notice I've checked out? What would happen if I just stood up and said I'm done? What would they do? Maybe I'll just walk out. How would their precious banter go then? They're so connected right now with their geeked-out probabilities of recovery that they wouldn't even notice.*

"I hope the book helps," Dr. Linn said, standing up to indicate the close of the session.

Deflated, she realized the moment to leave had passed. *Where's my coat? Maybe I can get to the lobby for a minute alone and avoid their wrap-up. Where is my coat?*

"I'm sure it will," her husband said as he held her coat up and helped her put it on exactly like he'd done for the last twenty-two years.

The intimacy of that simple gesture, as familiar as his face, reminded her of everything she had lost. A sharp pain seared her heart as she put her left arm in the sleeve and fought to hold back the tears that hovered below the surface.

3

BETH

Beth waited to hear the couple close the main office door before she ran down the steps to lock it behind them. Their intensity still hung in the air when the headlights from their SUV swept across the dark parking lot. She felt the wife look back at her through the side mirror, a question on her face. "She knows I'm not OK," she said out loud to the shadows in the empty room. Walking back upstairs to her office she tried to dismiss it, but she knew the wife had noticed. It was brief, but when she got to the bookshelf she had been transported back to a memory from her childhood and she felt small, like the little girl she was.

Back in her office she closed her eyes and took a deep breath. *We're OK,* she said to the fearful younger part of her who was crouching behind the couch.

Maybe I'm just not meant to be a couples' therapist, she thought. *I couldn't save my own relationship, so why do I think I can save theirs?* The flashback to her childhood, which seemed to be caused by the combined stress of Ben's request for the DNA test and the couple's similarity to her parents, had triggered her ever-present insecurity over her breakup with Nathan. She made a mental note to process it with her therapist before she made a blanket decision to give up all of her couples.

Six months had passed since Nathan moved across the country to sunshine and opportunity. In fairness to herself, she knew it was not a failure as much as a slow shift into neutral. Although Nathan had invited her to move west with him, she knew it was out of concern over the inevitable paternal criticism she would receive for a failed relationship and not from heartfelt desire. As predicted, her dad admired Nathan's choice to relocate for upward mobility but in an unexpected twist he also affirmed Beth's decision to stay at Serenity, where she had built a reputation in the community. He assumed they were both wisely choosing their careers. It was a flimsy cover, but their romance had cooled into a platonic companionship and they were relieved to resolve it without her father's judgments. When his job offer came it was an easy way to end what had already ended. Nathan didn't want to desert her, but Beth knew he wanted more for his life. So when she said *go*, he left that week. Five years of a relationship, just gone.

The hardest part for Beth was the loss of their day-to-day life. She missed Nathan's outrageous stories and his breakfast potatoes. He was her closest friend, and now he was three time zones away. Now, by the time he left work at night she was ready for bed. She wondered if she would have agreed to the DNA test if he'd been there to talk her through it. Would they have shared a bottle of wine and talked until she realized the cost was too great? Would he have helped her find a different solution? She would never know.

It was hard to write her case note about the couples' session with their energy still present. The wife's anguish hung in the air, reminding Beth of her inadequacy. She just wanted to finish her notes and get out of the office before she began to ruminate on anything else, such as how alone she felt. Motivated, she quickly finished and closed her laptop.

Aware that she actually was alone in the building, she relocked it for the night and began to make her way to Lola's, the Mexican restaurant in the square, where she would join some colleagues for dinner. They had embraced the Taco Tuesday movement to help alleviate the sense of isolation therapists often felt. They had only one rule: no work talk, which protected both their mental health and the privacy of their clients. The size of the weekly gathering ranged from three to fifteen. It was a guilt-free, no obligation event, but Beth had rarely gone when she was with Nathan. Her late hours had always been a problem for him, but now she was free to eat tacos any Tuesday she wanted to and tonight she felt like tacos and a margarita were exactly what was needed.

The thought of seeing her friends helped her to feel a bit lighter as she stepped over a pothole and crossed the street. Her stomach growled when the spicy smell of Lola's captured her senses and she realized her number-three combo still sat in the office refrigerator, uneaten. She grinned at the thought of the smell of tuna hitting Eleanor when she opened the refrigerator in the morning. *It can't rival the aroma of grilled pork chops*, she thought.

When she passed the post office, she tried to ignore the tiny version of her who sat on the steps with a worried look. She forced herself to focus on the LOLA's sign flashing above the heads of her colleagues seated in the front window of the busy cantina. She thought she saw her friend and former colleague, Peter, and hoped he was not an illusion. Tonight was not a night to trust her mind. She attempted to ground herself with the truth: the kit was gone. She was fine. Nothing bad was happening right now. She inhaled the textured layers of spices as she opened the door and let the sound of community wash over her.

"Hello all," she said when she got to the crowded table.

"Hey, Dr. Linn!" Michael called from the end of the table. "I'm sorry I missed supervision." Michael was the newest addition to the Serenity staff, and Beth had been assigned to provide his supervision for the next two years until he finished the required clinical hours to get his independent license as a psychologist, which meant she was also responsible for all of his clients.

"Oh god. No Dr. Linn," Beth said with a groan. "And no work talk! If you mention it again you owe me a margarita."

"Forgive me, Beth. New place, new rules." Before joining Serenity he'd worked as a teaching assistant while he completed his doctorate. He watched her face for approval, which made her laugh.

"Forgiven," she responded before taking her seat.

The camaraderie of the group helped Beth regain her balance. They were her tribe, a rare species who understood the balance between being authentic with clients while also being a blank slate. The isolation was unavoidable because being an ethical therapist meant holding people's secrets, but they could never really know you. Client safety had to come first no matter how lonely it was to be unseen.

"How is good old Serenity?" Peter asked when she met his gaze. His blue eyes never failed to unnerve her.

"You know how it is. That's why you left." She took a sip of her drink, aware of how the topic of Serenity had instantly affected her mood.

"No change?" His look of concern was unexpected. Beth had been prepared for him to brag about his own escape.

"Just staff. Meadows hired a chemical dependency counselor straight out of grad school who she wants me to supervise. I refused. She's frustrated with me but won't say it, so she takes it out on me in other ways. You know her."

"You could join me. You'd love my new—" he paused, grinning, "drama-free office.

"Drama-free and also client-free. You don't take insurance, and I can't do that right now." Beth leaned back in her chair and tilted her almost empty glass into her mouth.

"Can't or won't?" He leaned forward and took her glass and lifted it up so their server would know they were ready to order another round.

"That depends," Beth said. "Can you give me clients? Because you know I can't bring any with me. When you left it was like you were dead. We still don't mention your name in front of Meadows. When your old clients call, they get assigned to one of us. So the long answer is I can't." She paused to affirm she would like another skinny margarita from their server, aware that Peter wasn't taking his eyes off her.

"You underestimate yourself and your clients. They'll find you. Right now you're a willing hostage to Dr. Meadows's tyranny. Just think about it. I'll give you a good price on rent," he said with a wink.

"Don't let him schmooze you, Beth," said Julie from the seat beside her. Beth and Julie weren't just colleagues; they also went to the same gym and occasionally had coffee together after a workout. "He just hates being alone. You have to do what's best for you."

Beth wondered what was best for her as she nibbled on a chip and fantasized about how fun it would be to share an office with Peter. Maybe down the road, she thought. While she allowed herself to dream of what might be, her tiny young part jumped down from the post office steps, popped into the middle of the table, and scowled at her. Beth knew that this tiny part of her was panicked over the DNA test and needed stability, so her hostile rant about the irresponsibility of a job change wasn't a surprise.

Beth moved a water glass in front of the tiny terror. She didn't need to hear this right now. Tonight she would laugh, eat tacos, and enjoy this warm and cozy space without any critical voices in her ear, especially tiny ones.

4

THE DANCER

She forced her eyes open so she could find the off button on her Sonic Bomb alarm clock. Its blare barely woke her from the sedated sleep required to calm the demons that haunted her dreams. She hated how the drugs deadened her mind but if she skipped a dose she would spend the night in torment, screaming without sound, unable to identify the predators who stalked her. The specters lingered in the shadows of her mind even with her medications so she chose numbness over the horror show.

Half awake, she pulled herself up and crossed the room to her desk where her backup alarm was set to ring. She turned it off and leaned into the sunlight peeking through the curtain, hoping to clear her foggy brain but instead getting a full hit of adrenaline. Alarmed, she checked her pill pod. No, she had not missed a dose. Tuesday was empty. Today was Wednesday, which explained her anxiety. Wednesday was therapy day and it disturbed her at a subconscious level. She wished she could blow it off, but something about Pastor Dan intimidated her. He insisted she see Dr. Linn and on his dime. Or the church's. She was not sure who paid but she knew that every Wednesday one of his many minions came at 12:30 to collect her. Sometimes they were men she knew from growing up in the church, but often they were people she'd never met. No matter who showed up, they always returned her to her apartment with a meal or a bag of groceries and were generally harmless, so she decided she could tolerate it if she never had to actually see the pastor.

She doubted they would cross paths. He had sent a text to set it up, never a call, and his administrative assistant followed up. She assumed his motivation was to alleviate his guilt but she had no one to ask. Only the two of them knew he was the cause of her self-harm and she definitely had no desire to dredge it up now. He had not mentioned their arrangement to her parents and neither had she, so now it was just easier to show up and stay quiet.

When she bent over to pick up her cat, Sasha, the singular being who never seemed bothered by her illness, she felt the tightness in her quads that longed to be stretched. Her entire body felt uncomfortable with the added weight from her meds, but the average person on the street would never have guessed she had an extra ounce of fat on her body. Even her studio apartment gave the impression of thinness, with her narrow twin bed pushed against the wall so that she had space to do yoga each morning. Sun salutations had become a gentle replacement for the stress of medical school after she dropped out, and her Wednesday morning musings often led her to question her decision to give up dance for medicine in the first place. She wanted to believe staying in dance would have stopped the onset of her illness, even though she knew it wasn't true. The signs had been there years before her psychosis took over her mind.

On non-Wednesdays she went to work at the coffee shop down the street from her apartment where she made lattes and stocked shelves. Life in the city had freed her from the expectations that smothered her in her hometown. Question marks hung in the air when she encountered people from her past, but not in her new life. Here she felt comforted by the colorful array of people who frequented the shop; the indigent and the wealthy shared the space together. The sense of community enveloped her like the rich aroma of the coffee greeting her each morning. She embraced the orderliness of the workday and the regulars who knew her name. It was good. Every day but Wednesday. Wednesday ignited an instinct to run away and it took work to tame the reaction.

It's going to be OK. I look cute, she thought as she glanced in the mirror on the way out the door. She got to the street just in time to see someone attempting to wedge their car into a spot that was clearly too small. Assuming it was her driver, she knocked on the window to rescue him. Startled, he hit the brake too hard and his head slammed back against the seat. She heard a string of non–pastor-approved expletives.

"I think you're here for me," she yelled through the closed window.

He nodded back at her.

"I didn't want you to hurt yourself trying to get into that space!" She opened the car door with a spark of curiosity. *Today might be fun*, she thought suddenly.

"I think it's too late for my pride. It's definitely wounded," he said and laughed.

"I can't parallel park either. I'd rather ride a Harley. It's never hard to park a bike." She wondered how he'd react if he knew her first Harley ride had led to a cross-country trip with a guy she'd just met during her first manic episode.

"Me too. Unfortunately, the church expects me to provide a car for your transportation. Just between us, I agree a Harley would be better even though I've never ridden on one." He slowly began to pull out of the much-too-small space.

She breathed in the new car smell as she hooked her seat belt. "Tell your boss that, because I'm down for it."

He paused to merge into the flow of city traffic. "I could but I doubt he'd agree. He doesn't exactly seek my input. You know how he is."

"I do." She paused to observe the pedestrians in Highland Square, her neighborhood in Akron, and felt grateful she lived far enough away from her hometown to feel like she could breathe but close enough to see her family.

As they drove down the ramp onto the highway she was reminded of a different time when a guy like him would never have kept her attention.

"So are you from here?" she asked after a few minutes.

"I grew up on the west side of Cleveland about forty minutes from here. My parents moved to the suburbs when I left for college. What about you? Have you always lived here?"

She turned to look at him to gauge his reaction. "Pastor Dan didn't tell you about me?" She noticed her heart rate begin to increase as the landscape changed from the high rises in the city to the cookie-cutter shapes of suburban sprawl.

"Nope. He just gives me a schedule and I follow it. Why don't you tell me about yourself?"

She considered him with his khaki pants and his economy car. He seemed too safe.

She kept her eyes on his face. "I'm not sure you can handle my story."

"Now I'm intrigued. Do you think I'm too sheltered, or you're too dangerous?"

She continued to watch him, fascinated that his eyes never left the road. "A bit of both. Plus my parents attend Sunday services at The Chapel's main campus so I don't want you to feel awkward if you run into them. What about you? Why are you here?"

"Nice deflection," he said, smiling. "I plan to start an inner-city mission like The Chapel's satellite near you and I thought it would help to see how things work."

"Find out anything interesting?"

"Kind of. I've realized it's a lot more complicated than I imagined. I'm not sure about any of it anymore."

"Fascinating," she said as they pulled into the parking lot at Serenity. "I'd like to hear more but I guess I have to go get probed."

"I hope it's not as bad as it sounds," he responded.

She wrinkled her nose and exited the car. "See you in an hour."

Stop flirting. He's from your old reality where parents can protect their children from scrapes and bruises. That's not your life anymore, she reminded herself as she walked into the building. A memory of her mom at the counter of the grocery store bakery popped into her thoughts and she could smell the sugar icing. She could not count the number of times her mom had bought her a cookie to stop her tears and it made her wonder what her mom would think about Dr. Linn's theory that she should let her tears flow.

In general she avoided thoughts of her life before her illness, but going to therapy in her hometown made it hard to block them out. Just the sight of the town's welcome sign made her feel like she had a fifty-pound weight pressing on her chest because she knew she no longer fit in with the shiny people who lived there. A combination of anger and embarrassment seeped into her consciousness as she climbed the stairs to Dr. Linn's office. She recalled their first meeting, when she was sure Dr. Linn was part of a plot to poison her. She wondered if it upset her to be falsely accused. *I've said a lot of strange things and she never reacts*, she thought. *Maybe she's not real. Stop. Redirect. It's just paranoia. Get up the steps. She's completely real. OK. You made it to the lobby.*

She went directly to the seat farthest from the door. It had become her go-to spot. The back corner of the lobby rarely filled up, which helped her to avoid contact with anyone. No need to get preemptively agitated. *You're safe*, she told herself. *Focus on something neutral.* When the door opened she watched Dr. Linn lead her current client from her office to the stairwell. *Does she ever take a break, or does she always pick up her next victim on the return from her sunny send-off?* Such a control freak. *If I beat her to her office maybe it'll shake her up*, she thought, but by the time she grabbed her bag and stood up she was one second too late. Dr. Linn was walking toward her and greeted her with a smile.

"Come on back. Can I get you a glass of water?"

"No, I'm good." She followed obediently and plopped down on the couch. She wondered how many people came through this door every week.

"How are you?"

"I freaking suck," she said, shocked at how quickly her mood had shifted from the car.

"Then it's a good day to have a session. Did Dr. Zhu make any medication changes last week?" Dr. Linn picked up a file from her desk and made her way to the chair in front of the window, apparently unscathed by the negativity that had just landed on her couch.

"Just a tweak to my mood stabilizer to help with the depression. I asked for an SSRI but apparently the only person who enjoys me manic is me." She drew her right leg up under her and reclined into the corner of the couch, pillow on her lap.

"I know that's hard. Any improvement with the tweak?"

"Not yet."

"Give it time. How'd you do with your goals? Have you started walking?"

"Nope. Not walking. Not running. Not biking. I intend to and then I just don't. My yoga practice is consistent but that's not because of a goal, that's just survival." She watched the traffic below in the reflection of the mirror to avoid any look of disappointment on Dr. Linn's face. She was good at the whole nonjudgment thing, but everyone had their breaking point, even Dr. Linn.

"It's hard to force yourself to do anything when you're depressed even if you know it could help. Try to release the criticism and remember that a lack of motivation is part of the illness." She watched Dr. Linn's eyebrows furrow as though they could help her mouth to effectively communicate its uncomfortable message. If only those brows could help her mind to stabilize so she could absorb Dr. Linn's words and believe them.

"I get it but I'm still sick of myself. We talk about the same things every week and I commit to them and then I don't do anything." She turned her body toward the window to avoid eye contact just as the sun rose above the roof of the bell tower. For a moment she was blinded, but when her eyes adjusted she noticed the big hand of the clock was only on the three, which meant the end of the session was nowhere in sight. She had put her phone away for this exact reason; tracking the time in counseling always made it drag on and on.

Dr. Linn waited for her to turn around before she responded. "You do some things, you just don't realize it. I see progress."

"Really? Because it feels like nothing has changed. I'm numb from the medications. I feel nothing. I have no passion. I just exist." She turned her body to fully face Dr. Linn.

"Medication compliance is progress. It's huge that you're choosing mild depression to avoid mania."

"True. Mania is awesome," she said. She felt a tingle of excitement quivering at the edge of her consciousness.

"Until it isn't."

"When I'm manic nothing matters. I'm super creative and my thoughts have literal colors. You don't understand. When I'm manic I can laugh and connect." *If I could just get some cocaine,* she thought.

"And you think people are trying to kill you."

"Not all the time." She crossed her arms, remembering how often she'd thought her parents were trying to kill her.

"You think you're God and demons are after you." Dr. Linn looked smug, like she'd played her best card.

"Not every time."

"You get scared of your family. And me."

"Sometimes I don't." She knew she was reaching, but she couldn't give in.

"But sometimes you do. And then you trust people who hurt you."

"At least I feel alive when I'm manic." Tears began to form and she tried to hide them.

"So what I'm hearing you say is taking your medication is progress since you prefer to be manic?" Dr. Linn leaned forward with her usual look of reassurance.

"I guess." She sat back, exhausted.

"That's kind of huge. Any news about the clinical trial?"

Nice redirect, doc, she thought. "Not yet, but if I get in maybe you can get Pastor Dan to send my driver from today to take me. I can tell he thinks I'm hot."

"Tell me about him." A smile hovered close to the surface even though Dr. Linn tried to look neutral.

"He's the pastor's newest proselyte. He wanted to take me on a ride on a Harley if I could skip therapy."

"What did you say?"

"That I better not disappoint you and the almighty pastor." She stretched her arms over her head, enjoying the thought of her waiting driver.

"You know I don't have anything to do with him, right?"

"Really? I figured you were on his payroll, too."

"Absolutely not. He's friends with Serenity's owner, but I don't know him and I wouldn't talk about you with him if I did. I'm not on anyone's payroll. That would be unethical." The furrowed brows were back.

"Don't freak out. Pastor Dan seems to control everyone in this town, so I just assumed you were no different. No big deal." She looked back out the window, uncomfortable with Dr. Linn's unexpected intensity. She seemed to have hit a nerve.

"I don't want you to worry about confidentiality. Do you understand how important trust is for your therapy?" More of the serious face from Dr. Linn.

"Yes. Fine. I get it. New subject. Did you hear about the drama at the high school yesterday? Supposedly an anti-religion group is behind it."

"No. What happened?"

"My dad called me on his way back from picking up my brother because he was afraid I'd hear about it and flip out. I guess it was just a hoax but there was a bomb threat. So dumb. Who isn't religious in this town? I don't know any atheists. Do you?"

She hoped Dr. Linn would take the bait and stop her therapy talk. She had made it a game to see how quickly she could get her to talk about anything besides her mental health. It rarely worked, but this topic seemed to get her attention. Self-sabotage or not, at least she could avoid the more painful topics.

"No, not really. I'm curious how you reacted to the call."

"Fine."

"No fear?"

"Can we talk about something other than fear?" She looked back out the window, hoping she could completely avoid transition from the weekly update to EMDR.

"We can talk about whatever you want."

"I don't want to talk about anything," she said as her mind drifted to her last EMDR session, where she had started to work on a trauma from the hospital. *Maybe I should just talk and avoid EMDR,* she thought, but she knew Dr. Linn would encourage her to focus on the bad memories and follow the lights. This was the moment she dreaded the most every week, even though she knew the science behind eye movement desensitization and reprocessing was solid. Solid or not, she found the process of adaptively reprocessing her traumatic memories to be painful and at times scary. She hadn't gotten to the point where the benefits outweighed the process, and she wasn't sure she had the courage to get there.

Dr. Linn stood up and moved the light bar in front of her. "Here are your tappers," she said as she gave her the handheld buzzers that were calibrated to vibrate in conjunction with the light as it moved from left to right. "Let's just jump in. We're in the middle of your hospitalization target. I know it's horrible for you, so let's help it process and move into long-term storage. You certainly don't need it to pop up as though it's happening in the present anymore."

"Fine, if focusing on it for a short time today will help the flashbacks stop, I guess it's worth it," she said as Dr. Linn handed her the headset, which was also calibrated to the movement of the light bar. Dr. Linn assured her that the fully immersive approach was best because it would keep her from getting distracted and help her focus on her traumatic memories, which would then allow the bilateral stimulation to adaptively reprocess them. All she had to do was focus on the original memory for a moment and it would quickly flash by as the light moved back and forth and then the bilateral stimulation would help her to access all the other memories linked to it, and once they were all reprocessed she would have a reduction in symptoms. The scientific studies supporting EMDR were the only reason she agreed to try it, but she wasn't convinced it could help her. Out of ways to avoid the inevitable she put on the headset, resigned that her avoidance of treatment was probably not in her best interest.

"How disturbing is the image of the ambulance ride right now?" Dr. Linn asked, sitting down with her remote control to start the light show.

"A ten. It's always going to be a ten."

She noticed a brief, almost imperceptible shadow of sadness fall across Dr. Linn's face and she felt a bit of guilt for her response, but she did not want to access that memory.

"Do you think we could skip EMDR today? I had a pretty good drive over here. I didn't have nightmares last night. I just don't want to drag stuff up."

"Of course. It's your session." She paused while Dr. Linn stood up and gathered the light bar, the tappers, and the headset and moved them back to their place on the other side of the couch. She relaxed back into the couch and waited for Dr. Linn to sit down before she spoke.

"I was able to talk to my overwhelmed part last night and I think I helped it. I tried what we did in session. I closed my eyes and focused until I could sense her. She was curled up in a ball until I started to talk to her and then she seemed lighter."

"That's beautiful." Dr. Linn smiled an encouraging smile.

"I told her it was OK to feel overwhelmed and that we have other parts that can help. I introduced her to my organized part. She was so relieved she wasn't alone that she helped me to clean my apartment *and* make dinner."

"That's great. How did it feel to connect to those parts?"

"Amazing." She felt a warm feeling in her chest.

"You're doing powerful work."

"I guess so. Whatever. I tried," she replied, uncomfortable with the praise. Shame had become her normal. Praise felt much too vulnerable. She avoided direct eye contact with Dr. Linn. All of sudden it was too much.

"You tried and you succeeded. See? Progress."

"Whatever." She shrugged and looked back out the window.

"Look at me for a minute. I'm very proud of you. Bipolar disorder is never easy but your cycles have been exceptionally intense. It usually takes years to accept this diagnosis, but not for you. You've accepted it and you're here. That's major progress."

"I want to believe you but most people don't think like you. They judge me or pity me. I hate the look in people's eyes." She realized in that moment that Dr. Linn looked at her with respect no matter what mental state she was in, and she was taken back by how much that had come to mean to her.

"Most people don't understand the chemical imbalances involved or the medications that help stabilize your brain. Would you feel shame if you needed medication for anything else?"

"No, but it's because people don't judge other illnesses. If I had cancer nobody would judge me." There went the brows, deep in thought, preparing their argument.

"They might if you smoked. Have you noticed people look relieved when they find out someone who has cancer smoked? They correlate it. '*Smoking leads to cancer. I don't smoke so I won't get cancer.*' It's flawed reasoning, but it's what people do."

"I guess you're right. People judge everything."

"That's right, so don't let other people's judgments define you. If you do, you'll spend all your time living up to everyone's expectations except your own."

"Easier said than done, but I'll try."

"This week I want you to keep a record of your successes so you can see the payoff for all of your hard work. Maybe then you'll see how brave you are."

"Fine. I'll try."

"Great. So tell me more about your driver," Dr. Linn said as she leaned back for the first time during the session, apparently comfortable with the direction of their work.

She knew before too long Dr. Linn would ask her about her delusions and how she was managing the paranoia, but for a few more minutes she was happy to talk about her day. By the end of the session she had cried, laughed, and released some trauma. As she walked down the stairs, after the customary Dr. Linn pep talk and perky goodbye, she noticed she felt a tiny skip in her heart when she opened the door and saw her driver. She paused to acknowledge this unusual feeling. He was not dangerous. He did not have drugs. He appeared to be a responsible person. A year ago she wouldn't have noticed him at all so this seemed like progress. When she got home she would write it down, but right now she just wanted to feel this new feeling. Was it hope? Maybe, she thought, as she pirouetted her way across the parking lot all the way to his very reliable car.

5

BETH

Beth stayed in her office with the door closed until she had no choice but to go downstairs to the mandatory Friday morning staff meeting. She felt suffocated in Dr. Meadows's office, which had previously served as the dining room of the house. At first glance it seemed spacious, but not after you packed the room with ten therapists and coffee and pastry. She was grateful for the bay windows overlooking the bell tower because the people who gathered there provided a distraction if the meeting became tedious. Beth's gaze often drifted from Dr. Meadows to the activity around the tower, which had served as the symbol of the town from the time it was built in 1829. It was a reminder of the era when farms covered the landscape and the bell rang to warn the townspeople of danger. While the cities to the north and the south expanded, this small town had stayed quiet and preserved, untouched until the suburban sprawl from both Cleveland and Akron eventually spilled over into its idyllic space.

The bell tower was both a popular meeting place for people to congregate, and the main landmark the Serenity staff used to direct new clients to the office. As she waited for the clock to chime the full eleven times so Dr. Meadows would start the meeting, Beth wondered how many times she had heard Eleanor say, "If you're coming south you'll turn right into the driveway directly across from the bell tower, or if you're coming north you'll turn left into the driveway directly across from the bell tower."

Dr. Meadows always waited for the eleventh chime, and as it finished sounding, she thanked them for being prompt, while sweeping her eyes around the room to establish control. "We have a lot to cover, so let's get started. Our first action item is energy efficiency. I've created a list of ways you can contribute. Please look at the third page of your agenda."

As the group began to page through the electronic document, Beth noticed Michael's leg bouncing aggressively under his laptop. Could he be mad about the annual thermostat lecture? It had become a tradition, like a fall wreath that marked the change of seasons, but she realized this was his first time hearing it and made a mental note to explain it to him during supervision.

"Dr. Linn, can you comment on the safety concerns the front desk staff have in regard to your late hours?"

"I'm sorry I've worried them," Beth said. "I don't plan to continue being here that late. I didn't do it intentionally."

"It needs to stop, especially since you've been extending sessions without billing the clients."

"I've had two crisis situations that aren't ongoing. Client safety was my priority in both circumstances and it wasn't appropriate to bill for the time." Beth looked down to try to hide her frustration.

"Let's be sure these isolated incidents don't become regular events. I'm sure you've apologized to the staff for inconveniencing them, but a reassurance that it won't happen again would be appreciated. Moving on. Who has the *Psychology Today* report?"

Beth bit her tongue. She hated to back down, but an argument would put her under more scrutiny and it wouldn't help her clients. She had to appease Dr. Meadows until she could get out from under her rules, which meant keeping her thoughts to herself until the end of the meeting. When they finally dispersed, Michael stood back to wait for Beth in the hall. "Do you have a minute?" he asked.

"I do."

She felt him tense up as Dr. Meadows walked past them, and Beth assumed he was upset over the thermostat. Or at least she hoped it was something that minor.

"What's happening?" she asked, after they walked to his office and closed the door.

"I'm afraid I'm in over my head with one of my clients and I didn't want to wait until Monday's supervision to talk to you about it. I hope that's OK."

"Of course. I'm glad you didn't wait. That's why you have supervision." She sat down in the chair closest to his desk.

"I think he's involved with the bomb threat at the school." Michael sat down behind his desk and searched her face for a response. His confident demeanor gone, he looked younger than his twenty-six years.

The weight of his words landed on Beth with the full magnitude of their potential. She wished she could walk away and pretend she hadn't heard them. "Has one of your clients told you they're involved?"

"No. Not directly, but my client alluded to membership in a fringe anti-religion group and he said he wants to help them blow things up."

"Literally?"

"I'm not sure. He said he wants to blow up the system and that the Jews, Muslims, and Christians need to pay."

"Any history of violence?"

"He's had a couple of school suspensions for being aggressive, but nothing criminal. You've probably seen him in the lobby. Tall, skinny kid with hair so blond you can't see his eyebrows. He always has a big set of headphones on and a graphic t-shirt with some questionable band lyric that doesn't seem appropriate for the high school."

"I think I've seen him but I'm not sure," Beth answered. "Did you ask him directly if he was involved?"

"No, but I think he wants me to ask. He's definitely trying to get a reaction out of me. He brings up sex scandals in the church and how he's sure I know about it and don't do anything. He blames religion for all of the evil and violence throughout history." Michael stood up and walked over to the window facing the parking lot. "Half the time the kid's right. I don't even disagree with him, but he still scares me."

"He worries you because of his intensity, not because he's told you of any plan, right?"

"Right. I'm concerned because he goes off on tirades with a lot of explicit language. He wants to purify the minds of the nation from the brainwashing that has controlled us for centuries. Those are his words."

Beth's heart sank as she thought of her client who had recently been harassed at the high school because of her faith. "We need something concrete to take any action."

"When I went to the lobby to get him on Tuesday, he was glaring at the girl in the chair across from him. She seemed uncomfortable. He mumbled something on his way past her and it sounded like he said 'hypocrite,' but when I asked him what he said he just grunted. She had on a St. Joseph's school uniform."

"Has he ever said he planned to hurt someone?" Michael walked back to his desk, apparently not getting any answers from watching the cars coming and going from the parking lot.

"No, but I felt sick when I heard the news Tuesday. I've barely slept the last three nights wondering if I should tell the police. What if he was involved, and next time he's successful?" He sat down but looked back at the window.

"At this point you've got nothing to report," Beth said. "His dislike of religion doesn't make him a suspect. If you don't have proof he's a danger to himself or someone else, your only option is to work with his anger."

"I've got a bad feeling about him," Michael insisted. He motioned toward the window and Beth followed his gaze. "Look out there and tell me you could sleep at night knowing he could hurt any one of the people you see out of my window. How many students from the high school walk into our doors each week? It could be one of them or any of the other two thousand students in that building."

Beth considered. "I hear you, Michael, there's just not much we can do at this point. Why don't we plan to meet after his next session so you can get a second set of eyes on the situation right away. Until then maybe you could contact his parents and see if they have any concerns they want you to address."

"OK, I'll reach out. I appreciate your help. I know I sound paranoid, but my dream last night was so real. There were reporters standing on the front lawn of Serenity shoving microphones at me and asking whether the killer was my client. I woke up covered in sweat."

"Gotta love the subconscious mind working out your worst fears while you sleep," Beth said. It was a feeling she knew well.

"I hope it's that and not a premonition."

"Do you have a lot of those?" Now she was curious.

"No, but there's always a first time."

"Call the parents and try to get some idea if anything is actually happening," Beth told him. "Just say you want to check on all of your clients who could've been affected by the bomb threat to make sure they're OK. If they say he's great, then there's nothing else you can do except go home and spend the weekend *not* thinking about work."

"I'll try," Michael said with a wry expression.

"Remember, self-care makes you a better therapist. Let me know if anything comes up. If not, I'll see you Monday."

When Beth left Michael's office she felt the weight of his burden shift to her shoulders, and Dr. Maya Healey's face drifted into her mind. Beth had only met Dr. Healey in person once at a conference, but they had often spoken on the phone when she was the treating psychiatrist for several of Beth's clients. Beth had valued her as a compassionate physician and colleague, so when the news hit that Maya Healey had been murdered, Beth was in shock. Like everyone else, at first Beth assumed it was a horrible but random crime. Every night Maya's ex-husband filled the airwaves with tearful pleas for information as he held up photos of their young children. Two months into the investigation test results revealed his DNA was found under Maya's fingernails, and it became clear nothing was random about her death. At the trial it was revealed she had made several police reports and asked for protection from her husband that she never got. His therapist, who had treated him for anger management, was forced to share his notes, which revealed he had repeatedly stated he wanted to kill her. The therapist testified he didn't report it because his client was a police officer and he assumed he was just blowing off steam. His defense was that the threats were clear in hindsight, but were murky in the moment.

Beth shook herself. She hadn't known Maya well at all, but the memory was still sharp. Thinking of what Michael just told her, Beth was acutely aware she could not let a murky sign go unreported.

. . .

Monday came much too soon for Beth to feel comfortable with her response to Michael's situation. Throughout the weekend she had considered every possible scenario and the appropriate response, but every one of them felt like a disaster so she forced herself to stop. Michael's nightmare concerned her because it was completely out of character for him to share it, which meant he was close to panic. Beth knew she had to share the information with her boss—but not before she had her thoughts in order.

"Good morning, Dr. Linn," Dr. Meadows said, breezing into Beth's office unannounced. "You're here awfully early for someone who likes to stay so late."

"Not tonight. I'm leaving early for a family meeting so I thought I'd get a jump on the day. What brings you upstairs?" Beth was startled by the abrupt intrusion, but she forced herself to remain neutral.

"I've been asked to speak at the high school to address anxiety over the bomb threat, and I'd like for you to go," Dr. Meadows said.

"With you?"

"No, alone. You seem to like teenagers and I'm completely booked tomorrow morning, so I need you to do it."

"What time tomorrow morning? I've got clients all day."

"Ten. I've already had staff check with your ten o'clock and they're fine with coming in at 8:30 instead, so you'll still have time to get over there and back before your 11 a.m. Here's the outline for what they want covered." She handed Beth a sheet of paper with some notes.

"Sure, I suppose—" Her 10 a.m. was the queen; Beth was surprised Eleanor had so easily gotten her to come in earlier.

"Thanks for making this work!" Dr. Meadows said, turning and walking out the door.

"Sure, no problem," Beth said sarcastically under her breath. She was angry they'd moved her client without asking, but there was no point in complaining. Her reasons for quitting expanded daily, but something held her there. She wished she could blame her father's illness or the breakup with Nathan, but she knew it was her unexplainable loyalty to the place that stopped her.

The morning came and went without drama. Michael brought her an espresso for their supervision meeting to soften her mood before he reported he had no new information on his client. His client's mother had not returned his call, so he assumed he had overreacted. Beth hoped they had both overreacted, but once again Dr. Maya Healey came to mind and the more she tried to ignore it, the brighter the warning became. Like a crimson beacon at a railroad crossing, it flashed of the danger to come.

When Michael left her office, Beth tried to connect to the intuitive part of herself that was trying to warn her. As usual her father's voice was louder, and insisted she'd overreacted. Her intuition restated its warning in spite of her doubts. *The truth lies in the middle,* she thought as the bell tower chimed six times, announcing that her distraught couple would be waiting in the lobby. She asked her fearful part to stay calm. She couldn't afford another distraction during a session with this couple.

6

THE COUPLE

ere we go again, he thought as he sat in the same seat he had sat in once a week for the last three months. Dr. Linn did her best to facilitate calm communication, but he knew she was not a superhero and his wife's rage had grown to a level that was impossible to contain. Her anger had been simmering under the surface her entire life, but he had now given her a reason to blame him for it.

Early in their relationship she had shared her story with him on the condition he would never ask about it again. This was at the beginning of their sophomore year of college, and they'd just been dating a few months. Even though they'd become intimate, he could tell there was something holding her back. One minute she would be all over him and the next she was cold and distant, apparently distracted by her coursework, but in time he realized that wasn't the only issue. She evaded his questions until he began to withdraw, which caused her to spiral and threaten to end it.

By the end of the semester, she told him he needed the truth to decide if he wanted to stay in the relationship. He'd naively agreed to bury it without considering the implications, and regretted the decision before she was finished speaking. In some twisted reality she believed it was her fault her father left, because when her mother caught him sneaking into her room in the middle of the night to molest her as he had most nights of her childhood, she threw him out. Her mother never acknowledged it or spoke of him again.

From that moment she blamed herself for her parent's divorce, because she never stopped her father from molesting her. At four years old, she took on the burden of her mother's tears and built a wall around herself. He'd noticed her reserve, but he didn't realize how impenetrable that wall was until after they were married.

Once they were married, she insisted she was fine and that *he* was the one with the problem, because he needed too much from her. He tried to learn how to support a survivor of incest but she had no desire for help. His attempts backfired, strengthening her wall. Somewhere along the way he gave up and started resenting her, which had landed him here.

His wife's monologue was so hatefully familiar that he tuned it out and turned his mind to his addiction. Dr. Linn called it a "paraphilia." Whatever it was called, he wished he could go back in time and not overhear the guys at the gym talking about the swing club. It had only made things worse.

"That was a lot, so let's break down your message into smaller thoughts so he can respond," he heard Dr. Linn saying. "Could you tell him how it feels when he distances himself from you and won't engage?" She watched for his reaction as she spoke.

"I feel like a child being punished," his wife said. "He makes me feel insignificant."

"I'd like you to address him directly and then he'll repeat what you've said so we know he understands your feelings. Try to use I statements like 'I feel angry when . . .'"

His wife turned to address him. "I feel angry when you treat me like a child that you've just put in time-out," she said. "I feel angry when you don't listen to me, like you've done for the last ten minutes!"

"I'm trying to listen," he said, repositioning himself in his seat.

"You stopped listening when you found your club. You don't even see me."

"Let's try to focus on the exercise," Dr. Linn interjected. "Can you repeat what she initially said to you?"

"Yes. She thinks I treat her like a child because I went to the club and I don't listen to her complaints about it."

His wife let out a sound of exasperation. "Oh my god, I can't do this any-more. I said you treat me like a child when you block me out and don't listen. The cheating just makes you a creep."

"I don't block you out until the tenth time you say the same thing. I can only listen to how repulsive I am for so long before I check out." He won-dered if Dr. Linn judged him too. Maybe he was repulsive.

"So you think it's OK to watch other people have sex?"

"Not if your partner's not into it," he said without making eye contact.

"*I'm* clearly not into it and you did it anyway, so why do you expect me to believe you never participated?" She raised her hands and held the sides of her head in exasperation.

"I'm telling the truth, so I expect you to believe me." Though he had to admit maybe there was a good reason she couldn't trust him.

"That's hilarious."

Dr. Linn jumped in again. "Can we pause the argument and try to do the exercise? It's your choice how you spend the hour, but if you continue to microanalyze the past you'll end up at the same place you were when you got here tonight. I can't be with you 24/7 to moderate your arguments, so noth-ing will change if you don't find a way to process your issues on your own. You don't need a referee. You need skills."

"Fine," they said in unison as Dr. Linn began to explain the directions one more time.

If I could just slink off this couch and out the door I could spend this hour at the bar so I could at least tolerate the ride home, he thought, but that would make him like his own father—and that was the last thing he wanted. What he wanted was to connect to his wife, but he struggled with her criticism of him when he saw no effort on her part to change. He had to try. His kids deserved it and she deserved it, and there was no reality where he wanted to be remembered like the quitter his father had been.

7

BETH

How much longer are they going to tolerate it? Beth wondered as she finished her notes on the couple and closed her computer. It was time to leave for her parents'. If her dad asked about work she'd definitely not tell him how hard her day was, or he'd remind her that he'd told her not to become a therapist. Convinced she was foolish to reject her place in the family's custom plastics manufacturing business, he never missed an opportunity to prove he was right. So Beth avoided giving him ammunition.

At the bottom of the stairs, Beth opened her umbrella and realized this was the first time in months she had left work when there were cars in the parking lot. Maybe her dad was right.

On the short drive across town her thoughts returned to the DNA test and how her secret was going to make her feel awkward with her family. *I'm completely alone*, she thought as she pulled into her parents' driveway. The light from the bay window illuminated her two sisters working side by side in the kitchen. Beth studied them as she walked up the path, aware of how much the three of them resembled each other. Same petite frames, same auburn hair, same hazel eyes. *Maybe I can tell them*, she thought when they warmly greeted her, but then she felt the stress in the air. Their father's illness had forced their mother to help him manage his workload in addition to her own, which left some of his care to them. Beth knew it was a lot, and she didn't want to add to their stress. The only sibling she could comfortably tell was Jonathan, the second youngest of the four, but he lived an hour away with his wife and two children and he rarely spent time with her. For now, she knew that this was hers alone to carry.

"Is he awake?" she asked as she shook the raindrops from her coat and closed the door.

"He's awake and in a mood," her sister Andrea replied. "Someone from the warehouse made a mistake and he's been fighting with the distributor for an hour. Mom won't be back from Pittsburgh until tomorrow, so one of us needs to sleep here tonight. Weather delayed the client's flight, a bad thunderstorm or something, so her meeting's rescheduled for 9 a.m. tomorrow. Can you stay?"

Beth felt her chest tighten in anticipation of what would happen if she said no. Andrea, the oldest, mirrored their father's authoritarian persona perfectly and would use the excuse that her husband and three children needed her to push Beth into staying. Carrie, whose gentle nature balanced out Andrea's bluntness, had two dogs at home and a firefighter boyfriend who worked overnight shifts so might not be home to take care of them.

She said, "I can stay, but I have a client at eight-thirty in the morning. Can Hilda come at eight?" Hilda was the caretaker who had been hired to help.

"No, she starts at ten tomorrow. Can't you reschedule? I'm doing 80 percent of the work around here and I need a break."

Beth was grateful that Carrie, the second oldest, handed her the open bottle of wine she had been sharing with Andrea. Beth poured herself a glass and tried to channel her mom's energy of peaceful negotiation before she responded.

"It's 7 p.m. I can't move a session that's scheduled for 8:30 in the morning and even if I could, I have nowhere to move it. Don't you drop the kids off at school by eight?"

"I have a spin class at nine and I'm not cancelling again. Carrie, can you cover?"

Carrie stopped stirring the soup and stared at them.

"Really you two? Can't this wait until after dinner?" She stopped what she was doing and put her hands on the counter as she looked from one to the other. "You realize this is the reason we're meeting, right? We can work this out much easier when we're all together."

"If Jonathan ever gets here I guess we can," Andrea responded. "He promised to be on time. I'm sure he'll have a traffic-related excuse."

Beth walked down the hall, wine in hand, to greet her father. He was deep into a negotiation, comfortably reclined in his chair with a tray table covered in papers and his laptop open on his lap. The person on the other end of the call would never have guessed how sick he was.

"I don't buy it, Lee. Let's be clear. Either you fix this or we're no longer partners on the project. I've done what I can to mediate. Let me know when it's fixed," her father said with a stronger tone than Beth imagined he could conjure. He put his phone down in frustration, mumbling about incompetence. It took a moment before he noticed his youngest daughter was in the room.

"I didn't see you there." Beth was relieved that he was dressed for work in his usual freshly starched white button-down dress shirt, even though it hung loosely from his shoulders.

"Hi, Dad," Beth said as she bent to kiss his cheek. She wished she could ask him the question that burned in her mind.

"Has your brother graced us with his presence yet?"

"No, not yet. Do you feel up to this meeting?"

"Would you? I'm about to listen to my children argue over who has to take care of me. I can handle cancer, but I can't stand all of your opinions about how to manage my health, especially those of you who won't let me have a cocktail. Jesus, Beth, how do you think I feel?" It amazed Beth that no matter how thin and frail he got, he still made her feel very small.

"Horrible, Dad, I get it. I'm not here to manage you, so if you want a drink have a drink. Here, have mine," she said, handing it to him.

"Aren't you afraid of your sister?" Beth knew he meant Andrea.

"I'm more afraid of you," she said, sitting down across from him.

"Good," he said, taking a sip and handing it back with a shaky hand. "Your grandma was a wise lady. She did it right. The morning she died she woke up feeling fine. She walked down the steps and surprise: she had an aneurism. No fuss. No worry. Just gone. She never had to feel like a burden. I'd check out now if it wouldn't kill your mother."

"Oh my god, Dad, please stop. You haven't even given the radiation time to work. And you aren't a burden. You're a pain, but you're not a burden." Guiltily, Beth wondered if this was really true. She loved him, but she also hated how he viewed her and she had grown tired of trying to prove her worth. Maybe he was right; he was a burden to her, but not because he was sick.

"You're the only one who feels that way. I know the rest of them complain to your mother about me all the time."

"That's Jonathan," Beth said, hearing the door open and her brother's voice intermixing with Andrea's and Carrie's in the kitchen. "We should join them." She was grateful for a way out of a conversation about her siblings. "We don't want to give them any more reasons to complain."

"I'll get there when I get there," her father said, struggling to stand.

"Something smells good," she said to distract her father from his obvious decline. It was hard to process that the weak person who shuffled beside her was the same man who had held court at their childhood dinner table. Back then, if you disagreed with him or had poor manners, God help you. A simple elbow on the table brought down his judgment, which would elicit a soliloquy about their lack of respect for his household. Now she had to guide him into his chair and place his napkin on his lap like a child.

"What would you like to drink, sir?" she asked with eyebrows raised once they were all seated.

"A bold cabernet would be nice," he answered, his eyes on Andrea, who simultaneously whipped around with the look of righteous anger she had perfected as a child.

"Seriously, Dad? If you fall and break a hip this whole thing is over. Do you think wine is going to help your balance?" She glared at him with a look similar to one he'd given them as children, and it almost made Beth laugh.

"I'm not sure about my balance, but it'll help my mood. Come on, Andrea, I let you drink when you were sixteen. You need to lighten up." He shook his head in disgust.

"We were in Italy and it was legal, so you didn't technically *let* me. Do what you want. I'm sick of this constant fight with you," she said, placing the tureen of soup in the center of the table.

"At least you were sixteen, Andrea. We had to spend that whole trip watching you have fun," Jonathan said. Carrie nodded in agreement.

Carrie passed the basket of bread to Jonathan. "I know. Do you remember sitting at the end of the table while Andrea thought she was so cool talking to Mom and Dad about the wine and how it came from the Chianti region in Tuscany? We were so jealous."

Jonathan poured olive oil on his bread plate and smiled at Carrie. "That was a pretty fun trip even without the wine."

As bowls were filled and wine was poured Beth felt a deep, familiar sadness in her chest. Although currently magnified by her father's illness, it had been her lifelong companion. The camaraderie the rest of her family enjoyed had always eluded her. *Focus on your food,* she told herself as the banter grew louder and her protective shields went up.

The ding of the iPad drew all of their attention to their mother's seat, where it sat perched on a stand where her plate would be. Andrea was seated beside it and answered immediately.

"Hello, beautiful family," their mother said when her face popped up on the screen. The light behind her glowed like a halo around her head.

"Hi, Mom," they responded in unison.

"I wish I were there instead of alone in this hotel. Hello, Henry. Have you been able to keep everyone under control?"

"That's an odd question. Didn't you tell them to control me?"

"Like we could ever do that," Jonathan said without making eye contact with his father. He turned in his chair to face his mom and placed his arm on the back of Carrie's chair.

"We should probably get to it, Mom," Andrea interjected. "Your overnight stay has created some issues here that we haven't resolved. We need to get a workable plan in place."

"OK, no chitchat, I get it. Obviously we all know what we need to discuss. Henry, do you want to be part of this or do you want to go lie down?" Celeste asked.

"I'll stay for my own damn sentence, Celeste," he said in a fiery tone. Even though his hands quivered and he couldn't hide his shaking, nobody dared argue with him.

"OK," Carrie said. "Let's get things figured out."

Beth listened while they talked about schedules and budgets. Who could take what hours on which days, and who would manage the corporate issues on the days Celeste needed to be at home. Beth said little and let her sisters and mother make most of the decisions, agreeing to cover that night but clear that she had to leave for work by eight o'clock in the morning.

She felt herself float farther and farther away as she realized how her career choice had alienated her. She wasn't a chemical engineer like her brother or an accountant like Carrie. She didn't care about marketing or tariffs like her mom or Andrea. When she chose to major in psychology, her father grudgingly gave his approval because he assumed she'd be an asset to their human resources department. She had hoped that by the time she finished her undergraduate degree he'd understand her disinterest in the business, but he did not. Unfortunately, neither did her siblings. They had each followed their father's advice and chosen majors that fit well into the company's corporate structure with the knowledge that one day they would inherit the business. None of them took her seriously when she applied for graduate school because there was an assumption they were all on the same team working toward the same goals, even though she'd never agreed in the first place. That didn't matter. She was seen as selfish. Even if they questioned her loyalty, she did care about her family. But there was no room for that conversation.

She wanted to excuse herself from the table and call Nathan, but she knew she had to disconnect from him. She couldn't be that person: the ex who wouldn't let go, who had no boundaries, who irritated every new person he dated because she still relied on him.

"Beth, could you stay with the conversation, please?" Andrea asked.

"I'm listening. I'm just thinking." She forced herself to focus. She knew that as the oldest Andrea felt pressure to take care of all of them, in spite of their lack of gratitude. Beth didn't want to reinforce her feelings.

She needed Andrea to cut her some slack for once. "It's been a strange day," Beth went on. "I was actually wondering if we could bring in another caretaker in addition to Hilda. You know I don't have flexibility. If I commit to a client, I have to be there to see the client. Nobody can fill in for me."

"Seriously, Beth. We know," Andrea said. She raised her hands in mock surrender. "We all know how important your job is but this is your dad. You honestly can't take time off? The company will compensate you if it's about money."

"It's not about money. It's about my responsibility to my clients. They expect me to show up. I can't just cancel on them at the last minute."

"I leave my children to be here," Andrea said.

"It's not the same thing!" Beth felt her cheeks flush with anger.

"Well, then we need you to commit to more in advance," Jonathan jumped in. He pushed his chair back and put his napkin on the table, apparently ready to be finished with the conversation.

"Is your job more important than your family?" Andrea demanded.

"Of course not," Beth replied, fighting to keep the tears from spilling onto her cheeks.

"You do expect the rest of us to make it work," Jonathan said.

"It isn't fair for you to compare my work with being part of the family business. You can all cover for each other. You're the owners. Who's going to fire you?"

Andrea rolled her eyes. "Just stop the drama, Beth. We know you're saving the world while we just make money and support capitalism."

Carrie finally spoke. "Enough, Andrea. Beth has a point. Hopefully Dad will recover quickly, but we don't have a timeline and none of us can leave work for weeks at a time without it affecting our careers, the company, or our personal lives. Mom, what do you think?"

"I think you're all doing your best in a very difficult situation. It would help if we all try to appreciate each other a bit more and complain a lot less. I'll talk to Hilda when I get home tomorrow," Celeste said. "Just let me see what I can arrange. Henry, do you agree?"

Woken from a micro-nap, Henry nodded. Beth watched her siblings—his children, who were so far from childhood now—and she wished she could help them understand why he'd fallen asleep. Their father would never normally nap during a meeting, especially one about him. He was fierce. Beth knew he'd fallen asleep to escape his despair, and she was the only one with a lens through which to see it.

8

CELESTE

As Celeste closed her laptop, exhaustion washed over her from her family's energy. She stretched her arms over her head and tilted her head from side to side to release the tension.

The sudden silence of her hotel room felt luscious. Soon enough Andrea would call to vent, which would be followed by Jonathan's rant on his long drive home. He'd critique the meeting and instruct her on how she should handle things. Henry would be waiting for her call so he could talk about work, and Carrie would send her a heart emoji to say goodnight. The one who needed her the most was Beth, and she was the one who would stay silent.

Celeste found it impossible to keep them all happy without sacrificing her soul, which felt ironic, because she believed she'd already sold her soul the day she decided not to tell the truth. *Whose fault was that?* she asked herself, as she wondered for the millionth time if she could have changed what had happened so long ago.

Henry. How could she ever explain her relationship with Henry? Did she even want to? The world saw what she intentionally created, a gorgeous, social media post of a life. In the background she masterfully hid behind a curtain of fantasy. If anyone ever tried to step through the veil they'd hit the wall she had built to hide the tangled threads of deception. She had become the protector of her family without any help from Henry.

Their dance had begun forty-five years ago with all the sparkle of a New York City romance. The hotel where they met was in the theater district, near Hell's Kitchen, where Celeste was living for the summer with a friend. She'd secured a job as a tour guide and each of her groups gathered in the lobby to begin their excursions. The big tips and interesting people were much more fun than a temporary administrative assistant job would have been.

In complete contrast, Henry walked through the door of the bohemian hotel with no understanding of flow. Out of place in the dimly lit lobby, he looked like he was late for an important meeting on Wall Street but had somehow landed at a poetry reading. He quickly scanned the room until his eyes landed on her. He smiled, and it was his smile that had intrigued her.

"You wouldn't be Randy Amherst, would you?" he asked.

"Unfortunately, I'm not," she said. He seemed to be beside her in an instant.

"Then I need to know your name."

She took a moment to observe him. "Why do you need to know my name?"

Matching her pause, he held her gaze. "Because I can't live one more minute without it."

She tried to maintain both her own space and eye contact. "That sounds serious. I'd hate to see you die over not knowing my name."

"It would be tragic."

His dimples distracted her, but she held her ground. "Don't you think you should find Randy Amherst?"

"He's lost my interest. I told you. I have to know your name."

She paused again. She had no use for players. "Do you use that line on everyone you meet?"

"I've never used that line in my life," he said with a look so earnest it was impossible not to believe him.

"You're quite serious, sir," she laughed, completely disarmed. "My name's Celeste. Now I'll need your name."

"Henry Linn. Engineer. Entrepreneur. And your future husband," he said, reaching out to shake her hand.

In retrospect, Celeste could see the warning signs. She should have been cautious of such a charmer, but his vulnerability had intrigued her. He was different from the boys where she'd grown up in New Jersey, so when he invited her to drinks that evening she accepted and they met every night that followed for an entire magical summer. Unfortunately the current version of herself barely recognized that younger, carefree college student anymore.

She quickly turned her thoughts to the work before her and wondered how her client meeting in the morning would go. It was crucial for her to continue to hide Henry's illness until she got the contract signed. If Anastasia, the client, asked where he was, she had a solid alibi and he could call her later to answer her questions. His treatments had not yet affected his mind. For now, his forceful phone presence allowed them to keep up the facade that he was in charge, which was important to some of their customers. She could easily run the business even if she'd never wanted to be part of it. She regretted that she had been triangulated into it by the same charm Henry used to entice her to marry him, but it was much too late to change careers or marriages.

He was so different now from the young man she thought he was when they'd met. At twenty-three he had moved to New York from Ohio with a midwestern optimism she'd never experienced. He took risks and laughed easily. Her brothers constantly ripped on him because he was so easy to tease. In response she had trusted him, and that had ended up costing her a great deal.

She tried to finish her meeting preparations in the hour she had left before the inevitable calls started, but her mind continually returned to Henry and the children. She knew Andrea was upset about Beth's apparent lack of concern for the family and the company. She would try to mediate, but it was hard to deny that Beth was distant. She always had been. It didn't help that Henry drove her farther away with his criticisms. Henry. Always back to Henry.

For some reason the thought of him in that moment broke something open in Celeste, a combination of anger and grief, and she grabbed a pillow and began screaming into it. At first she felt uncomfortable but after a few minutes she started to laugh until the laughter became uncontrollable. *I'm losing it*, she thought, but then she put her face back into the pillow and screamed some more until the pressure in her heart began to subside.

Exhausted, she sat back against the mound of pillows on her finely made bed and closed her eyes, greedy for a little more time alone before she had to reengage. A sound on the street drew her attention to the window, where raindrops slid gently down the pane softly illuminated by light from the streetlamp. The beauty made her smile and reminded her she was only a few miles away from the last man she loved before she met Henry. They had remained good friends after their breakup, so when he saw red flags with Henry he tried to warn her. But she was too far gone. It felt ironic that she was now in his town, a few miles away from his house, and dealing with the repercussions of not listening to him so many years ago. Being in Pittsburgh did this to her. It brought her closer to who she could have become.

The buzz of her phone snapped her back into the present. Andrea's name flashed on the screen. She took a breath before she picked it up. Her daughter's intensity came through even in the ring.

"Mom! I can't do this anymore. How do you take it? They're all so ridiculous!"

"They seemed OK from my side of the screen," Celeste replied.

"Seriously, I don't have patience for them," Andrea said. "Any of them. I'm so angry. And I don't know what to do with it. How can you say they seemed OK? They're so selfish."

Celeste stood up and began to pace. "I see the bigger picture, Andrea. They're all afraid to lose your dad."

Andrea sighed. "I know. You're right. I'm sorry, Mom. You don't need my stuff piled on top of your own. I didn't even ask how you are."

"I'm OK; just ready to try to get some sleep," Celeste said. "Anastasia will come at me caffeinated and confrontational at 9 a.m., so I need to be on top of it. I'm sorry you had to handle the meeting tonight without me being there. Your siblings try. They just aren't you."

"Why do you always defend them?" This was a common refrain with her eldest.

She tried to patiently explain. "I don't defend them. I just see them in a way you don't. When your kids are bigger you'll understand. I know you want me to change your siblings, but I don't want to change them. I accept each of you for who you are, all of your differences. If you could accept them, you wouldn't get so angry."

"Whatever, Mom. I swear you try to be the family therapist. I love you, but I don't want to hear your psychobabble tonight. Dad needs help and I'm angry that I'm the only one who seems to care."

"Everyone cares, they just care differently than you do. Get some sleep and we can talk when I get home tomorrow."

"Fine. I love you."

"I love you, too," Celeste said as she hung up the phone and prepared for Jonathan's call. She wished she had a magic wand to make it better for all of them—including herself.

9

BETH

Henry's rough night translated into a worse morning for Beth. It took all of her patience to get him ready before she raced off to work, and on her drive she fantasized about a job where she could call in sick without creating chaos. In her daydream, Dr. Meadows happily covered the school assembly and all of her clients easily rescheduled while she made lunch for her dad. In this alternative reality she even had time to stay and make dinner, and nobody at work needed her—which was far from the reality of Michael's client and the danger at the school.

Beth wished Andrea could spend just one day at work with her and see the vicarious trauma that persistently nipped at her heels. Anonymously carrying people's pain created isolation. And now her loneliness was even more pronounced at night without Nathan to come home to. She wished she could share it all with Andrea. The coexisting sacredness and sadness. The insecurity she had to keep in check. The question of whether she actually helped at all.

Today her fears were fueled by her father's demands, which she somehow couldn't adequately fill. When he said he just wanted coffee for breakfast, she made sure he was dressed and got him set him up in his office so she could bring it to him there. But by the time she returned with his coffee, he was frustrated because she should have known that he needed food with his morning medications. She apologized and made him toast, but in the ten minutes she was gone his coffee slipped out of his shaking hand and spilled on his shirt. While she tried to clean him up, he blamed her for choosing the wrong coffee cup. For a moment she felt responsible, until she realized he couldn't tolerate how fragile he had become and needed a scapegoat. She let him rant for another few minutes about everything wrong in the world, told him she hoped his day got better, and headed for the door. Almost late for work, she had barely any time to prepare for the queen during her drive. Thank God she had a clear enough recollection of their last session. Arriving at 8:24, she had exactly six minutes to run up the steps and open her office.

A news update about the bomb threat popped up on her phone as she closed her office door behind her. *Not now*, she thought as she braced herself for the queen's arrival. Probably it would be about the abusive husband again, and his affiliation with the anti-religion group. *Just be a blank slate*, she told herself. *Don't think about Michael's client. Just do your job.*

She took a deep breath and opened her door. Beth tried to gauge if her client's scowl was attributed to her usual frustration or if it was the result of the news. *Stay blank*, she repeated to herself.

"Good morning, come on back," Beth said neutrally. "How are you today?"

The queen said, "I just got a text from my administrative assistant that our hot water tank is broken, and the maintenance department needs to know if I want to dismiss classes for the day. It's ridiculous that I can't leave that place for an uninterrupted hour."

Beth paused before she closed the door. "Do you need a minute to call them? I can step out."

"No. I just texted them to proceed with the day. I swear it's always something." The queen walked toward her normal spot on the couch, dropped her bag and coat on the other end. Today her outfit was stunning. Her tailored suit showed off her figure in a way that drew the eye and also respect.

Beth nodded and settled into her chair. "I'm sure the pressure at the academy is stressful enough without the added problems at home. How are things there?"

"My son has stopped having contact with most of his friends from church," the queen said. "I'm sure it's because his father makes so many nasty comments, but I can't do anything about it."

"Did you meet with the divorce lawyer?"

"Not yet. I know you think I'm weak, but I'm afraid of what he'll do if I try to leave. Anytime I question him he attacks me in front of our son. He's not the man I married. It's like a switch flipped in his brain."

"How would he know if you got advice from an attorney? It might empower you."

"I can do that but right now, I'd rather rely on you to get him arrested." She crossed her arms.

Beth considered how to respond as she processed her client's words. She needed to stay sharp and toss it back into her court.

"If I had the omniscient power to see the crimes he's committed I'd be happy to alert the authorities, but unfortunately I don't have that type of power," she explained.

"I'm serious, Dr. Linn. I know he's behind last week's bomb threat. His propaganda is all over our house. He's dangerous." She raised two fingers to each temple and began to rub in circles, as though Beth were giving her a headache.

"If you believe he's dangerous, then you're responsible to report it." Beth held eye contact to meet her client's challenge.

"So are you."

Beth paused, aware that the queen had successfully lobbed the ball of responsibility back to her.

"Am I?" she asked her client. "With no proof? All I have are your vague accusations. Unless you're hiding information that would prove his involvement?"

"Of course I'm not. Do you even listen to me? I've told you my son has changed under his influence. I've told you everything. His meetings are very dark." She lowered her eyes.

Listen for tone. Stay clear. Without proof, you can't do a thing. Not one thing. She wants to push you to do something but you can't. The minute he threatens her son then it's your time to act. And you will act. You would never allow a child to be hurt. "I don't know what you think I can do. I can't get your husband arrested based on your intuition."

"What if I find evidence he was behind the bomb threat last week?" The queen tucked her hair behind her ear and tilted her head.

Beth held her breath. What did the woman mean? "You just said you don't have any proof."

"I said I don't have it *yet*," the queen said, relaxing back into the couch.

"What do you mean by yet?" *Stay blank, Beth. Stay blank.* She kept her posture erect and her features smooth.

"Let's just say I know there's no way he can get away with it. It has to be him. I've seen the change."

"Explain."

"About a year ago things got intense," she said, staring out the window. "We have a friend who just got back from Afghanistan. When they're together it's worse. They're obsessed with religious fundamentalism. It gets explosive."

"Does your friend have PTSD?"

"Definitely, but he won't go to therapy. He's just angry, and my husband can match his anger pretty well."

"Did something happen to your husband to trigger this anger?"

"Not really. His brother died in the Twin Towers, but that was a long time ago."

Beth's investigative part snapped to attention. "You never told me about his brother. Were you close to him?"

"Not really. He adored me, but we didn't see him often. He was killed early in our relationship and I was absorbed with work. I rarely went into the city with my husband because he was there on business so they had a lot of time together. They were pretty close." She looked pensive, as though this was something she hadn't thought of in a long time and hadn't considered.

"How did he handle it?"

"He didn't talk about it much after it happened, but that wasn't unusual. The whole world was in shock. I don't really remember the details, it was a long time ago, but I know he was really angry at the memorial service. Why do you ask?"

"It could explain the start of his anger toward religion." Beth wanted to give her client a way to connect to her husband. It was the best way to protect herself and her son.

"I guess so. I never thought about it." She looked at Beth with curiosity.

"Has anything happened recently?"

"Not really. His father died last year, but we expected it."

"That could have stirred up the trauma response from his brother's death. His emotional reactivity could be a symptom of PTSD," Beth said. "I can't diagnose him, of course, but if you want to schedule an appointment I could have one of my colleagues assess him. If he got help all three of you would be safer."

"He won't go to therapy, Dr. Linn. He thinks it's for weak-minded people. PTSD or not, it won't matter. He's volatile. You'd diagnose him as a sociopath if you had cameras in our house. Maybe then you'd understand my fear that he's going to do something horrible. I'm not overreacting."

"Tell me how you chose sociopath for his diagnosis."

"Can you just read my notes from last week so I don't have to go back through it? I want to talk about my son. I think he's in danger, too."

Beth focused to regain her balance. She wanted to follow the clues about the husband, but that wasn't what her client wanted from her. She felt uncomfortably pushed.

"What do you mean by danger?"

"Maybe you'd like to hear his rant from last night?" The queen picked up her cell phone and hit play.

A brutal tirade burst from the phone and filled the room with vitriol from a man Beth now felt grateful to never have met. She looked up to offer compassion, but her client's look of satisfaction was as disturbing as the audio.

"I think I've made my point. He's dangerous. Any more questions?"

Beth shook her head, confused by the triumphant look on her client's face. "No questions. He's clearly abusive, and I know that has taken a toll on you."

"I told you," the queen said as she stood and picked up her things and then turned with a smile. "See you next week," she said as she walked out the door.

"OK. Be safe," Beth said, unsure how else to respond to the abrupt departure but grateful for a few extra moments to gather her thoughts and her notes for the speech she had to deliver in thirty minutes at the high school.

Why did I say be safe? she wondered on her walk to her car. She was so shaken by what she had just heard that she began to question her speech. How could she walk up on the stage to offer support to students who might be the target of her client's husband's hatred and not do something to stop him?

She drove the few blocks to the school with too many questions and not a single answer. She parked on a side street and hoped the walk to the building would give her time to pull herself together.

When she opened the door and walked into the security station, she was met by a familiar smell of unknown cafeteria food that was exactly the same as when she had been a student there sixteen years ago. It was comforting. And the officer seemed relaxed enough and in control, so maybe she was overreacting to what the queen had told her. She took a deep breath and watched the students pour out of their classrooms and into the gym.

"Hello, Dr. Linn, so glad you could be here today," said Paul Anderson, the new principal, as he emerged from the crowd.

She shook his outstretched hand. "Thanks."

"Do you have any questions before we begin?" he asked.

"I'm wondering what concerns you've heard from students?" She was curious about what he would say.

"Most of them seem to think it was a prank, except for those who've been targeted," Paul told her. "It's actually encouraged some of them to come forward to make reports about other things that have happened to them lately. Apparently threats have been made through notes left on lockers and stuck to cars. We plan to install security cameras so that we can better monitor the campus. I can tell you more after your talk."

"Do you have a motive for why specific people were targeted?" Beth asked, aware that several students looked up when they heard her question. She was grateful for the flow of traffic that kept them moving down the hall.

"Possibly religious beliefs, but it's not clear."

Beth felt pressure in the front of her head. She wanted any other answer than that one.

"Do you think there's an organized hate group here?"

Paul said, "I've heard rumors but I haven't witnessed any activity. The only physical evidence we have is antisemitic graffiti in one of the women's restrooms." He guided Beth back toward a wall to let more students pass and she scanned the surge in the hopes of seeing her Jewish client who had been harassed.

"OK," she said. "Is there anything else other than what you sent over to the office that you want me to say?"

"You could bring in your ideas about the psychological effects of bullying you shared in your workshop last month for the district. Most of these kids don't identify as a bully to anyone. My hope is that you can get them to see that with some conscious effort they can make changes that will allow them to protect and support each other to make this a safe place for everyone, even if they don't feel like they're part of the problem."

"Sounds good. I can do that," Beth responded as he guided her through the double doors and onto the stage, where three people already sat in folding chairs directly behind the podium. She nodded at them and took the empty seat on the end nearest to the bleachers with a clear view of the students seated there.

The other three speakers were staff from the school: a security officer who covered the installation of additional cameras to monitor the building, a guidance counselor who outlined the options for groups or individual sessions for students who needed support, and the vice principal, who would wrap up the assembly after Beth spoke. When it was her turn at the podium Beth focused on the sea of young faces as she let her words glide gently over them. She was comfortable talking to a crowd, and tried to say things that would connect to them emotionally. *Maybe everything is OK*, she thought until her gaze landed on a familiar figure at the edge of the bleachers motioning to someone out of her view. It was a boy, wearing a black hoodie, the edges of his white-blond hair a sharp contrast to the black stocking cap pulled down over his ears.

Seconds later the fire alarm sounded and she watched him slide back up into the bleachers. Everyone else stood up and began moving toward the doors. A security officer ushered Beth and the other speakers out of the building and into the parking lot with everyone else, so she didn't see where the student went. The teachers around her didn't know if it was an emergency or a drill, but nobody seemed worried. They reassured her she could go back to work because the next period started in twenty minutes, so even if it was a drill the students would still be sent to their third period classes and not the auditorium. Beth looked for Paul to be sure, but she didn't see him in the parking lot. Unsure of what to do, Beth felt certain that the kid she saw was Michael's client, but she wasn't sure if that even mattered. Maybe it was just a drill.

When it became clear no information was coming, Beth walked to her car. It was only 10:25, which gave her a moment to breathe and consider what she had just witnessed. Curious, she drove back toward the school instead of returning directly to work. Two police cruisers were in front of the building, but the students were still calmly milling around the parking lot. Beth decided to pull over and call Andrea. Her kids went to the elementary school, so if something had happened she would have gotten an alert from the district's emergency alert system. Andrea answered on the first ring.

"Oh my god. Are you safe? I was just about to text you. Aren't you at the high school? I just got an alert that the school's on lockdown because of the threat of an active shooter." Andrea sounded frantic.

"Oh no! That's why I called you to see if you knew anything. I just left. I'm in my car a block from the school." Beth looked back but saw no new activity.

"Wait. How did you get out? The text said no shots had been fired but the threat was being taken seriously and the school would remain on lockdown until the building was secured."

"That's so weird. I just left and nobody said anything about a shooter. The fire alarm went off at the end of my speech and security escorted us all to the parking lot. I waited for a few minutes but nobody knew if it was a drill so I decided to go back to work. I just called you to make sure nothing actually happened." Beth pulled back onto the street.

"That makes no sense. Why would they send an alert about a lockdown if there's no lockdown?" Beth wished she had an answer.

"I have no idea, but I'll let you know if I find out. Maybe the district got misinformation. There were two police cars there when I just drove by so maybe you'll get an update once they check the building. Could you let me know if you do?"

"Of course. I'm glad you're safe." Beth noticed her hand was shaking as she thanked her sister and ended the call.

In order to get through the rest of the day, Beth tucked away what she had seen and focused on her clients. But on the drive to her parents' house that evening she found herself more and more troubled that she hadn't told anyone what she saw. She hoped for time alone with her mom to talk, but she also didn't want to add to her burden. Before her father's illness Beth's relationship with her mom had been effortless. Unlike the rest of the family, Celeste had encouraged Beth to become a therapist. Beth longed for time with her mom now, as she walked up the sidewalk and peeked in the window. Maybe she'd find her alone. The kitchen was empty, so she knocked and opened the door.

"Anybody home?" she called.

No response. She took off her coat and shoes and made her way to the living room, where Celeste was on a call with a notepad and pen in hand. She smiled and motioned Beth toward the study. Beth found her father asleep there with a book in his lap. She quietly closed the door and went to the kitchen to pour herself a glass of wine to keep her company while she made dinner. The kitchen always smelled of garlic and olive oil, and it relaxed her.

"Hello, sweetheart," Celeste said, crossing the room to give her daughter a hug. "I'm so glad you're here. How are you?"

"I'm fine," Beth said. "The better question is how are you?"

"I'm glad to be home. I wish I could've been at the meeting in person. Are you OK?" she asked, taking a seat at the counter.

"Other than feeling frustrated that Andrea gets so mad at me I'm OK," Beth replied. "What can I do? I think she deflects her anger about Dad's illness onto me or maybe there are times when she just doesn't like me. I try to see her perspective but it's really hard, and I don't want you to be in the middle of it."

"Well, she's much edgier," Celeste said. "I guess it's put us all in a tailspin, hasn't it?"

"Definitely," Beth said, opening the refrigerator and scanning the contents to see what she could make for dinner.

"He holds a lot of power in this family and in the company. Your siblings are destabilized on both fronts, and I'm sure they're afraid even when they pretend they're fine." Beth turned to look at her, an assortment of vegetables in hand to make a stir-fry.

"I get that, Mom. I do. I'm sorry I haven't been more available to help, but I have a full client load and it's really intense right now. I'm in the middle of a situation that has me pretty freaked out." She bent down to get a cutting board.

Celeste looked at her in concern. "What's happening?" she asked. Even though she'd been preoccupied lately, Beth always appreciated that her mom was interested in what she did.

"I can't tell you specific details, but I think that a client of my supervisee might be dangerous and I'm not sure he isn't being influenced by one of my client's husbands. But it's all conjecture. I don't have any proof." She turned to the sink to put the red peppers and broccoli in the colander to wash them.

"What do you mean by dangerous?"

Beth paused and turned to look at her mom. "School shooter kind of dangerous."

"Are you talking about what happened today?" Celeste asked. "If you know something you have to report it, Beth."

Beth sighed. "It's complicated, Mom. The information I have came from one of my clients, and then I pieced her story together with something my supervisee told me about his client. The stories line up, but both situations involve confidentiality that I can't break without some form of proof. If I tried to report my concerns without any evidence the police would find my logic questionable. Anything I said would be based on assumption."

"I understand, but aren't warnings generally based on an assumption? Don't you have a duty to warn if there's a chance of danger?"

Beth paused to wipe away the cascade of water spilling from her eyes, a consequence of her vigorous onion chopping, before she replied. "Yes, I do if I know someone has a plan to hurt themselves or someone else. My problem is I don't know if there's such a plan and I have no way to find out." She opened the refrigerator to get the minced garlic and saw a container of leftover rice. "Can I use this tonight?" she asked, holding it up for her mom to see.

"Of course. I made too much the night before I left." She paused. "What about your supervisee? Can't you ask him to get more information?"

"I've tried, but I can't tell him what my client told me. It's a slippery slope. If I say even the slightest thing I could unintentionally break confidentiality. I shouldn't have even told you what I just did but I'm scared and very alone. It's a mess." She pulled the wok out from under the oven and placed it on the stove.

"Oh, Beth, I'm sorry. You know I'm here for you. Even if you can't talk about specifics." Celeste walked around the island and hugged her.

Beth hugged her mom for a bit longer than usual. "Thanks. I know." She noticed how thin her mom felt, and a new wave of concern washed over her.

"I thought about you on my drive back from Pittsburgh and how much I miss our morning runs," her mother said. "That seems like another lifetime, doesn't it?"

"It does," Beth said. "Which makes me realize how long it's been since you've gotten to go for a run at all. Let me come over on Saturday so you can get out. Dad and I could use some alone time so we can argue about my low-paying job and future dating prospects. It might give him a surge of energy." She laughed.

"You know your dad loves you. He just worries. He doesn't understand how you can afford to live on what you make and he thinks you need a partner. He's old. Give him a break," Celeste teased, picking up a knife and cutting board.

"I'm joking, Mom, but not about your free time on Saturday. It's on the calendar, so you have to go." Taking the knife and chopping board from her mother's hands, she said, "Now you need to sit back down and talk to me while I chop. Let me take care of you for a change." In a few minutes she rummaged up enough from the fridge to pull together a charcuterie plate.

"Here, have some of this," Beth said. "I can tell you haven't eaten a thing today, have you?" She started dicing up the vegetables.

"I made soup for your dad."

"I didn't ask what you made for Dad."

"That's fair. I haven't eaten," Celeste said, taking a bite of cheese and a date.

"I knew it," Beth said. "You need me!"

Celeste smiled. "I do. Wow. This is good. Did you bring these dates from home? They're delicious."

"Right! I told you they're good," Beth said. "I bought them yesterday so you'd finally try them. You should listen to me more often."

"I should. I'd probably have a lot less stress."

"You truly would, Mom," Beth said as she tried to gather her courage to bring up what was on her mind. "I forgot to tell you I saw Ben Kelly at the gym the other day. He said to say hello."

"How is he?"

"He's fine. Intense as usual. He wanted to know if Dad was up for a visit, so I told him to call you to check. He seemed upset." She watched her mother's face for a reaction.

"I'm sure he's worried about your dad, since his own father just died," Celeste said. Beth noticed a tightness in her mother's voice that hadn't been there a moment ago.

"I didn't get the impression he was worried dad was going to die. It seemed like something else." Beth paused her chopping to see her mother's reaction.

"Maybe you're right, and it's something else. Your father's a force, so it's hard to accept he's human like the rest of us. I don't think it's easy for him to accept either."

"What can't I accept?" Henry asked, leaning heavily on the doorframe to support himself as he walked into the room.

"That you aren't superhuman, dear," Celeste answered. She walked over to pull a chair out for him at the table. "Would you like some of this charcuterie plate? The dates are amazing. Beth knew if she paired them with wine, nuts, and cheese she'd finally get me to try them." Beth smiled as she watched her mother take the plate to the table so her father would sit there, which would be much more comfortable for him than a bar stool. Whatever else was happening, she couldn't deny the ease her parents had with each other: their marriage was a well-oiled machine.

"If I get the same deal, sure. I'm all in for a glass of wine," he said. "Don't suppose you'd pour me one of those would you, Beth?"

"Only if you explain to Andrea why I'm happily destroying your life," she replied, giving her dad a hug.

"She doesn't need to know about your evil plot," he said as he hugged her back.

"Hey, I was just telling Mom I saw Ben Kelly the other day and he wants to come over to see you. I told him to call Mom," Beth said. She poured a glass of wine for him and delivered it with a fresh napkin and plate.

Then she heard her phone ring. "My office answering service," she said, glancing at the screen. "I've got to take it." She walked toward the living room, unaware of the look that passed between her parents as she left.

10

CELESTE

Celeste caught Henry's gaze before turning away to bring her plate and glass to the table. Her alone time with Beth was over, and she felt the exhaustion settle back into her bones. She'd enjoyed listening to a few details of her daughter's life. It had been a diversion from her own concerns. Watching Beth chop vegetables and chat with her father, she knew that she had to do something soon before it was too late to protect her daughter's heart.

"No problem, just ditch me," her father joked as Beth left the room to take her call. But then he saw his wife's face and changed his tone. "What's wrong, Celeste?"

"Ben is the last person I want here to visit you," she said, arms crossed.

"What would you like me to do? Tell him my wife's uncomfortable with our relationship even though I promised his dad I'd be there for him?" Celeste felt the wall go up between her and her husband. She knew he would turn this around onto her, so she needed to try a different angle.

"I'm too drained to deal with him." Celeste kept her face emotionless, but she counted on Henry's need not to be a burden to her to get him to give in.

"I've put you through it," Henry said, placing his hand over hers and holding her gaze. "I'm sorry."

Celeste sighed. There was no use in reliving the past when there was no way to repair it. "Can we just focus on Beth tonight? She wants to spend time with you, Henry. She shared some serious stuff that's happened at work and she needs us."

"What's going on with Beth?" He sat back in his chair and released her hand.

"If she still wants to share, she'll tell you herself, but you have to listen and not give advice. You know she shuts down when you go into fix-it mode." Celeste decided to take advantage of Henry's subdued mood to try to get him to soften his tone toward Beth. Over the years she had learned when she could give him feedback without getting his overly defensive side to lash out at her.

"If she didn't need fixing, I wouldn't try to fix her," Henry said. His tone was gentler than his usual aggressive posture, so Celeste proceeded.

"Come on, you don't really think she needs fixing. You see how hard she works. Are you ever going to accept that she likes being a therapist?"

"It's a ridiculous job," he responded.

"To you, not to her. You might be surprised by her knowledge if you asked her questions instead of assuming you know what she does. I think you'd find her to be interesting if you didn't see it as a personal rejection of you." Celeste looked down the hall to be sure Beth was still on her call before she continued. "I think you need to try because it would be good for her to feel safe with you if Ben starts any problems."

"You're being paranoid. Ben's not going to start problems. He just misses his dad," Henry responded.

"I hope you're right, but can we agree not to include him in our family gatherings for right now, and just focus on our own kids?" Celeste knew she'd created a rare moment where Henry wanted to please her more than he needed to be right and get his own way.

"I'll see him on my own if that makes you more comfortable," Henry said.

"Thank you. I just need some space." Celeste picked up their used plates and walked to the sink to rinse them, ending further discussion between them about Ben. She didn't want Beth to walk in and hear them. In her gut she knew Henry was wrong about Ben; she had a sense he was looking for something, and she felt powerless to stop him.

11

BEN

Ben got up and walked around his apartment, determined to ignore his urge to call Henry. He appreciated the freedom his job as a sports journalist gave him, but right now it was torture. He had much too much time alone to think and too many ways to distract himself that weren't helping. For the last hour he'd tried to focus on writing his weekly column, but had zero words on the page and a waste of sixty minutes perusing the DNA site for new matches. The mystery of how Andrea was his half sister consumed him.

He felt bad about the curveball he'd thrown at Beth, but he saw no other alternative. Nobody else was safe to ask. His mom was still drowning in the grief of losing his father, so he refused to add to her pain. He doubted she knew the truth anyway, because he couldn't imagine she could hide something so huge for so long.

Memories of his parents rolled like a film through his mind as he sat back down at his desk. He closed his computer and just let them flow so he could look for clues within them. Nothing came. Nothing made sense. The rare flashes of conflict that came up were so short-lived they seemed inconsequential. The only fight he remembered was when his dad brought home a stray kitten and his mom said she didn't want another cat. His dad got upset, but he found a home for it the next day and that was it. No drama. Most of Ben's memories were of his parents being so close to each other they weren't always aware of him. He could think of many summer nights when he would leave the dinner table to go back outside to play and find them hours later still sitting there talking. It was hard to imagine what would have been different before he was born that could have led to an affair. It just didn't make sense to him. He opened his laptop, typed a sentence, and immediately deleted it.

Henry knows something, he thought, standing back up to get away from the blank screen. High school football just wasn't holding his attention long enough for him to write anything. If only he had an answer to the DNA question he knew he'd be able to focus, and he felt fairly confident the answer was in his dad's history, not his mother's.

Do not call him until Beth gets her results, he said to himself, putting his phone in a drawer so it would take an extra step to get to it. He'd told her he would try to give her time to investigate before he upset anyone in her family, and he wanted to keep his word. He felt guilty when he remembered the shocked look on her face when he asked her to take the test, and he didn't want to make it worse. At least not yet.

So many things felt awkward to him now, especially that he had almost asked Beth out in high school. He could not shake the thought that she was also his half sister. It was more palatable to him to think his father was Andrea's dad, since she was born before his parents met. No matter what the truth was, he was glad he hadn't dated Beth back then, because it would have put Henry in the middle of his personal business. He had no desire to be under that kind of scrutiny from Henry, who was critical enough without an actual reason to be. He wondered if one of the adults involved would have stopped him from asking her out if he had gone through with it. Surely whoever knew would have done something—at least he hoped they would have.

What a mess, he thought, as he pulled the garbage bag and recycling container from the bin. *You're a selfish ass. You knew she'd wonder if the coffee was a date, but you invited her anyway. You wanted answers no matter the cost. You didn't care about her feelings at all and for Christ's sake, she might be your sister! You charmed her to get what you want. Maybe Henry is your dad after all. He pulls shitty stunts like that all the time,* he thought as he tied up the bag.

I need to redirect. Get outside and get a grip. He pulled on a hoodie and slipped on his running shoes.

The walk from his apartment to the complex's disposal area got him out of his head long enough to gain perspective. Beth was just as affected as he was. He had to involve her for both of their sakes. He had to be patient. His answer was coming. He could wait a few more weeks.

12

MICHAEL

Michael paced from one side of his office to the other in an effort to
expend his nervous energy. Beth had helped him rehearse his client
assessment, but he still felt unsure that he would detect a real threat
if there was one. For the past three nights the same nightmare had haunted
him. Reporters on the lawn. Accusations and threats. Death. Shame. He was
afraid to fall asleep because the dream felt so real. A part of him worried it
foreshadowed his future, which caused him to compulsively check for news
on his phone. If the dream was prophetic, he believed it meant he was at fault
for missing the signs that his client was capable of murder.

I just need to quit my job, he thought. *Walk away.* But since he couldn't
ethically do that, he decided he should record the session so Beth could listen. *Get a grip*, he told himself. *It's too late to get permission and even if there
was time, what's my reason?* It was two minutes until 3 p.m. He was out of
options. He had to go to the lobby and get his client.

"Come on back," Michael said. *Be calm.* His client appeared to look up
from his phone, but his eyes were hidden behind the white-blond hair hanging in his face.

"You need a bigger waiting room," his client responded, clearly uncomfortable with the couple seated beside him.

"How long have you been here?" Michael asked in an attempt to keep
him under control until the door closed.

SLOW SLIDE INTO THE TRUTH

"Five minutes. Five minutes too long."

"I thought your mom wanted to talk to me today. The front desk said she left a message for me that she wanted to come to the first few minutes of your session."

"I told her everything was great and she didn't need to come. I don't get why you called her anyway," he said, slouching into the farthest chair away from Michael.

Michael sat down quickly. He wanted a view of his client's reaction before he responded. "I decided to check in with all of my clients who could've been affected by the bomb threat," he said.

"Really? The bomb threat? That's a joke." The boy smirked and for a moment Michael questioned himself before he pulled it together.

"Huh. Tell me why you think it's a joke." Michael leaned forward in his chair.

"I just know it was." There was the smirk again.

"Do you know who did it?" Michael held his gaze.

"Maybe."

"Do you know why?"

"I told you. It's a joke." He pushed his hair out of his face and stared back at Michael.

"If you know who did it, don't you think you should tell someone?"

"Why do you care? Do you get a bonus for outing kids?" He laughed.

"No. I don't get a bonus for outing kids," Michael said in a patient tone. "I called because I was concerned you might be afraid to go to school." He realized he was pressing too hard, and needed to move the focus from the bomb threat to his client's mental health.

"Yeah, no, I'm not afraid." The boy looked out of the window.

"Good. I'm glad you know it's a joke and you're not afraid. Let's move on. How's your rage been this week?" he asked as he leaned back in his chair. *Be cool, Michael. Jesus, just calm down.*

"I didn't want to kill my mom for dragging me here, so I guess those buzzer things did something. I'm still pissed, though." He looked away from Michael.

"About therapy?"

"About everything. Sometimes it hits me hard. Knocks me on my ass out of nowhere." He glanced back up but then avoided Michael's eyes.

"Give me an example." Michael felt the tension in his body start to ease.

"OK. Just now. I got here early. I'm in a good mood. I just wanted to sit in the lobby and listen to music for a few minutes before I came in. You know, to calm my mind like you said. When I got to the top of the stairs, and saw it was full of people, I got mad and just wanted to go back down the steps and leave. What the fuck?" he questioned as he moved his foot away from a spider crawling across the carpet.

Michael saw a glimmer of vulnerability and fear. "Was it anyone specific in the lobby?"

"Not really. I had school bullshit all day and I just wanted to sit and chill before I had to come in here and get drilled." He let out an exasperated breath.

"Is that what therapy feels like? Getting drilled?" Michael thought he saw a crack in the kid's armor.

"Isn't that your job? To figure me out." He looked up.

"My job is to help you understand yourself so you can manage your anger. Your mom brought you here because you said you hated your life. I want to help you to not hate it." Michael again held his gaze.

"I just told you I feel a little bit better. I just wish people would give me some space." A moment of connection occurred between them.

"Like who?"

"My parents. My dad is mostly cool, but my mom always asks me about stuff. She's so intense about college. She stresses me out. I wish I'd never told her any of it." His eyes went back to the ground. The spider was moving back toward the wall.

"Could you ask her for some space?"

"Maybe, but then she freaks out."

"How did she react when you told her not to come in today?"

"She looked relieved." Michael thought he noticed a tone of disappointment in his client's voice. Maybe the kid did want help.

"You could ask her for space when you need it. She probably just wants to be sure you're OK." Michael hoped his client was really opening up.

"I'll try, but I think she'll just bug me."

"You can report back and we'll see who's right. Hopefully it's me," Michael said in an attempt to lighten up the mood. "So tell me how the thoughts are that we worked on last week. Any better?"

"Those are, but I have other ones."

Michael stood up so he could reach his light bar and slide it in front of his client. "Want to tell me about them?" he said as he handed him the tappers.

"Can we do the sand thing instead?" Michael pushed the light bar back into its spot against the wall.

"Sure. You know where the figures are. I'll set it up," Michael said. While he opened the sand tray table, he watched his client methodically sort through the miniatures in his cabinet. Michael wondered if the tray he created would reveal something, or if his client just planned to waste time until the hour was over. He hoped the kid would try to help himself and do the work.

One by one he arranged a tray full of soldiers facing the top left corner, where he half-buried a small group of random figures and enclosed them in a circle he drew in the sand. Michael watched the intensity on his client's face grow as the soldiers got almost close enough to touch the circle, but didn't cross the line. For a moment both Michael and his client stared at the tray in silence and then his client sat back in his chair and stared at Michael.

"Intense," Michael said.

"Yeah."

"What's happening?"

"A lot."

"Want to share?"

"Not really." He looked directly at Michael.

Michael paused for a moment to give him space. "Can I ask about the figures that are half-buried?"

"They're trying to escape."

"From the soldiers?"

"From the anger."

"Can you help them?"

"Nobody can help them."

"Do you want to?"

Silence.

"Are you thinking?"

"No."

"Do you feel like those figures?"

Silence.

"Can you tell me about the soldiers?"

"They do what they're told."

"Whose telling them?"

Silence.

"Does this feel like the lobby did today?"

Silence and a smirk.

"We only have a few more minutes. Any thoughts you want to share?"

"I like this tray."

"Care to say more?"

"Time to go, Doc," his client said as he stood up to leave. He crushed the spider under his foot.

"Have a good week," was all Michael could get out before his client slipped out of the door.

Michael's heart was beating in his ears as he snapped a picture of the tray to put in his client's file. What the fuck did it mean? Michael held his breath until the picture was uploaded and he could analyze the scene. He pulled each figure out and laid them side by side and took another photograph. Each figure had a religious undertone. A priest. A woman kneeling in prayer. A buddha. A Christmas tree. A person holding a song book. He was glad he was going to talk to Beth now, especially after seeing the boy smash the spider.

"Those must be some interesting case notes," Michael said as he knocked on Beth's half-open door.

She looked startled and quickly closed her laptop, and then looked at her watch. Clearly she'd forgotten it was time for his supervision.

"Fascinating," she said in an all-business tone. To Michael, it seemed like she'd been thinking about something else entirely.

"I've got a pretty interesting one too. Take a look at this," he said, sharing the photos with her. "That's his sand tray from today."

"Is he baiting you?" Beth asked.

"I have no idea."

"Want to tell me about the session?"

"Sure. When I approached him he was agitated because of the crowded waiting room, but he evaded my question about why. He said the bomb threat was a joke and the person who did it is too smart to get caught, but he wouldn't say if he actually knew who it was. He thought it was strange that I cared who did it. I had to back off. Then he asked to do a sand tray. He created this and he was done. Out the door. No processing."

She looked from Michael's phone back to Michael. "What do you think?"

"Anything I think at this point is conjecture." He took his phone back and sat down across from her.

"I get that, but do you think he's involved?"

"Maybe."

"You want to be more specific?"

"He knows something. He was super intense, but I don't know if he knows something or if he did something. I just don't know."

"OK, then we have nothing to report. Just keep me up-to-date if anything changes."

"Yes, ma'am," he said as he opened the next client file for them to discuss and tried to push the uneasiness of the sand tray out of his mind.

13

BETH

On her Saturday morning run, Beth's thoughts buzzed like a swarm of bees. Every attempt to focus on one thing caused the other thoughts to get louder. Exasperated, she politely asked them all to land on a hydrangea bush with a few remaining flowers so she could listen to them one at a time.

Ben. Let's listen to the bee that's buzzing about Ben first, she thought as she whispered thank you to the others for being patient. She knew her clients would worry if they saw her on a run, talking to imaginary bees, so she was careful to keep her inner world to herself and her eyes open for possible clients on the path.

When she tuned in to this anxious part of her she was amazed by how quickly it shared its concerns.

"You thought it was a date!" the bee scolded. *"What if he's your brother? You could have kissed your brother! That's disgusting!"*

"I wasn't going to kiss my brother. Calm down. And he's probably not my brother. Can you wait for the results before you freak out?" She sidestepped a puddle.

"Your parents are going to find out, and they're going to be so mad! You should've said no."

"Mad at me? They're the ones with a secret. Nobody can be mad at me. I should be mad at them." She increased her speed.

"That's a laugh. You don't get mad at anyone. You just do what everyone wants you to do, which is why you took the stupid test."

"I did that for me." She turned the corner into the sun, and the brightness made her eyes tear, the drops slipping down her cheeks.

The bee lowered its voice. *"Did you? I thought you did it for Ben."*

"Fine. At first I did it for Ben, but in the end I did it for me." Was that true? she wondered.

"Whatever you want to tell yourself," the bee taunted.

"You're impossible. Can you try to relax until I get the results?"

"If you stop flirting with your brother."

"I did not *flirt with my brother. And he's not my brother. Well, maybe he's not my brother. Can you just stop? I wasn't flirting."*

"You hoped it was a date," the bee said accusingly.

"So what if I did? I don't want it to be a date now, that's for sure."

Beth shook the voice out of her head. Thankfully, the other bee voices seemed to have quieted. Had she flirted with Ben when she'd met him at the coffee shop? She played their meeting over in her mind.

She remembered feeling relaxed by the smell of coffee when she arrived. She'd heard Ben say her name from across the room. He was at a cozy table. *I remember smiling*, she thought. *Did I smile too much? No.*

"I got you a black coffee," he'd said as she sat down. She was happy he remembered. *Did I think he was flirting? Maybe for a minute. Did I like it? Kind of. Maybe*

"How is your dad?" he'd asked.

"His treatments are hard but we hope they'll work," she'd answered.

"Glad to hear it," he replied, pausing. "Have you ever taken a DNA test?" Shocked, she'd said, "No. Why?"

"Andrea is my half sister."

"That's not possible."

He reached down to the computer bag at this feet, pulled his laptop onto the table, and opened it. He turned the computer toward her. She was looking at his DNA results. The name of one of his matches jumped out.

"Maybe it's a different Andrea Mitzo," she'd said. His brow furrowed. "It could be," she'd insisted.

"How many Andrea Mitzos do you think there are in this world?" he'd asked her.

"Hundreds," she'd replied. Then he showed her a screen shot of Andrea Mitzo's results, which had her picture. It was her sister.

After sitting a while in silence, she'd asked him, "Do you think she knows?"

"I don't think so. When I got the email with my results, I opened it right away. As soon as I saw her name, I took the screen shot I just showed you, then made my account private so no one searching the website can see my matches."

"Look, I'm in shock too," he'd said. "I only did the test for the health report, because my dad died so young. I wasn't looking for long-lost relatives."

"When did you find out?" she'd asked him.

"Last Monday."

"How can this be?"

Sitting in the coffee shop with Ben, relief that Andrea didn't know had washed over her. *Why was I relieved?* Beth thought to herself now as she jogged along. *That's weird. Do I think I can stop her from finding out? She has to know. He's her brother. Oh my god, he's her brother. Why has that just sunk in?*

In the coffee shop, she and Ben had sat across from each other and discussed the possibilities.

"Either my dad had an affair with your mom or my mom had an affair with your dad," he'd said.

"My mom would never do that," she'd replied.

"Mine either."

"What now?"

He'd put a box on the table between them. "You can help me figure it out by taking this test," he'd said. Beth had stared at the box, a roaring sound filling her ears.

"Are you OK?" he'd asked. She kept staring at the box.

"If you won't do it then I'll have to ask Carrie or Jonathan, because all of my other matches are too distantly related," he'd said.

The roar got louder. If she'd said no, then it could be ugly. Carrie would keep it private but then she'd have to see the family at work every day and act normal until she got her results. That seemed like too much to ask of her.

On the other hand, Jonathan would get angry and make a huge scene, which also seemed like too much.

Beth hadn't wanted her parents to have to deal with all that, so she'd agreed to take the test. She remembered grabbing it and hiding it in her bag. At that point there had definitely been no flirtation at all. *I didn't look in his eyes*, Beth recalled. *I felt nauseous. Like a traitor to my family. Why did I agree? Why? I wasn't thinking about what could happen, and now it's too late. The test is mailed and I can't un-mail it.*

They'd entertained other possibilities: maybe his dad had gotten someone pregnant and she didn't want kids, so Beth's parents rescued the baby and adopted her—adopted Andrea. If Beth wasn't his sister, that would rule out her dad having an affair with his mom. That's what Ben thought was probably the truth. He'd asked if there were pictures of Celeste when she was pregnant with Andrea. *What did I say? I said I'd check.* Beth hoped there weren't. Adoption was a good answer, especially since Ben's dad was dead. It would be easier. It would make her dad a wonderful best friend who helped out Ben's dad. *That's what I want to be true.*

Beth paused her replay to check her heart rate and pace, which were both faster than she realized. She gave herself a moment to just focus on her run before she went back to processing what had happened in the coffee shop that morning.

Ben had said, "My counselor was right to have me talk to you."

"Who's your counselor?" she'd asked.

"Michael Ellis." She was stunned. Could this get any worse? Her supervisee is counseling her possible half-brother?

"The Michael Ellis who works in my office?" she'd asked in a high-pitched voice.

"How many Michael Ellises do you think there are doing therapy in this town?"

Absolutely not flirting then, Beth told herself as her feet beat a rhythm on the pavement.

"Did he tell you to talk to me specifically?" She winced at the memory of how panicked she had sounded.

"Of course not," Ben had said. "I'm not an idiot. I didn't tell him your name. He told me to talk to the woman I had told him about who I grew up with who is the youngest sister of my half sister."

She'd taken a breath then. *I'd felt spinny*, she recalled. He'd said he didn't want this to get out either. She could use initials or something for the test, he'd told her. "Just make sure you add me as a connection, but only me. Pretend you're a private eye, like you did as a kid. Remember how you were always sneaking around spying on people?" *OK, so I laughed. It wasn't flirtatious.* Her grandmother had bought her the spy set.

"I remember," she'd said. "I wonder if my grandmother knew what happened?"

And that had been it. Beth was sure. Ben had said thank you, they'd had a friendly hug, and she'd said she would call him soon. He'd said that sounded good, and apologized for dragging her into this, but felt he had no choice.

I'm letting this go, she told herself. By the end of her run she was able to release the memory and she chose to leave the rest of her chaotic thoughts in the hydrangeas. Her next stop was her parents', and she wanted to arrive with a clear, calm mind.

• • •

"Anybody home?" Beth called out when she got to her parents' house. It was unusually quiet. *That's odd*, she thought as took off her shoes in the kitchen and took inventory. Something felt off. No radio. No TV. No food on the stove. The kitchen door unlocked. *Don't panic, he's just napping*, she told herself, but when she found her father's office empty, she ran up the stairs and knocked on the closed bedroom door.

"Come in," her mother responded.

When Beth opened the door she saw her father tucked into bed and her mother kneeling on the bathroom floor wiping up water.

"Your father wanted a bath."

Beth looked from her mother's exhausted face to her father, who had a grin from ear to ear.

"How did you get her to let you take a bath without someone here to help you get out?"

"I'm charming. Even in my weakened state."

"Not so charming, Henry," Celeste said. "Annoying is a better word. You're relentless. I couldn't listen to you beg for one more minute."

He pushed himself up into a seated position so he could see her reaction. "You love it when I'm charming. You can't hide it."

"You'd be surprised what I can hide. You just know I always give in," she responded.

"Have you two had lunch?" Beth interrupted.

"No. She won't feed me because she's so taken by my charm that she can't leave my side. She's really smitten."

"Oh yes, watch me swoon," Celeste said, drying her hands.

Beth realized as long as they had an audience, this was not going to stop. "I'll let you two battle it out while I make you lunch. Any requests?"

"How about a gin and tonic?"

"Dad, seriously."

Her mom crossed the room and gave her a hug. "Anything you make will be great. He still has to do physical therapy, so take your time. We'll be awhile."

"Try not to give Mom a hard time," Beth said as she kissed her dad on the top of his head and left the room. On her way down the steps, she realized she had a perfect window of time to look at photo albums. She could get some good smells going in the kitchen to cover her sleuthing. Adrenaline rushed through her when she opened the freezer. *Yes! My pasta sauce.* She was grateful her meeting last week with Ben had sent her into a cooking frenzy that led to bags of frozen sauce. *If I pull out stuff for salad and leave it on the counter then I'll have an excuse if they come down and catch me. I'll just say I was in the bathroom. The smell of the sauce will throw them off while I search.* Within five minutes she had sauce on the stove and a mess on the counter, and she was off to the study.

When she walked in her burst of energy stalled as she stared at the bookcases full of photo albums. Where should she start? Logic says Mom would organize chronologically, so start at the top. She pulled down an album and was greeted by her grandparents smiling back at her. *Help me,* she said as tears filled her eyes. She could use her grandma's wisdom right now. Breezing through the pages, she realized the photographs were of the first year of her parents' marriage. Too early. Three albums later she struck gold as she followed the thread from a baby shower with her very pregnant mother in the center of the gifts to the hospital with her mom holding newborn Andrea and her dad all smiles in the background. There's no way they could fake a pregnancy and a birth, she thought. She took a photo of the photo with her cell phone and texted it to Ben.

There's our proof, he texted back immediately.

Proof of what? she texted back. No answer. She tried to analyze the faces and body language in the photos. Were there any clues that would tell her the truth? Then she heard her parents' footsteps upstairs. Startled, she dropped the album, dislodging some loose photos and an envelope from an inside flap. She grabbed the envelope to put it back but the unfamiliar handwriting drew her attention. It was addressed to her mother, and the postmark was dated a few months before her parents' wedding. Beth opened the envelope and pulled out the letter inside.

> **My dearest Celeste,**
> *Please reconsider. I know you think you're happy, but I don't see you in that life. Why would you settle? Why would you give up your dreams? I won't ask again. I will respect your decision. I just need you to hear my words one more time. You were made for bigger things than this path you've chosen.*
>
> > **With a forever and embracing love,**
> > **G.**

Beth sat down on the floor and took a photo of the letter and the address on the envelope before quickly returning it to the back of the album where it had been hidden. Intrigued, she hurried to the kitchen with more questions than answers.

14

THE COUPLE

The sound machine's crashing waves had pushed her nervous system to its edge. Her eyes were glued to the ticking clock in the waiting room. Ten minutes early was ten more minutes of torture. Dr. Linn had suggested they each find individual therapists but neither of them had, so they were early and noncompliant and she had ten extra minutes to question why. It concerned her that no one else in the lobby seemed bothered by the noise. They just stared at their phones or read magazines like the sound of the waves was just what it was, a brilliant sound barrier and not a plot to make them crawl out of their skin.

She didn't consider that the sound had become linked to her husband's dark secret, a secret that had consumed her thoughts for the last seventy-two days. Seventy-two days of not being able to keep food in her body. Seventy-two days of being overwhelmed with the desire to walk into the lake with rocks on her ankles so she could sink to the bottom and not think anymore. She didn't want to die, but she did want to stop feeling this razor-sharp pain. She wished she could hand it all to him. Let him have the intensity of it. That would be her best revenge.

She watched the clock turn to 6 p.m. at the exact moment Dr. Linn's door opened. The routine, the commonness, caused something inside of her to snap. Angry flames danced in her mind screaming *He's a liar! He never loved you! And nobody cares!* She tried to ignore them, but that made them get louder. *He loves therapy because he loves the attention,* the voices taunted. The more she tried to ignore them the meaner they got. *He's a liar. He fakes his sadness so she thinks he's sorry, but they both think you're the problem.*

"Hello you two, come on back," Dr. Linn said with a hopeful, chipper tone. "How was your week?"

"We had a great week," he answered, walking to his usual spot on the couch.

"We had a great week if you're fine with a husband who won't answer a simple question like whether he took days off work to go to the club or if he ever touched anyone. It was a great week if you think it's fine to avoid all of your wife's questions," she responded. She sat down as close to the other edge of the couch as she could and put her purse between them.

"So we have different ideas about the week. Let's start there. Did you use the communication exercise when you asked your questions?" Dr. Linn asked her.

"I tried your method, but he won't answer a direct question. He says that isn't the point of your exercise because facts aren't going to help and we're supposed to focus on our feelings. My feelings are focused on the facts. My feelings are feelings of anger that my husband has a fetish and he isn't open about the details. It's my life. I deserve to know what happened," she said.

"Do you agree that the week went the way she just described it?" Dr. Linn asked her husband.

"I guess," he answered. He sat back and rubbed his temples, eyes closed.

"Can you explain why you don't want to give your wife the answers she needs? Last week I recall you said you would do anything to regain her trust and repair your marriage. What's changed?" she asked.

"I don't see the point," he said. "I confessed. It's over. I won't go back. Every detail I give her is just one more thing for her to obsess about, which drives her to ask more questions. What does it matter? I watched people have sex and I won't do it again. Why do I have to give the intimate details? It just makes it worse."

Dr. Linn turned to her. "Would you like to answer him?" she asked.

She fought back angry tears. "Yes. It's my life! I need to know what was happening in *my life*. When I drove to Columbus to see our daughter at college, were you at the club? Did you call me from the lobby? Did you bring a couple to our house? To our bed? You did this, not me. You blew things up. You destroyed my security and my future. I deserve to know the details of what you did while I made your dinner and slept with you. I deserve to know."

"I want you to focus on what your wife just said. Tune into her feelings. What do you see that wasn't there prior to your confession?" Dr. Linn looked at her husband again, who ran his hands through his hair then held his head in frustration.

"Insecurity. Hurt and insecurity," he responded.

"How does it make you feel to see her pain?"

"I feel like a piece of shit. I feel like I don't deserve her anymore and that if our kids found out they'd hate me," he replied.

"Is that why you avoid her questions? Because it makes you feel like a piece of shit?" Dr. Linn asked.

"Of course it is. Every time I have to describe what I did I have to look at it and see what a horrible, selfish person I was. Every answer breaks her a little bit more. I hate to see what I've done. I hate to keep hurting her."

Does he really feel that way? The room was silent. "I didn't know," she finally said, aware she may have missed something important by dismissing everything he said.

"What did you think?" he asked.

"I thought you missed it and you were angry I made you stop going." She sank back into the couch.

"I do miss it sometimes, but not as much as I'd miss you if you divorce me. I want to be with you," he said.

"It would be good to start our communication exercise right here, if you both feel comfortable to explore it now." Dr. Linn handed the wife the wooden owl to give her the first turn to talk.

"OK. I guess what I want you to understand is that my questions come from a place of fear, not as a way to punish you. Now I'm constantly afraid I'm missing something and that whatever I'm missing will cause me more pain. Like your fetish has. The fact that I had no idea is why it's been so scary." She passed him the owl.

"I just repeat what I heard, right? No response until she feels that I understand her message?" He looked at Dr. Linn, who nodded in agreement.

He held the owl and looked into his wife's eyes. "What I'm hearing you say is that you need answers to feel safe. My secret betrayed your trust and it blindsided you because you thought you were safe. Now you need to know everything, so there's no question about something under the surface that could unexpectedly come up."

"That's close, but there's a little bit more. Did you understand that I'm not trying to punish you?" She noticed a slight shift in his disposition as he leaned into the exercise, which encouraged her to continue.

The hour passed as they stated and restated their feelings and for the first time in seventy-two days, she was able to calm the screaming banshees of anger and distrust enough to hear him. In their absence, she saw a tiny spark of hope that had been desperate to ignite.

15

BETH

For the entire couples' session, Beth had been distracted by the image of the letter she'd found. The handwriting on the note and the image of the signature—G.—materialized in her mind and she'd struggled to stay focused. For once the couple had communicated well, which must have relaxed her enough to let her own thoughts emerge.

Now, after the session, she sat in her office and pondered the possibilities. What if her mother had had an affair? What if it had started as a night of drinking and sharing too much and then she had fallen in love? What if it was just one of those things that happened, a best friend and the wife sneaking around for a lifetime to keep the peace, suffering in silence and never talking about leaving their spouses? What if G. had been onto something? Maybe her mom had never been happy with her dad, and Ben's dad had made her happy. They certainly had lots of family events where all of them were together. What if all that time they had been staring longingly at each other at game nights and barbecues?

Beth got up from her desk and walked to the window. The town below her, her hometown, looked like it always had. Small changes happened, sure, but she could count on the bell tower and the green, the pedestrian traffic and the deli, the pace of life here, to stay the same. That consistency had drawn her back after grad school. That and her father's insistence that if she wasn't going to join the family business, she could at least live nearby.

Ironically, it was one of the few times she didn't mind his persistence, and now her presence here might be the reason his life would turn upside down.

It was too bizarre for Beth to accept the possibility that Henry wasn't her father, but she had to admit that it was in the realm of possibility. Andrea being Ben's sister was one thing, but if both the oldest and youngest of Henry's children shared Ben's DNA, that would be too much. Soon they would know, and then the conversation would shift. Right now the truth was that these two factors created questions with uncomfortable answers and if the obvious answers were correct, then Beth's mom had lived a double life. What if Ben kept pushing for her to get her mom to tell her the truth, and the truth was an affair? Would he tell her father and risk affecting his health? Beth couldn't imagine how hard that would be for her dad when he was already so weak. She wanted to call Ben and tell him to stop being so selfish, but a part of her needed answers as badly as he did.

The questions kept coming, but Beth decided it was a waste of time to contemplate the what-ifs when she still had notes to write from earlier in the day. She reluctantly left her perch beside the window on the arm of the couch and returned to her desk. When she opened the next note she needed to write, Pastor Dan's name popped up on the screen as payor. Beth cringed when she saw it, remembering her slight overreaction when her client had brought him up in session. She had just wanted to be clear she did not report to him so her client would know her privacy was safe, but for some reason she had sounded defensive, and she wasn't sure why. Since Eleanor handled billing, she rarely thought about how her clients paid for their sessions, so she wasn't sure why it bothered her that Pastor Dan made arrangements to cover this one. All she knew was that it made her uncomfortable. Maybe it was because she had heard stories about him all her life, even though she'd never actually met him. Her parents hated him, especially her father, and he mentioned his dislike every time they saw him around town. He didn't talk details, though; those were hazy, but she knew that when her grandfather died her father had found evidence that the pastor had pressured him to make donations he couldn't afford. Beth remembered her parents arguing about it and she knew her father had confronted him, but that was all she knew.

In a moment of clarity, she realized Pastor Dan was the least of her problems. She needed to put her unease aside and get back to work.

When she finished writing her case notes she decided to peruse the DNA website one more time before she left the office. She was desperate to see if she could find a reasonable explanation for the situation, so Ben had given her his password and access to his profile while she waited for her results. The list of DNA relatives tied to both him and Andrea immediately overwhelmed her. In fact, everything about the website annoyed her. There was no way for her to take off the privacy setting without Andrea seeing his profile, which limited her ability to dig any further into his matches. Several things remained clear. Andrea was his sister. There was no way to deny it. Beth did not know any of his other close relatives, but he said they were all on his mother's side, and none of them were surprises. The majority of his matches were distant relatives with no identifiable markers to help her in her search. It felt unreal, like she was going to wake up and realize it was all a mistake. Yes, clearly there had to be a mistake. Even if the mistake was a drunken night with her dad and Ben's mom that led to an unplanned pregnancy, that would be much better than the alternative of her mom lying to her and everyone else their entire lives.

She felt an intense pressure in her chest and her breath became shallow as the full potential of the realization hit her. *Oh my god, what if it's my mom who did this to us? She's the person I trust the most.* If it was true Celeste had hidden an ongoing affair, then Beth knew the ripple effect on her family was going to be much more monumental than she could imagine in the moment. She needed to stop the thoughts and get out of the office for the night. She'd somehow missed the sound of the bells at seven o'clock. If she didn't leave soon she'd again be the last person in the building, and this time the only reason would be her own racing thoughts.

16

THE DANCER

Her quiet mind felt oddly familiar, like someone from her distant past she almost remembered. Familiar, like a comforting stranger. She had wanted to believe Dr. Linn when she said she could help her find that part of herself again. Dr. Linn and her dreaded meds. Maybe they had both helped.

She couldn't remember much of the last three years and most of her knew that not remembering was a blessing. She felt haunted by the remnants of her psychosis that seeped back through any time a crack formed in the protective wall her psychotropic medications created. Today Dr. Linn had helped her to leave her fear of those demons in a container on the shelf in her office. The hope was that this would allow space for the spark of life she had recently connected to. She was surprised to feel a sense of lightness as she walked down the steps and into the parking lot to find her ride.

When she spotted her driver she sent up a little prayer he wouldn't talk about her family all the way home. Luckily on the drive into Serenity he was on a call with one of his daughters, so he whispered an apology when he dropped her off and said he'd be done before she came back out. She hadn't seen him in a few years, but he was an active member of the church and knew her family, which meant he might have heard gossip about her. Most people had no idea what had happened when she got sick, but she was never sure and preferred to avoid any conversations about it. She knew her family didn't blame her for her behavior during the worst moments of her illness, but she was ashamed of how much suffering it had caused them.

"I'm all patched up," she said as she opened the door to the car and hopped into the back seat.

"You're welcome to sit up front," he said.

"It's OK. I like to pretend you're my chauffeur when I sit back here. Like I'm famous or something," she said with a laugh.

"Fine by me," he said as he pulled out of the parking lot.

"Could you drop me at the middle school on 10th Street instead of my apartment? I have a recovery meeting there. I'll be early, but I'd like to have some time alone before people arrive."

"Tough session?"

"No tougher than any other." She watched his face in the rearview mirror.

"It's good you go." He looked up and they locked eyes.

She looked away. "It is."

"I saw your parents and your little brother last week and they seemed good. How's your older brother? He's overseas, right?"

"He's in France, but he'll be home for the holidays. He finishes grad school in May and then who knows where he'll go. Somewhere fabulous, I'm sure."

"What's he study? The wife thought he was in medical school, but I told her that was you. She was glad to hear I'm driving you for the pastor today. She's always liked you kids. Thought you were smart and all. She actually sent you a bag of cookies she made. They're on the front seat so don't forget them."

"Please tell her I said hello and thank her for me. I always looked forward to snack time at Vacation Bible School because I knew she'd bring her sugar cookies with sprinkles. To me they were the best part of the week, but don't tell the pastor."

"He'd hate that, wouldn't he! But I don't think you're the only kid who showed up for the cookies. She made so many that she'd ice for hours every night before VBS." He glanced back at her again in the rearview mirror, but her gaze was far away.

"Please let her know they were greatly appreciated and that my brother studies art history. He wants to teach in a university. And yes, I was the one in med school. I had to drop out after the first semester."

"Do you think you'll go back?"

"I have no idea. I guess if I don't my little brother will have to be the hero and be the one the family brags is a doctor. Right now I'm OK to just make coffee. This is a perfect place to drop me," she said as they exited the highway onto Main Street. The conversation had begun to puncture her tiny balloon of hope.

"Are you sure?"

"Yeah . . . this is perfect. The school is right down the next street and the meeting starts in an hour. It'll give me some time to journal," she said, gathering her things.

"Well OK then, don't forget the cookies," he said, turning and handing her the bag. "You take good care of yourself now."

"I will. Thank you again." She closed the door and gratefully ended the conversation.

His questions had ripped away the veil of anonymity her new life provided. She needed the walk to refocus. Here she could be the slightly unusual neighborhood barista and not the fallen rock star medical student she was in her hometown. Her driver's well-intentioned attempt to treat her normally simply shined a spotlight on the dichotomy of her two worlds.

When she arrived at the middle school, she realized the janitor down a faraway hall was the only other person there, and she relaxed. The appeal of the almost empty school helped her to shift back into a happier space. She breathed in the familiar school smell as she made her way toward the auditorium. She could almost feel the presence of her four-year-old self in a sequined tutu with all of her dance mates, their teacher off on the right side of the stage guiding the tiny troupe through their first recital.

The memory brought a smile to her face as she pulled herself up onto the stage and dropped her coat and backpack on the floor. She was careful not to let the cookies spill as she removed her shoes and pushed her belongings to the back wall. When she stood up, her limbs began to move to a faraway melody and the dance began to reconnect her spirit to her body. Her mind felt clear as her bare feet glided across the wood of the stage. A glimmer of freedom.

Growing up in a "nice" midwestern family, there were accepted rules. She was supposed to work hard, go to church, respect her parents. Be kind and friendly. She could have her own identity as long as she followed those rules. It was OK if she got a little crazy as long as she apologized and still liked normal things like football. She could question those rules as long as she respected the boundaries. There was a line. A clear, defined line that was embedded in the collective unconscious.

Somewhere along the way she'd lost sight of the line and then the line disappeared into her mental illness. Now the only thing that held her to earth was a bunch of pills and her sheer determination not to continue to blow everything up. She knew if she ended her life her family wouldn't recover, and that was a line she was desperate not to cross. No matter how painful it had become, she fought for ways to create meaningful moments.

Captivated, she lost herself in the power of her muscles as they engaged, awakening a joy long asleep in her body. Slowly, purposefully, she floated across the floor. Fully there. Fully herself. Every past shadow gone in that moment in time. All the future fears momentarily silent. Her essence connected to the music in her heart and it gave her the space to just be.

She danced freely, unaware that anyone saw her, even though the janitor had passed by a few times without a sound.

17

THE QUEEN

When she scheduled her appointment for the end of the day, her intention was to get Dr. Linn to relax and trust her. Apparently she wasn't a morning person, since their last session had been awkward after abruptly being moved to 8:30 a.m. There was no more time for awkward. She needed an expert witness in court and she had to convince Dr. Linn her son was in danger. There was too much at stake for her to let her therapist ruin it. Today it was do or die.

She was desperate for movement. Change. Work had become unpleasant with the drop in both alumni gifts and applications for enrollment. She blamed the propaganda for the school levy that touted the district's high test scores and college admission rates. People in the community had begun to question why they needed to pay tuition when the public schools were top-notch. Her only choice was to redirect the media to all the concerns in the public schools.

She observed the people who were obviously parents in Serenity's lobby and wondered what would scare them. None of them made eye contact with her, so she assumed they found her intimidating. If she could make them feel like they had failed their children, enrollment would skyrocket.

She shifted her focus to the therapists greeting their clients and wondered if they saw them as dollar signs like she saw her students. She doubted it. They seemed much weaker than she was. So calm and compassionate.

If money was a motivation she'd know how to manage Dr. Linn, but it seemed her driving force was her empathy button, and today she needed to hit it hard.

Speak of the devil, she thought, glancing up just as Dr. Linn led an emotional couple out of her office. When she caught the man's eye she recognized him immediately as one of her husband's colleagues. Uncomfortable, she quickly looked down at the magazine in her lap to regain her composure before Dr. Linn took the two steps back to her. She hoped he had the discretion not to mention seeing her to her husband.

"That's gorgeous," Dr. Linn said, referring to the landscape on the open page.

"Portofino, one of my favorites." She closed the magazine and placed it back on the table.

"I can see why. Come on back. Can I get you some water?" she asked.

She held up her coffee cup. "No thanks. I came with my fuel to power me through to the end of the day."

"How's your week been?" Dr. Linn asked after she closed the door behind them. She took her usual seat opposite the couch.

"Tough. I'm terrified for my son and work's unbearable. My staff has no grasp of the fiscal side of education or how to help me increase profits to the level that the board expects."

"Are their expectations realistic?" Dr. Linn asked.

"Probably not but I'm so distracted by my sociopath husband I can't trust my judgment," she said, twisting sideways on the couch to look out the window.

"No improvement?"

She turned back sharply to emphasize her point. "None. He lost it Saturday morning when I asked him not to go to an anti-religion group rally organized by a radical offshoot of the national organization. The actual organization has warned people to avoid these extremists, but he doesn't care. He was so furious with me he put his hand through the wall in our kitchen on his way out the door. Of course the local news covered the rally. Luckily he wasn't in the footage. Sunday morning he insisted our son go to breakfast with him instead of church with me. When I confronted him, he said I could choose to be brainwashed but he won't allow our son to go anymore. He's so bizarre. It's like an alien has taken over his brain."

"That's what you said last week. I'm interested in what happened to cause this drastic change?" Dr. Linn tilted her head and narrowed her eyes with a look of curiosity.

The queen lifted her hands in exasperation. "I don't know. He's agitated. Paranoid that he has a target on his back. Last night at dinner I corrected him about some minor thing and he slammed down his plate and left us at the table."

"What did your son do?"

"He never even looked up. He just finished his food and left. I think he blames me," she said, pushing her hair behind her ear.

"For?" Dr. Linn looked confused.

"All of it. His dad's anger. The problems in the world. My inability to fix it."

"Would a family session with just the two of you help?"

"Maybe. He saw your colleague, Dr. Andrews, but he won't tell me what they discussed and Dr. Andrews is a closed book. Maybe you can ask for me." She hoped that Dr. Linn would take the bait.

"I would need a release from both parents to talk to your son's therapist. You know I'd like to meet with you and your husband together anyway so maybe this would be a way to facilitate it," Dr. Linn said, reaching for her water on the end table beside her.

"Absolutely not. He doesn't know I see you and he won't know until we go to trial."

Dr. Linn paused to take a drink and returned the glass to its spot. "So it's final—you're done with the marriage?"

"Would you continue to live with this man?" Sometimes she truly wondered what Dr. Linn was thinking.

"Is that important to you?"

"Maybe." She wished she could read Dr. Linn's thoughts so she could either inspire her or guilt her into helping.

"It's impossible for me to answer that question," Dr. Linn said.

"Fine. Would you live with someone who was abusive?"

"I don't think it's healthy for anyone to live with someone who's abusive."

"Good," she said. "Then you'll support me in court." This *had* to convince Dr. Linn to help, she thought.

"Let's hope you can work this out without a mess in court."

"You don't know him at all, or you'd know he won't work anything out and his abuse won't stop until I'm away from him. He'll fight me on everything, so I need to know you'll support me in court."

Dr. Linn looked at her with a concerned expression. "I'll corroborate what you've told me, but it will just be a repeat of what you've already said."

She decided to try another tactic. "I don't think you want to see my photo on the local news: 'Local educator found murdered in her office. No suspects, although the husband has been held for questioning. Rumors are circulating her therapist knew of her husband's violent threats but did nothing to protect her. More details at 11 p.m.'"

"No, I don't," Dr. Linn said. "Which is why I'd like you to schedule a couples' session. Maybe I can help him with his rage or at least witness it, so I have something to say if I need to testify."

"He'd laugh at you and mock me. The thought of him in this room is out of the question," she said, glancing around to emphasize her point.

"Do you want to schedule a time with your son to come in? Maybe I could help him to communicate his feelings to you."

"No. I can't put my son at risk. I'd have to tell him not to tell his father I see you, and secrets are never good in my house. My husband is hypersensitive to lies and if he had any idea something was up he'd make life unbearable until he knew the truth. It would be awful. My son would feel torn between us and I can't make him choose to take sides against one of his parents just to prove to you things are bad."

"I understand things are bad," Dr. Linn said in a reassuring tone that exasperated her.

"I don't think you do," she insisted. "Look at this bruise on my arm." She pushed her sleeve up. "I didn't want to tell you, but that's where he grabbed me yesterday to make me shut up. I'm embarrassed I've let my life get this out of control, and humiliated, but I need you to know I'm not safe and nobody else is safe with my husband."

"Has he hurt your son?"

"Not that I know of, but he'd never tell me. Remember, he idolizes his father and takes his side against me. He'd feel like a bad son if his dad got mad enough to hit him. He'd hide and blame himself. He's too smart to fight back. Nobody can win against a sociopath."

"It's good you got him into therapy. If he's in trouble and shares it then Dr. Andrews will have to report it."

"That's a huge if. I just told you he won't betray his father and I can't count on Dr. Andrews to pull information out of my son. I need you to be there for me in court," she stated, mentally checking off a win for herself as she saw concern overtake Dr. Linn's consciousness just as she had planned.

18

BETH

Beth arrived early for the Friday morning staff meeting in the hope that Dr. Meadows would start on time and wrap up quickly. She chose her favorite seat with a view of the square just in time to glimpse Michael walk past the tower on his way into the office. She wondered where he'd been and hoped it was a good sign he was on a casual stroll through town. Her mind relaxed with that hopeful thought.

She felt the energy increase as her colleagues began to enter the room, so she quickly switched from her work to her personal email to check for her DNA results. She considered closing her laptop to avoid disappointment, but she couldn't resist the temptation to check one more time just in case the results had arrived. The minute her inbox refreshed she saw the DNA website logo with the message "Your results are in." Her heart pounded as she moved the cursor to the message. She looked at the time. 10:52 a.m. She had eight minutes before the meeting started. Did she dare open it now? How could she wait? Most of her colleagues were still outside the door getting bagels and coffee, and Michael had just crossed the street. She had time.

She closed her eyes and hit the RESULTS tab, which launched the app before she could rethink her decision. She felt her heart skip as the list of relatives flashed before her face.

Andrea Mitzo: close relative, sister. *Breathe, Beth. Breathe.*

Ben Kelly: close relative, first cousin, half-brother or uncle.

No. No, no, no.

Panic gripped her and her body felt numb. *This can't be right*, she told herself. *Wait. Why is Ben's profile public? He was supposed to stay private until I got my results. We were going to go public together for just long enough to see if we matched. What's he done? Oh my god, how do I make my profile private now?* She searched for the privacy settings. She knew that if Andrea logged on now and saw someone that with the initials MJ matched as her sister, she would lose control of everything. She couldn't let that happen.

Focus, Beth, focus.

Move the cursor.

Find account settings.

Hit the private button. OK, done.

As her colleagues filled in around her she felt a numbness settle over her. She wondered if anyone could sense it. She felt pale. *Surreal*, she thought as she tried to shake herself out of shock. She knew Dr. Meadows was like a bloodhound who could smell fear, so she willed herself to look normal. She didn't want to draw any attention.

Touch fabric, she told herself. *Ground. Breathe. Be in the moment. Smell the coffee. Close the DNA website window. Do not look for more relatives. Be Dr. Linn.*

Her ears started ringing as she closed her laptop. Her head tingled. The only explanation for her genetic connection to Ben was that her father must have slept with Ben's mom, who just happened to be his best friend's wife. What was she supposed to do with that information? For the first time she felt anger. She wanted to scream at her father and make him answer her. She wanted to force him to tell her the truth for the first time in his life. She was frantic, like a bird that had flown through an open window and could not find its way back out. She didn't want Dr. Meadows to see her distress, but she couldn't push it back into a box. She was trapped. She had to do something, so she texted Ben and asked him to meet. He responded in seconds and said he'd leave work as soon as she was free. She felt relief. She wasn't alone.

The next hour passed in a blur. Beth felt like she was under water, unable to comprehend what was said around her. Nobody questioned her, but she heard nothing until the bell tower chimed twelve and everyone dispersed. She felt the vibrations of the bells as she escaped up the steps and straight into her office to text Ben.

I'm out. Meet me at the hike and bike trail next to your office in half an hour.

She got there early and just stared at her results. Nothing made sense. Nothing at all.

"Hey, big sis," Ben said as he walked toward the bench where she sat.

"Do you want the world to know? What's going on with your profile?" she asked, standing to greet him.

"Sorry about that. I made it public this morning to check and got a call and forgot to switch it back," he said, giving her a side hug.

"We're only a month apart," she said, looking up at him with a new perspective.

"That's creepy."

"That's just the tip of the creepy iceberg, don't you think?"

"It's a lot," he responded, stepping back to look at her.

"I think I'm in shock. My hands are shaking, the top of my head is numb, and my ears are ringing. I'm not right. How about you?" she asked as they began walking.

"I'm OK. I've tried to avoid the site until we got your results because I don't want to become a DNA stalker, but I can't stop looking. When I saw our connection today all of the original feelings rushed back at me. Thank God you texted me. I needed to talk to you about something else anyway."

"I'm still trying to grasp that you're my brother," she said as they started to walk up the rocky trail. She wanted to get ahead of him. All of a sudden she needed some space.

"I get it," he said. "It's a lot at first. I had to give myself time to absorb that Andrea's my sister before I talked to you. This is different. I was prepared to find out about you, so it's not as hard for me. I want to talk to you about one of my matches, though. You OK?"

"I'm OK," she lied, picking up her pace.

"I found out that I have a distant cousin I didn't know about on my dad's side. We're genetically connected through my dad's lineage. That couldn't be true if your dad's our father, unless he's also my dad's distant cousin."

"Weird. Could it be a married name?"

"Maybe. I'll sort it out. I could message her, but I'm afraid to be open with any of this story right now." He took a long stride to try to catch up to her.

"Yeah . . . let's not go public," Beth said. She felt as though she needed to escape and run away from all of it.

"You OK?" he asked her again.

"Yeah, it's just a lot."

"Are you trying to burn off all of your adrenaline? You're almost running up this hill," he said with a laugh as he ran to catch up.

"Sorry," she said, trying to control the anger that had suddenly overtaken her.

"I'm sorry I had to bring this to you when your dad's so sick."

Beth shook her head. "No, I get it. You needed help, but I won't lie: right now I wish you'd gone to Carrie or Jonathan instead of me. I don't even know what to say about this new match of yours, which makes no sense. How could my dad be related to your dad's second cousin?"

"What if he's not?" Ben asked. "What if my dad is *our* dad?" he asked.

"You actually think my mom had a lifelong affair with your dad and gave birth to four children without my dad's knowledge?" She stopped to look him in the eyes.

"Stranger things have happened. I think I look like my dad and actually so do you," he said.

"Both of them are Irish, so of course we look a bit alike. My dad is half Irish, and I remember your dad bragging he was two-thirds."

"True." Ben didn't look like he was buying into her logic.

"Our parents are the only source of the truth," she said, beginning to walk again.

"Are you going to ask your dad?"

"I can't. I'm too angry. And hurt. I feel stupid." *And exhausted*, she thought but did not say. Ben didn't know about everything else that was going on.

"Why?" he asked.

"I'm not sure." She sat down on a bench at the overlook on the top of the hill.

"Whatever else happened before we were born, we know our dads were best friends for our whole lives, so this is—complex. Complex and awful," he said.

"Exactly. And I'm mad about it. We deserve an answer to a question we shouldn't even have to ask," she said, staring out at the view.

He sat beside her and they looked at the trees. "Yeah, we do, but how can I ask my mom if she had an affair with your dad?"

"How can I ask my dad if he had an affair with your mom?"

"No clue." He looked down at his feet.

"And clearly neither of us can just forget it." Beth stood up to start back down the path. For the next several minutes neither of them spoke as the heaviness of the truth settled on them like a cloud.

"I wish we could just enjoy being siblings," she said with a half-smile.

"I'm really sorry I had to involve you," Ben said. He sounded sincere. "I thought the results might be different. I wasn't ready for my mom to be the one who cheated," he admitted.

They rounded a bend and almost ran into another group of hikers. Beth jumped, startled by the chance someone they knew could have heard them. Then she relaxed. No one was familiar.

"It's OK. We're in this together," she said. "I'll start to investigate matches in our family tree who have recognizable names and try to see if my dad's genes show up." She picked up her pace to climb another hill.

"Is this a race?" he asked.

"Yes. The winner buys the drinks!"

"I can't let my big sister beat me," he said, running to catch her.

"That sounds so odd. I've never been a big sister," she replied. Her journey had just taken an unexpected turn, and it was one she knew she couldn't escape.

19

CELESTE

She cleared the breakfast dishes with the hope this would be her final domestic task before she could dive into the mound of work beckoning to her. The goal of working from home had been to reduce stress, but it had only created more. She could never escape the drama in her personal life. The one person who could help her probably wasn't willing, but she decided it was time to ask him.

"Henry, we need to talk," she told him.

"One second, let me send this email," he said. He slowly scanned the screen to ensure it was accurate before he gave her his attention. "OK, what's up?"

"Ben has called me four times asking to come over, and I feel bad I haven't called him back."

"Then call him back," Henry said. "You're the one who doesn't want me to see him."

"Can you call him and tell him you aren't up to visitors?" she asked as she wiped off the final crumbs from their meal.

"No. I'm not going to lie to him because you're paranoid. The boy just misses his dad and he's afraid he's going to lose me as well. Let him come over. We'll make chili and watch football. Invite all the kids and grandkids. It's almost Halloween. We'll make it a Halloween party."

"You infuriate me, Henry Linn," Celeste said without her normal anger.

The threat of his death had punched holes in her rage. On the one hand she needed Henry to understand her concerns, but on the other, she wanted to just ignore the threat and forget about Ben for awhile.

"Don't forget how charming I am." He winked at her and went back to work.

Celeste stared at her computer screen and tried to avoid the question of how to deal with Ben. Not today. She just couldn't today.

"Do you want to play hooky?" she asked him suddenly, inspired.

"Are you serious? It's not nice to tease a guy when he's down."

"I'm not kidding. Let's go for an adventure. Drive through the park. Have an extravagant lunch. Ignore work for once." She closed her laptop.

"I'm in," Henry said. "It's a gorgeous day, but can you really go?" He looked concerned.

"How many sunny days will we have before the leaves fall?" she asked, knowing they both wondered how many days he had left at all.

"It's Northeast Ohio, darling. We might not see the sun again for months. I believe the leaves are calling us." He looked at her with something of his old spark.

"Then let's go." She turned away to hide her sadness. When the doctor suggested the clinical trial, he had been clear that Henry had a slim chance of survival. With the trial, he had a 50 percent chance of getting the placebo. Every day felt like borrowed time.

If it's borrowed time I want to live every bit of it, Celeste thought as she packed a bag with his pain meds and a snack. She felt a tiny surge of excitement at the thought of escape.

"Do you need my help?" She grabbed a blanket in case he got cold.

"No, I'm good." He slowly made his way toward the car.

Celeste checked her phone once more before they left the house and then forced herself into the present moment. The part of her who was afraid Henry would die wanted her to be responsible and stay home in case something happened. So she gently placed that part of herself in the trunk with the blanket, to make space for her rebellious part to drive off on an adventure with her husband beside her and the sun in her face.

20

THE DANCER

Her dad's ringtone startled her awake. He rarely called without warning. "Hi, everything OK?" She struggled to orient herself to time and place. It was her day off, and she had slept in unusually late.

"Your brother's been injured. He's in an ambulance on his way to City Hospital. I told the paramedics you'd meet them there," he said. While he continued, she could hear him open his car and start the engine. The radio startled her before his phone switched over to the car audio.

"What happened?" She tried to control her instantaneous panic.

"An explosion at the school. I'm not sure what his injuries are, but I know he's OK. Apparently someone planted a homemade bomb in the hallway near the restrooms and he walked by right as it detonated. He and a girl were injured but they're both conscious and stable."

"How do you know he's OK? Did you talk to him?" she asked. Her voice broke at the thought of her little brother injured and alone.

"I didn't, but I could hear him talking in the background. I'm sure he's OK. I just don't want him to be alone when he gets to the emergency room. I just got on the highway but it'll take me awhile to get there. Your mom is in a meeting with her phone off."

"Mom's phone is always off. Can't you call her office?" She had put her phone on speaker so she could get dressed, and she realized she was shouting.

"I will, but right now I'm counting on you."

She sighed. "I'll leave now and call you when I get there." She grabbed her bag and headed to the bathroom to brush her teeth and throw her hair in a ponytail.

The thought of City Hospital made her insides vibrate like a tuning fork. A slideshow of images from her involuntary psych hospitalization played in her mind and she couldn't make it stop. *You have to go*, she told herself. *You can't leave him there alone. Just put on your shoes. He needs you. Get out the door.*

On the bus ride to the hospital she saw a headline on her phone about the attack. RADICAL ANTI-RELIGION GROUP MAY BE RESPONSIBLE FOR LOCAL SCHOOL VIOLENCE. She wondered if there were specific targets. Most of the students probably practiced some form of religion or other, so maybe that was it? The video on her phone wouldn't play, so she let her imagination run wild. By the end of the quick bus trip she'd convinced herself she was to blame, and her paranoid part was committed to that delusion.

The hospital smell accosted her when she walked through the doors, triggering more memories from her time in the lockdown unit. She forced herself to quell the panic so she could focus on why she was there. *Look up at the signs. Find your brother.* The arrow pointing to the ER helped her ignore the flashbacks. *Be brave, be brave, be brave,* she chanted over and over to herself until she turned the corner and almost collided with an EMT pushing a gurney.

It was her brother on the gurney. She gasped when she saw the blood splattered over his face and chest. Their eyes met and his relief was evident when he saw it was her.

"Hi there," she said as she matched the EMT's pace and reached for her brother's hand.

"Hi." He squeezed her hand tight.

"You OK?"

"Yeah, I think so," he answered with a catch in his voice. "Where's Mom?"

"Her phone's off. Dad's on his way. He's super worried."

"Tell him I'm just cut up, but I don't know about Sarah."

"Who's Sarah?" she asked him. She squeezed his hand again.

"My friend," he told her. "I think she's OK too but she was in a different ambulance." He looked around, but they were moving too quickly.

"What happened?"

"I was walking to my second period class with Sarah and someone bumped into her. I stopped to help her pick up some papers and I heard a loud pop and something hit my forehead. The last thing I heard was someone scream there was a bomb, then I guess I passed out."

"Oh my god. So it was a bomb?" She felt a sick feeling in the pit of her stomach. Somehow she knew this was her fault.

"I guess. It felt like glass hit me." He gestured to the medic in front of him, who nodded in agreement. The paramedic steered the gurney toward an exam room and pointed her in the direction of the front desk.

"Check in there and they'll keep you posted," he said. "We can't let you back here just now. The police will be here soon to ask him some questions."

"OK. Thank you." She gave her brother's hand another squeeze. "Hang in there, buddy. I'll call Dad and let him know you're OK."

She watched him roll away before she walked outside to call her dad. Her hands were shaking uncontrollably, but after she finished the call she forced herself to go back in and check in at the desk. *Just stay calm, breathe, focus on your heart rate, you can lower it.* The lobby was crowded. Too crowded. So much activity. So many smells. *Distress tolerance*, she told herself. *Think distress tolerance.* But it wasn't working. Paranoia about her mother overtook her. *Why's her phone off? Is she involved? Is she part of the conspiracy?* Objectively she knew these thoughts were just part of her illness, but they were strong. *None of it is true. No, no, no.* She focused on her breath to distract herself.

You aren't going to win this time, she said to herself. She dug into her backpack for her phone to call Dr. Linn's emergency number.

A sudden sense of calm washed over her as she stood outside and spoke to Serenity's office manager. Eleanor reassured her that Dr. Linn would call as soon as she was available. She offered to let her speak immediately to one of the available therapists, but it had to be Dr. Linn, she told Eleanor. It helped her feel more solid. She had support. The voices were just thoughts, not reality. She could feel her feet on the ground. See the color of the sky. Smell the dampness in the air from an earlier rain.

She decided to position herself so she could see the television and the door. Maybe there would be something on the news. Nothing. She waited. Where was her father? Her fear of a conspiracy against her family began to seep in, so she dug her nails into her leg to get back into reality. *Ground, ground, ground,* she told herself. Stay in the present.

Just when she thought she might have broken the skin on her thigh, she saw her father walk through the door. He looked ashen. Like he'd been in a tomb. Like a vampire. *No,* she told herself. *Stay grounded. It's just dad.* She watched him frantically look around the large room for her. Stand up, she said to her frozen body, but she couldn't move. Her feet felt like granite. Her hand cooperated enough to wave in his direction. Catching his eye, she motioned for him to go to the nurses' station.

Breathe.

She was relieved she had an awareness of the two tracks her mind was currently running on. One track knew everything was normal and she was safe. The other track believed everyone was out to hurt her—even her own family. She tried her best to keep herself on track number one as she watched her dad talk to the nurse.

Then the news came on with a headline she strained to see. SCHOOL BOMBING . . . ANTI-RELIGION GROUP . . . JEWISH STUDENT. She couldn't hear what the newscaster was saying, and there were no more headlines. She sat frozen in place. It was her fault. She knew it was her fault, and no one was going to convince her it wasn't.

21

BETH

An emergency notification popped up on Beth's phone near the end of session so she wrapped up quickly, walked her client down the stairs, and bolted to the front desk. She could tell by the look on Eleanor's face that it was bad, but there were too many clients in the waiting area to ask questions. Eleanor handed her a note and motioned toward Dr. Meadows's office. When Beth saw the client's name on the note her heart sank in fear. It was the dancer. Had there been another suicide attempt? Why else would Dr. Meadows want to see her?

"Come in," Dr. Meadows said when she noticed her.

"What happened?" Beth asked. She hoped it wasn't as bad as she feared.

"Sit down." Dr. Meadows closed a folder and shifted in her seat. "We've got several issues to discuss. Apparently your client's brother was hurt in an explosion today at the high school and now she's experiencing some paranoia. You need to call her immediately and stay late tonight to see her."

"Of course," Beth answered. *Thank God*, she thought. It was bad, but it wasn't as bad as she'd thought it might be.

"The second issue is that Michael's client has been taken in for questioning about the bomb and his mother has called to see what Michael knows. Since you're his supervisor, we need to talk about what you know as well. Serenity will be liable if there's any indication Michael thought his client was dangerous and did not alert the authorities."

Beth felt weightless, and the top of her head began to tingle. "How many people were hurt?"

"Two students were injured. No fatalities. The bomb apparently failed to correctly discharge so fortunately the damage was minimal. The bigger issue right now is our liability, so I need to know if you knew Michael's client was dangerous."

A shift in the clouds allowed sunlight to pour in through the window and cast a shadow over Dr. Meadows's face that masked her expression. But it was clear in her tone she felt no compassion. This meeting was about business, and Beth needed to be careful. "I knew Michael was concerned his client could be involved, but he had nothing concrete," she said. "The kid's angry, but as of last week he hadn't indicated he might hurt someone. Michael asked for my oversight on duty to warn, but there was nothing we knew of to report. The client seemed to know Michael suspected him and became very evasive. There was nothing for us to do at that point."

"Did you document this in your supervision notes?" Dr. Meadows asked, looking up sharply from her own notes.

"Of course," Beth said. "Michael wanted my input when he had his first concern. He's been vigilant to make sure he did everything he could to protect his client and anyone his client might put in danger."

"I guess he failed," Dr. Meadows said.

Beth was astounded. "Are you blaming him?"

"You'd better go make your call. We have a lot of exposure with this, and we need to make sure that at least your client is stable and calm. Pastor Dan has a lot invested in her. You know his referrals are vital for us." Again, there was no compassion whatsoever in her voice that Beth could detect.

Beth got up to leave. She couldn't understand Dr. Meadows's focus on liability when students were injured and an entire town was on edge. But what else could she say? Something with Dr. Meadows always felt a bit removed, but Beth expected at least a normal amount of human compassion in this situation. She had no idea how to ask her boss to care.

"Fine," she said. *First things first*, she told herself. Make sure your client is really OK.

"Keep me posted," Dr. Meadows said as she left.

Stay focused on what you can do, Beth said to herself as she went back into her office and made her call. By the end of it her client had a safety plan to get her through until her emergency session that evening. "You're finally going to meet Pastor Dan. He insisted on driving me tonight to be sure I'm safe," she informed Beth with a nervous laugh before she hung up. The thought of the pastor made Beth uncomfortable. She needed to shake it off and go find Michael.

"Knock knock," she said as she leaned into his office. "Do you have a minute?"

"I do. I guess you heard?" Michael was sitting at his desk, head in his hands, clearly distressed.

"I just talked to Meadows. Any thoughts?" She crossed the room and sat in the chair across from his desk.

"It looks like he was involved, but I have no way to know what happened," Michael said. "His mom's already interrogated me and I've got nothing. Meadows wants me to cover my ass in case it all comes back on me somehow."

"Liability's her biggest concern," Beth said in disgust. "I know this has been horrible for you."

"Thanks. I'm feeling pretty shitty, and now she wants me to protect Serenity," he said, holding up a document from their liability insurance company. "She told me to contact them immediately."

"I guess that's wise."

"I know, but she's so cold. I guess I expected some human emotion," he said.

Beth had hoped for the same. "How can I support you?" she asked Michael.

"I'll make the call, but I also need a therapeutic plan to deal with my client and his family."

"Well, your therapeutic plan will be determined based on the facts we can piece together, since your client won't talk. We can start with the day I spoke at the school. I saw a student leave the auditorium right before the fire alarm went off and I saw him here yesterday. If that's your client, then I have evidence I might have to share. Right now it's still circumstantial," she said.

"I saw him yesterday at 2 p.m."

"Then that's him," she said.

Michael rested his head in his hands. "Fuck."

"You have to figure out how to get him to tell you what happened. If he's involved then he's a very disturbed young man and he needs your help. His mom had a right to question you today."

"You know I've done my best to handle this case, right?" His question had a hint of desperation to it.

"I do. Just keep me in the loop, OK?" Beth stood up and walked to the door. She tried to sound reassuring, but at the moment she wasn't sure how well either of them were handling the situation.

"I will," he said.

· · ·

At 6:55 p.m., Beth saw Pastor Dan walking up the sidewalk with her client. The sight of him made her uneasy because of Dr. Meadows's reminder of how important his friendship was for Serenity. *No pressure,* Beth thought as she watched them enter the building. The sound of their voices in the stairwell suddenly made the quaintness of her small town feel oppressive. She stepped into the lobby with the hope she could quickly usher her client into her office and send him on his way.

"You must be the infamous Dr. Linn," the pastor stated as he reached the top of the stairs and immediately reached out to shake her hand. He was taller and younger than she expected, with just a hint of gray in his sandy blond hair.

"I am," she said, glancing over at the dancer with a smile.

"I'm Pastor Dan. It's good to finally meet you. I remember your parents from your grandfather's funeral, but you were out of the country on a school trip when he died, weren't you?" he asked, staring directly into her eyes.

"Yes, unfortunately," she responded, uncomfortable with the topic but even more uncomfortable about discussing a personal issue with her client there.

"I'm sure you miss him," the pastor went on. "He was an amazing man." He smiled again and paused, looking at her client and then back at her.

"Well, I'll let you two get to it. I'll be right outside until you're done," he said, turning to leave.

"Thanks," Beth responded, curious why he was bringing up her grandfather when he knew how angry her parents had been with him at the time of his death. Was he intentionally trying to upset her, or did he think she didn't know?

"You weren't kidding. You really don't know Pastor Dan," her client said the minute the door was closed.

"I really don't. Did you think I lied to you about it?" Beth asked.

"I'm paranoid, remember?" her client said with a nervous smile.

"Tell me what's going on with you," Beth said, motioning for her client to make herself comfortable in a chair. "Is your brother OK?" She hoped she'd recovered her professional demeanor.

"He's OK," her client said. "It's just surface cuts and bruises, and he's emotionally shaken. It could've been much worse. But I feel like it's my fault. I know it's the paranoia, but I can't get it to stop." She pulled a pillow onto her lap.

"Let's process how it could be your fault," Beth said gently.

"It sounds crazy, but I keep picturing the psych unit and this guy who was there with me. He kept whispering that he was a Satanist but he acted normal around the staff. As soon as no staff were there he'd hiss and call people horrible names, but he was nice to me so I talked to him. I shouldn't have talked to him. I should've stood up for the other patients."

"So you think that because you were nice to a mentally ill person who claimed to be a Satanist during their inpatient treatment that your brother was a target of the school bomber?" Beth had helped her client process delusions before, so she felt confident they could work through this paranoia together as well.

"Yes. I think he read my mind and knew I was angry with him for being cruel because he worshipped Satan, so he's trying to punish me for being fake. I should've done the right thing. I'm a horrible person." Her client stared at the floor, her hands trembling, clearly afraid.

"Let's separate these two things for a minute," Beth said. "You were in the hospital to get well, not to manage the other patients on your floor. Your role was to heal. To take care of you. The hospital staff was responsible for the safety of everyone on the unit, including you, and they did not expect you to do their jobs. You would've put yourself at risk if you confronted him. He was there to get well, just like you, so his thoughts were not stable either."

"You can say whatever you want, but I still think my brother was punished for my mistake."

"Do you know the patient's name from the hospital?"

"No," the client said, without making eye contact.

"Did he know your name?"

"Probably not. We were only there for part of a day together."

"When were you hospitalized?" She hoped that prompting her client to recall how long ago it was would help her confront her irrational thought process.

"Thirteen months ago."

"OK. So do you think that a guy you met thirteen months ago, who didn't know your name, went to a school with over one thousand students and strategically planted a bomb to go off in the exact spot where your brother was walking with his friend?"

"If he could read my mind, then he could know where my brother would be," her client insisted.

"Do you have proof he could read your mind?" Beth knew she had to be methodical here, and also tread carefully. Working with this client had challenged her in ways she hadn't anticipated. Maybe it was the similarities in their backgrounds combined with the severity of her psychosis, but Beth felt something akin to survivor guilt with her. It was an uncomfortable emotion that she knew could interfere with the therapeutic relationship if she allowed it to surface, so she felt doubly responsible to be at her best with this client. Her personal best and her professional best.

"No."

"Did he say he was mad at you?" Beth watched for any sign of irritation to know how far she could go with her questions.

"No."

"OK. So he was not nice to other patients, but he never showed anger toward you. What was the last thing he said to you?"

"When I was discharged, he said, 'Nice to meet you, blondie.'" She looked up at Beth with a quizzical expression as though she hoped Beth was on the right track.

"Does that sound angry to you?" Sensing she had found a way to break through, Beth relaxed a bit in her chair.

"No."

"Do you think we could soften up on the belief that this is your fault based on the logical process we just did to sort it out?"

"Let me think for a minute." Her client rubbed her forehead with her right hand and squeezed the pillow with her left one.

Beth sat quietly while her client absorbed the information and hoped they'd shaken the delusion enough for her to at least partially return to reality.

After a few minutes, her client said, "OK. Maybe he couldn't read my mind." Now she sounded open to the possibility, which gave Beth a chance to further dismantle the delusion.

"Which means it can't be your fault that someone set off a bomb that hurt your brother, right?"

"I guess not. I think I got paranoid because when I got to the hospital I remembered that guy, and for some reason I connected him to what was going on. It scared me really badly." She looked at Beth wide-eyed.

"Of course it did," Beth said. "It was a scary day. Your brain's extra sensitive, and it needed to find a reason. It's uncomfortable not to have answers, so if the answer is that it's your fault, then it gives you control to stop it from happening again. Does that make sense?"

"I guess so." She looked a bit unsure, but Beth noticed a shift in her mood.

She continued walking her client through the day. "Tell me what happened when you got to the emergency room."

"I was overwhelmed by the smells and my thoughts started to race. I just wanted to run. Like fight or flight, you know, but I was more in flight mode until I saw my brother and then my fear for him was bigger than my need to run. When they took him back to the exam room I knew he was OK but I still felt anxious. My dad was on his way and nobody had been able to contact my mom. She frustrates me. She just left me there scared and alone."

"When you felt alone where did your thoughts go?"

"I started to think about all of the cameras around the lobby and how somebody who monitored the cameras might think I had a bomb. I told myself they were just thoughts, but it was hard. I tried to ground myself but that smell made me think about the unit and how it was just six floors above me. I can't go back there." Tears began to stream down her face.

Beth handed her a box of tissues. "I know. It's OK. Nobody will send you to the unit for your fearful thoughts. Today was a really hard day. Let's try to help your nervous system back to a calm place. Would that be OK?"

"Yes, please help me calm down," her client said, pausing to blow her nose. "I haven't felt this bad for a while. I can't slip back. Not now."

"Let's do some breath work," Beth suggested.

"OK," the client said. Her hands clenched the pillow in her lap.

"Breathe in deeply. One . . . two . . . three . . . four. Now hold your breath for four . . . three . . . two . . . one. Exhale . . . one . . . two . . . three . . . four and let all of the air out at the bottom and hold the breath out for the count of four, three, two, one. Excellent. Now continue to breathe slowly and deeply as we lay all of these thoughts out on the floor on these sticky notes. They're just thoughts." Beth went to her desk and picked up a pad of light blue sticky notes to help her with the externalization.

"I see the guy I met on the unit who called another patient a towel head," the client said.

Beth placed a sticky note on the floor. "What else?"

"I see myself as I looked away. It was lunch time and the staff told him not to use racist language." She hugged the pillow.

"So staff saw that he was inappropriate. What happened next?" Beth sat on the edge of her chair, ready for the next thought.

"He laughed and walked out."

"Did he talk to you?"

She paused and took another deep breath. "No. He didn't even know I saw it, because I was around the corner."

"How does it feel to think of the thoughts as far over there on the square of paper?"

"It feels OK. Like a memory." She let out a long sigh.

Beth paused and let her take a deep breath in before she continued. "Excellent. Now what comes up?"

"I see the lobby today and the security cameras. I can smell the place and I can feel the fear I had that the people in the room think I'm bad and that the people on the other side of the camera think I have a bomb." She pulled the pillow back into her chest.

Beth pulled another sticky note off and placed it on the floor. "Do you see anyone who looks upset with you?"

"No. Nobody is looking at me at all. They all look worried about their own stuff."

"What else do you see?"

"I see my little brother as he reached for my hand. He looks relieved to see me and I see the paramedic who spoke to me." Another deep breath.

Beth again gave her a moment to exhale. "How does that feel?"

"Good. It feels like I'm there to help." She was breathing a bit more steadily now, Beth noticed. Good.

"Continue to focus on your breath and the good sensations you feel and try to connect those good feelings to your breath," she went on.

"That feels nice," her client said. "Light."

"Good. What else do you see?"

"I see my dad walk in and he looks pale, like a vampire."

Beth placed another sticky note on the floor. "Do you have any evidence your dad is a vampire?"

"No, just my delusions from when I first got sick. I was sure he was a vampire then."

"How are those thoughts now?"

"I know we decided they were delusions, but right now they feel real." Her client sounded frustrated again.

"Let's help your mind to deconstruct it, then," Beth said. "Focus the thought over here on this sticky note."

"OK. It's over there."

"Great." Patiently, she walked her client through the steps of visualization until she was calmer again and could jettison the thoughts that were scaring her.

"How's your breathing feel now?" she asked after a while.

"It's good," her client said. "I feel a little bit better. I just hope I can stay better."

"Of course." Beth joined in with the breath work, hoping it would manage some of her own anxiety about the events of the day. She had no idea how to untangle her own thoughts about the bomb and her lack of action, even though she knew there was no real way she could have intervened. Logically she knew that, but just like her client, she struggled to stay in the reality of the situation. She had no information, no client who had expressed a plan, no knowledge of any group targeting the school—and yet somehow she felt like she'd let everyone down.

22

BETH

By the time Beth got home, she was ravenous. She'd been too distracted to notice. And she hadn't had time to do any DNA research at all. Grabbing a container of cold leftovers from the refrigerator, she opened her laptop and went to the DNA website. She scanned the screen hopefully, but every new match linked back to her mother's side, which did nothing to help her. The relatives that appeared to be on her paternal side were all so distant she couldn't track anything to either her dad or Ben's.

She was desperate to prove Ben's theory that his dad was all of their dads was wrong, but she needed proof quickly in order to shut him up before he tried to get answers from her parents. Frustrated, she was ready to close her laptop when Ben's face appeared beside a text bubble.

Hi, he said.

Hey, she replied.

Meet for a drink? I have some news.

Just got home. Super tired. Can we video chat instead? She really was exhausted. Did she want to see Ben now?

If you're tired I'll pick you up. See you in ten minutes.

Before she could respond, he logged off. *I guess I don't have a choice*, she thought.

She just had time to respond to a text from her mother: a dinner invitation for Sunday, another family meeting. She didn't want to have to deal with it with Ben around, or have to explain. And she also didn't want to explain to her mom she was with Ben if she happened to call to see why Beth hadn't responded. Best to get it out of the way.

When she stood up to put her coat back on, she caught a glimpse of her eyes in the mirror. She always thought she had her dad's eyes. Now she had no idea whose eyes she had.

"Thanks for picking me up. It's been a day," she said as she climbed into Ben's passenger seat.

He grinned at her and she noticed how much his cheekbones resembled her own. "I have a lot to show you, so let's just go down to the Jac. Nobody will be there on a weeknight after eight. Have you had dinner?"

"Not really. A few bites of leftovers," she said.

"Me either," he said. He pulled into a front spot in the almost empty parking lot.

The host had barely seated them when Ben pulled out a folder and put it in front of Beth. He looked uncomfortable. She stared at it with equal trepidation.

"We share a dad," he said as he pulled out the first document. "But as I suspected it's not the one we thought."

"What do you mean?"

"I mean that my dad is our dad," he answered.

"That's impossible," Beth responded. The letter signed by G. came to mind.

"Just look." He pushed the folder closer. "I found more relatives for both of us that are only through my dad's side. How could that happen if Henry was my dad? I've done the research and I have proof that our parents aren't related even if you go generations back."

Beth opened the file and started to read. She felt faint and she wondered if Ben shared her sense of shock.

"What are we going to do?" she asked finally. It was true. It was all right there in front of her.

"I thought you might want to talk to your mom," Ben said.

Beth shook her head. "I can't," she said. "Not now. My dad's too sick. Between taking care of him and running the company, it's already too much. I can't confront her right now." She lowered her voice as the server approached. She waited for Ben to order before she decided what to have. As hungry as she'd been an hour ago, the thought of food wasn't appealing. She ordered a salad and waited until the server was out of earshot before she continued. "I just can't, Ben."

He took a deep breath in before he responded. "Don't you think it already haunts her?" he asked. "She knows what she did."

"I get that, but she doesn't need to know that I know. I need to think. What if I asked Andrea and Carrie and Jonathan to take a DNA test? I could say it'd be good to get tested to see if we have any genetic cancer markers. They'd probably go for that. Maybe that would scare my mom into telling us before we found out ourselves."

"Or she might try to dissuade everyone from taking the test for some reason," Ben said.

"Maybe," Beth said. *I just want to stall on this right now,* she thought. "What about you? Have you contacted any of the other relatives?"

"No," he said. "I wanted to talk to you first. And now I'm wondering about my dad. What the hell was he doing before I was born?"

"Have you asked your mom anything?"

He shook his head. "I'm not going to ask her until we give your mom a chance to explain," he said.

"OK. You're right. I'll talk to her," Beth said. "I just need to think some things through first." She realized there was no way to get the ball out of her court.

Nothing made sense. How could they put Tom Kelly and Celeste Linn together? Beth's memories of Ben's father—her dad's best friend—were upended. Had he been in love with her mom? Had they been in love the whole time and hidden it?

She managed to reassure Ben she'd figure out what to do soon. On the drive home, she wondered how different her life might have been if her mom had been with Tom. She didn't share that thought with Ben, who'd always seen his parents as the idyllic couple. But everything was different now. For both of them.

23

CELESTE

Celeste scrubbed the broccoli much longer than she needed to, but the cold water on her hands gave her a sense of calm. Her entire body felt hot, like she had a fire deep within her, fueled by her anger at herself for all the years she had protected Henry. She expected him to be difficult, he always had been, but today his critical nature had hit a new level of agitation and his frustration was all directed at her. Why hadn't she hired a better plant manager? Why hadn't she negotiated a better deal? Why was his soup cold? Why was she exhausted when he was the one with cancer?

They'd had a lovely time playing hooky, driving to the park and enjoying the fall day without talk of cancer or work. She insisted they limit their conversation to topics that wouldn't lead to an argument, and to her surprise Henry was agreeable. It was a good day for him, but now he had regressed to an even less pleasant mood than usual and she knew it was directly correlated to his current feeling of weakness.

She wanted her children around her today. She wished she could tell them the truth about their father. Her mom would have helped if she was still alive, but right now all she had was cold water and broccoli. Her mom would have let her vent or cry or throw a fit. Having big emotions was as much a part of her family's traditions as cooking with wine was. Her mom taught her to be comfortable and strong, just like she was. She said they came from good northern Italian stock. She also said that tears were productive and cleared your energy so you could see the truth. Celeste wished she could ask her mom what to do with her emotions now.

As she dried her hands, she remembered the first day she had cooked in this kitchen. The kitchen she and Henry had hoped to fill with children. When they moved in they opened all of the pots and pans first, because they were so excited to christen their new home with a traditional Italian meal. They walked to the farmer's market and carefully chose tomatoes and zucchini. They chopped them up together and created a pasta like her grandma used to make, and they paired it with a bottle of wine they had saved for that day. They pulled apart Italian bread and laughed and ate and felt invincible. Forty years later the bread and wine still flowed, and their table was filled by children and grandchildren. They had created their dream life—but Celeste wondered what the cost had been.

She heard voices: they were all arriving now. She allowed herself to savor their smell, their essence. The shoes that piled up against the wall reminded her of all the years that backpacks and gym bags filled the entryway. She remembered the smell of the outdoors and of locker rooms, especially when Jonathan wrestled. It had been impossible to calm him down before a match, and the smell of his nervous sweat clung to the wrestling clothes when he forgot and left them in his gym bag overnight. He still had nervous sweat when he was put on the spot. She watched him talk to his sisters. Andrea was his complete opposite: she had washed her running clothes and her bag sat neatly at the door, ready for her to leave each morning. Carrie's backpack usually had a pom-pom that had lost part of its fluff, and Beth's bag had too many books in it and one inevitably slid out onto the floor. Henry always left his racquetball clothes in his gym bag and expected them to magically make it to the laundry room, and Celeste always made sure they did. He was the worst but she knew she had created him, so how could she complain now?

She wished she could go back forty years and warn her younger self of what was to come, like the ghost of Christmas future. *It's a bit late now,* she thought as she observed Beth and wondered what she knew. Ben's behavior concerned her, especially after she learned he'd contacted Beth.

As they all gathered around the table, Celeste and Henry held hands and asked their children to toast to the family. Celeste saw the questions in her children's eyes so she stood to explain.

"Your dad and I have decided it's time for us to have an adventure," she said. "We don't want to burden you, but we also don't want to waste the precious days we have left together. I'm officially stepping down from the company for as long as I need to and I'm putting the three of you in charge." She nodded toward Andrea and Carrie and Jonathan, who were exchanging glances.

"Wait, what?" Jonathan asked.

Celeste continued. "Beth, if you want to get involved you're welcome to, but we know you're busy. Dad and I just want some freedom. We want to take unplanned trips or watch movies until late at night and not have to get up for meetings. We trust you. So cheers, to our capable children," she said, raising her glass.

Jonathan looked indignant. "Mom, you can't—"

"Yes, I'm stepping down," Celeste said and took a sip. "I'm joining your dad in his pause from work."

"You can't," Jonathan said again.

"I can. You and your sisters are fine. Actually, you're great." Celeste watched as a smile began to form on Andrea's face. She had a feeling her oldest would be on board with having more power. Carrie was a bit harder to read; her face showed no sign of emotion until Celeste made eye contact with her and she gave a slight nod of approval.

"Dad, you can't let her do this," Jonathan said, turning to Henry.

"I asked her to do this," he answered calmly.

"Why? We need her," Jonathan said. Celeste could hear his panic.

"I need her too. I want time with her. We've spent the last forty years being responsible for this family and the company and now we want some freedom."

"What about us?" Jonathan asked.

"What about you? There are three of you. You can handle this while we take a little break." His voice was clear, his tone forceful. He was not backing down.

"I think it's great," Andrea interjected. She sat up straighter in her chair. "We've got this, Jonathan. They've handed us a company, so I think the least we can do is run it."

"How? How are we going to run it? You don't even have your kids in day care," Jonathan responded.

Celeste noticed Jonathan's response seemed to make Beth uncomfortable as she watched her youngest completely disengage from the interaction.

"That can change," Andrea said with a shrug.

Carrie said, "Leave her alone, Jonathan. We've all enjoyed a great deal of flexibility, but we can step up now and make this work. Thank you for trusting us." Celeste smiled at her as she raised her glass to them.

"Thanks for being trustworthy," Celeste responded. Jonathan still looked frustrated, but he appeared to appreciate her compliment.

"What happens now?" he finally asked.

"We'll work out the details soon," Henry reassured him. "But not tonight. Tonight we eat. We laugh. We toast." He raised his glass once more. "Cheers!"

"Cheers," they all said. Celeste soaked in the moment as she watched her family, with all of their passions and flaws, clink their glasses in solidarity.

24

MICHAEL

Michael watched his client squirm as he avoided eye contact. It was his tell, the clear sign of a lie, but Michael had no way to confront him. The boy had curated a persona that made it difficult for Michael, or any adult, to connect with him. Earbuds still in, hoodie up, shoulders back and hair falling across his right eye, everything about him said *don't mess with me*. Michael knew his client wasn't about to implicate himself intentionally.

"Tell me about the police officer who questioned you," Michael said.

"He was a jerk," his client said. He crossed his arms and leaned back.

"Can you tell me more?"

"What more do you want me to say? Some prick accused me of setting off a bomb." He glared at Michael.

"Did he say why he thought you were involved?" Michael asked.

"Apparently I've got a reputation for hating God."

"Do you?"

"What do you think?"

"I have no idea what you think about God." He wanted to see if his client would offer anything up.

"I think religion is the opiate for the masses," the boy finally said, removing his earbuds and putting them in the case. Michael wondered if that meant he'd gotten his attention.

"Big Karl Marx fan, huh?" Michael tried to make this a bit light.

"Not really," his client said. "But I'm sure you are."

"Why would you think that?" Michael tried to maintain his composure.

"You seem like a communist. You clearly don't care about how much money you make if you're a doctor, and you're working in this dump." He glanced around the office as if to prove his point.

"I do this work because I care about people."

"So you're on a mission from God, right?"

Michael kept his expression neutral. "No, I just care about people's mental health. Does caring about something have to be a mission from God?"

"In my family it does. All my parents talk about are their callings. My brother, too. He moved to Haiti to teach people to grow crops so they won't starve. He thinks God called him there." His tone had changed, and Michael wondered if there was something here to pursue.

"When did he go?" Michael asked.

"Last year. It's almost four. Are we done?" He abruptly pulled his hood around his face.

"I'm sure it's hard to not get to see your brother," Michael continued smoothly. *Maybe I can draw him back in.* "What got him interested in Haiti?"

"He went on a mission trip in high school and decided he needed to go back after college to make a difference in the world," the boy said sarcastically. "He could make a difference here too." He emphasized with air quotes and an exaggerated eye roll.

"That's true. Have you talked to him about it?" Michael started to see the pain behind his client's anger.

"What, tell him I think he's stupid? I don't think so."

"No, have you told him you miss him," Michael asked, hoping for an opening to connect.

"He cares more about them than me. I'm not telling him anything." There it was again. Michael saw the pain.

"Just think about it. You might be surprised if you asked him about his work. I'm going to guess he cares more about your family than anyone else in the world. You should ask him."

"Whatever. I'm over it," his client said. Michael could hear the pain behind the anger, but he decided not to push him any further.

He decided instead to return to his original question. "Do you want to talk about what happened at the police station before we end our session?"

"No. Can I just go?" the boy asked as he stood up to leave.

"Sure," Michael said. He had to make sure his client felt he had some control. It was the only way to build trust and have any chance of helping him. "I'll see you next week." He rose to lead him out.

Michael tried to make sense of the session as he walked back to his desk. He suspected his client was involved, but he still didn't have anything definite. He might have discovered a motive, since the kid clearly hated religion, but he wasn't sure how to write that in a case note.

He wanted to ask Beth for guidance, but he didn't want her to overreact. Not that she had so far, but he sensed in their last meeting she was on edge and he didn't want her to force him to contact his client's parents. He would if he had no choice, but he knew that would break the small amount of trust he'd built. If he asked Dr. Meadows for advice, she would make him close the file and refer the client out. All she cared about was the risk of a lawsuit.

He decided to do nothing until he could get out of the building and clear his head. Two more sessions. He had to focus.

His next client bolstered his confidence. The kid had gone from complete silence in the first session to bringing his notebook with his finished homework each week. And he smiled a lot now. And he had asked someone out, Michael learned during their session. Definitely progress.

His final client reduced his anxiety even more when she shared how much he had helped her.

"I sat with a group of people at lunch today for the first time since I started high school," she told him, beaming.

"Tell me how you did it," Michael probed.

"I did what we practiced last week and it worked."

"Great job. How did it feel when you sat down?"

"Amazing. And I could eat and everything." She raised her arms and did a little dance in her seat, which caused Michael to chuckle.

"I'm proud of you," he said as he flipped open her chart. "Should we pick a new goal for this week?"

"Definitely. I think I want to try out for the musical," she said, beginning a long story about her best friend moving away and how she just realized that's when her anxiety had started. The session flew by as they pieced together the past and put together a plan for the week.

By the time Michael walked her out he was feeling much better: two clients who were making progress. Maybe he did know what he was doing. Beth escorted a client out of her office and he noticed her serious expression.

"Long day?" he asked.

Beth nodded. "How about you?" she asked.

"Same. You going to Taco Tuesday?"

"I'm not sure," she said. "Are you?"

"I am. You should come," he responded, even though he knew it would blow his chance to vent to Peter.

"Promise not to talk about work?"

"It's a requirement," he said with a grin. "Give me fifteen minutes to close up and I'll walk over with you."

"Sounds good. Thanks for the nudge."

His ambiguous feelings about Beth frustrated him. He liked her and was grateful she had agreed to provide his supervision; if she hadn't he would have had to report to Dr. Meadows, which would have been much worse. But for the first time, he realized he was irritated he had to report to anyone at all.

Write your notes, he said to himself as he stared at his screen. *Keep it light. Be vague. There's nothing to say.* Even as he thought this, the vision of his dream nagged at the edge of his consciousness.

He typed, *What if the kid does hurt someone?* in the summary section of his note before he realized he was recording his concerns and not his verifiable observations.

Beth popped her head in his door. "Ready?" She looked happy to be done with business for the day.

He pressed delete and closed his laptop. "Ready."

Michael locked the main door behind them as Beth chatted about the rain that had begun to spit gently onto their faces. *No work talk*, he reminded himself as they walked to the restaurant. He was grateful she hadn't mentioned the bomb. Maybe she was depleted from it too.

"It's eerie tonight, don't you think?" Beth asked.

"What do you mean?"

"The wind is eerie. See how the leaves are sideways and you assume it's from the rain but it's just misting so it's clearly not. The raindrops are like tiny fairy kisses. The wind is the actual threat." He looked up into the trees, surprised by her accuracy. The leaves were blowing sideways.

"Tiny fairy kisses?" He laughed.

"Don't make fun of me," she said. "I've lived here my whole life and these nights always take me by surprise. I think fall is going to go on forever, and then one night a storm takes it away while we're all asleep. I remember a night in grad school that felt just like this one. I had a late class and when I walked to my car the wind was just like it is now. Like Halloween."

"It's funny you bring up grad school," he said. He felt a bit uncomfortable, as if she'd suddenly shared something too intimate. "Today I had the thought that maybe I should have stayed in the classroom."

"Why?" she asked. They were walking by the deli and Beth waved to the owner, who was locking the front door for the night.

"Less risk than direct client care."

"Sure, but also less growth," Beth stated emphatically. "We learn a lot from our clients. They shine a light on our weaknesses. Wouldn't you miss it?"

"I'd miss the clients," he admitted. "But not the stress."

"We agreed not to talk about work so I won't, but if we did I'd say that our current issue is much more stressful than normal. It's very unusual, so try not to gauge your job satisfaction at this moment," she said. Now she sounded more like his supervisor again.

They had almost reached the restaurant, and the rain began to pelt them.

"Your fairy kisses have turned to the kisses of an orc," Michael said, jogging ahead to open the door.

"I told you these nights sneak up on you," Beth said, waving to the familiar group already seated.

He felt a bit of relief. "First one to order a margarita wins," he said.

"What's the prize?" She took off her coat and shook the water off.

"An alibi to miss the next staff meeting?"

She laughed. "Bartender, I need a margarita!"

Michael took a seat at the other end of the table and watched Beth greet their colleagues. He felt off-balance. Like the day he'd seen his third-grade teacher at the beach. It hadn't crossed his mind that she had children or a life outside of the classroom, and he realized he'd done the same thing with Beth. Until now.

He watched the leaves swirl and drop outside the window with the force of the rain. A change from the peaceful sprinkle that had barely been perceptible on their skin just minutes earlier. His positivity felt equally fragile. The calm of this moment would quickly shift with another dream about reporters tracking him down for a story.

Peter's laughter disrupted his rumination and he found himself pulled into a story about hot yoga and Peter's ignorance about its intensity, which had led to him passing out in his first class. The yogis at the table were concerned, but Peter continued to laugh. Michael followed along even if his heart wasn't quite in it. He wished he could be more like Peter: less serious, more fun.

Beth patted Michael on the shoulder when she left and thanked him for encouraging her to come out. He watched her go and wished they could stay out all night. Sleep meant dreams, and he wasn't in the mood for another nightmare.

25

BETH

Beth dug through her drawer in search of her reflective vest so she could run outside. She'd been startled awake by an anxious dream, and the thought of human interaction at the gym was too much. *I need to be in nature*, she told herself as she took her first step into the dark morning mist. She paused to notice that all of the leaves were gone, just like she'd predicted to Michael. The bare trees stretched up into the darkness and guided her eyes to the moon still hanging in the lowest corner of the sky. She breathed in the quiet beauty of the morning and tried to reassure herself she would be OK. Most of the houses were still dark, but as she ran past, lights slowly came on as her neighbors began their days. She remembered sitting in the back seat of her parents' car when she was a child, entertaining herself by making up stories about the people inside the houses they passed. She'd liked to imagine grandmothers with cookies about to come out of the oven and big fluffy dogs in front of a fire. *If I could just talk to my grandma now,* she thought, *I know she would help*. She tried to push those thoughts away, but the more she tried to avoid it the more her ache grew.

What should I do? she whispered into the darkness, desperately seeking her grandmother's wisdom.

"Trust your heart," she heard clearly in her grandmother's voice.

My heart is confused. She tried sending her thoughts out in hopes of receiving a response. *Ben wants me to talk to my mom but I can't. I can't hurt her. I can't hurt my dad either. But I do need to know who my biological father is. Who am I if my family isn't what I've always thought?*

Silence. She could no longer hear her grandmother's voice no matter how hard she tried. The only sound she heard was a car slowly easing out of its driveway and onto the street.

What's the point in any of it? she wondered. Her pace increased and her feet pounded harder on the pavement. *Ben might not be so eager for this talk if his dad were still alive.*

She had to face it: her father was dying. What if the so-called work hiatus was his final chapter? *Maybe it's his last big moment and they just don't want us to know,* she thought. What would she do when he died? What if he didn't die, and she had to tell him about Celeste and it broke his heart? *How could I do that to him?*

She also worried about what would happen if Ben went to them without her. She'd promised to get back to him soon, but she didn't think she could count on him to wait. *How am I supposed to feel about any of this?* It struck her again that she wished she could have grown up with Tom as her father. It made her feel like a traitor. But he'd always asked questions about her and seemed interested in her choices. It was easier than trying to convince Henry that the way she wanted to live her life was right.

The sun peeked above the horizon at just that moment and made the path more visible. She clearly saw her feet as they hit the ground, and when she looked back up she saw a deer who looked back at her. She smiled and felt sure the deer smiled back. *Namaste,* she whispered. *You probably don't know who your dad is either, and you're fine.* The deer held her gaze for a moment before it bent down and continued grazing.

When Beth came around the next bend, she was startled by the sight of two people on a bench across the lake. *It has to be a mirage,* she thought. One of them looked just like the queen, and the other one looked like Michael's client who was now a suspect.

No, she told herself. I must be really stressed out. She tried to shake it off, but when she looked up again they were still there. Alarmed now, she moved closer to the trees and kept her head down so they wouldn't see her. What was going on?

It's not them, she said to herself as she hid behind a tree so she could peek around and get a better look. *Please don't let it be them*. But from her new angle, she was easily able to identify them. In the same moment she realized she was trapped, and would have to wait for them to walk away before she could move.

Now she felt rage. What could her client possibly be doing on the bench with this kid, who was apparently aligned to her husband's violent ideology? Was she a pawn in some twisted game? There were no good reasons Beth could think of for the queen to meet this particular young man at daybreak in a deserted park.

She kept still. The two apparently hadn't seen her. She couldn't hear anything, but then they both stood up and left the bench. She watched as they walked in opposite directions until it was safe for her to run back home.

· · ·

Only three hours later, Beth greeted the queen in the lobby where she sat waiting for her session. "Good morning," she said, keeping her features neutral. The queen was definitely wearing the same coat as the one she had on that morning on the bench. So she hadn't been imagining things.

Keep your cool, Beth, she told herself firmly. *Be Dr. Linn.*

The queen glided over to her normal spot on the couch. "Is it a good morning?" she asked in an accusatory tone. She smiled as she spoke, but Beth felt an undercurrent of something other than cordiality.

Beth smiled back at her. "Apparently not for you," she said. *Stay calm*, she reminded herself. *Let's see if she reveals anything.*

"Not at all," the queen said. "He was at it again before I even got out of bed today. He threatened me. I barely got here on time because I had to lock myself in the bathroom until he left for work. Our son was late for school because I was too afraid to come out and drive him."

Beth paused to process the boldness of the lie.

"Is your son OK?" she asked. *Stay blank.*

The queen shrugged. "He's mad at me, but he's fine. He didn't hear any of the fight. By the time I left the bathroom he'd already overslept. I had to call the principal and explain I had an emergency and it was my fault he was late. It's not a big deal. The principal knows me."

"I think it's time for me to meet your husband and your son," Beth said.

The woman sighed, sounding annoyed. "Have you listened to one thing I've said to you?"

"I've listened to everything you've said to me," Beth told her. "I'm not sure how to help you except to directly confront the situation."

"I've told you my husband is dangerous. How do you think a direct confrontation with him is a way to help me?"

"The only way I can help is to either get you out of the house or get him to stop his abuse. You don't seem ready to leave, so my only choice is to address his anger. He's the abuser, so maybe I could get him into therapy if we do an intervention." The queen's lie had flipped a switch in Beth.

"I think you've lost your mind," the queen said.

"You've asked me to help you survive. Every week you tell me how afraid you are of him. Every week you ask me to report him. I can't report someone without proof." Beth tried to hide her anger, but she could hear the edge in her own voice. She felt like a pawn in a dangerous game her client appeared to be playing, and she was trapped with no way to address it.

The queen was visibly irritated now. She stared at Beth with a look of disgust. "You could do the right thing and call Children's Services and tell them you suspect my son is in danger," she said.

"You know I can't do that without evidence."

"I'm not bringing them here. It's not safe."

Beth looked down as if to read her notes. She needed to regroup. "Fine. Let's focus on your options. Have you made any progress on the plan for a divorce?"

"I haven't done anything. I have a board meeting next week and our numbers are still down for midterm enrollment, so I'm focused on generating interest."

"I would've thought the violence at the high school would've created lots of interest."

"That's a fascinating concept, Dr. Linn, but I'd like to think students come to the academy for the excellent education and not out of fear. I'm offended you'd even mention such an idea considering we both know my husband's associates are most likely responsible for the violence. It would destroy me to gain students at the cost of those two innocent young people who were injured."

"The authorities have said it was a random act of violence and that it wasn't the act of an anti-religion group," Beth said. She knew what she'd seen in the park, and now she had to dig for answers.

"I doubt it was random," the queen said. "Someone is angry."

"Apparently they are," Beth responded as she contemplated how much further to push. "If you really believe your husband has orchestrated the violence then I'm sure you're devastated that those kids were injured and the community's on edge."

"I'm absolutely devastated. My husband's evil."

Beth waited in silence.

The queen looked past Beth dismissively. "I may write an anonymous letter to Pastor Dan so he can warn his members that there are dangerous people in this town. It might scare my husband if he hears his group has been called out from the pulpit. The people of this town need to know the truth."

"I guess that's an option," Beth said, recalling her recent interaction with Pastor Dan and wondering how he would handle such a letter.

"You don't seem eager to help me, so maybe he will," the queen said.

Somehow, they got through the rest of the session. The queen started on another example of terrible things her husband had said and Beth let her go on without interruption. She tried to stay calm, hoping she could hide her suspicion that every word her client said was a lie.

When the queen left, Beth sat back in her chair and chose not to walk her out. A heaviness pressed down on her as she watched her client walk back across the street. When she neared the bell tower she stopped to talk to a woman Beth recognized as a client of Dr. Meadows's, who brought the staff pastries at the holidays. She sighed. The town felt too small. Much too small.

The sound of blaring sirens rattled the window panes. *They must be close,* Beth thought. What was happening? She watched her client rapidly take a phone call and then bolt across the square while the woman she had just greeted waved awkwardly. The sirens seemed to pass, and there was no further stirring among the other people she could see on the street.

OK, everything's fine, Beth told herself, turning from the window to focus on work. It was her lunch break. She felt the urge to call Nathan again but she knew that was a bad idea. Maybe baklava would help, she thought, so she grabbed her coat and walked down the stairs.

Michael was two feet ahead of her on the sidewalk when she emerged onto the street so she called out to him, unsure if he wanted company. He turned and waited, seemingly glad to see her.

"Going to lunch?" he asked.

"If baklava is lunch, then yes."

"Rough day?"

"Strange day. How are you?"

"I'm OK. I'm grabbing food to take back to the office because I think I'll be here late tonight. I got a call from the high school about one of my clients. She found a threat in her locker this morning. Her family is pretty active in the local mosque. The guidance counselor asked me to see the whole family and I think that's wise."

"Very," Beth said as her phone buzzed simultaneously with Michael's. It was an emergency tag from Serenity summoning them back to the office. Beth leaned against the building as she read the message. "There's been another bomb threat at the school," she said.

"I heard the sirens a few minutes ago," Michael said.

"Me too," Beth said. "I hoped it was nothing."

"This is out of control," Michael said. They hurried back to Serenity and went into the main lobby.

Eleanor motioned for them to go to the back office. "Dr. Meadows is waiting for you," she said.

No explosion had been reported, apparently, but a portion of the building hadn't been evacuated, Dr. Meadows told them. The sound of sirens continued to fill the air. All three of them looked out the window. People were dashing into buildings or to their cars. It was suddenly much more frantic than it had been only a few minutes before.

"I have an update," Eleanor said, walking into the office. "Right now it seems to be a false alarm. The bomb squad is there and they'll do a full sweep of the building. No students or faculty are allowed to return until it's clear." The sirens stopped, though Beth could see flashing lights pulsing in the distance.

"How do you know?" Michael asked, looking visibly shaken.

"I talked to my sister-in-law, who's an assistant principal there," Eleanor said.

"I think you can both carry on with your appointments," Dr. Meadows said. "Let's not create unnecessary panic."

Beth nodded and rose to leave. Her next client was probably already waiting.

"You OK?" she asked Michael.

"Sure," he said, going to his own office and avoiding eye contact. Beth kept thinking about the queen and what she had seen that morning, but there was no time for further speculation. She saw her next client in the upstairs lobby and so she turned the thoughts off. Her client must have heard the sirens too. Time to be Dr. Linn again.

26

THE DANCER

On the way to her next session, she forced herself to engage with yet another new driver and his boring analysis of the cloudy weather to avoid her own thoughts. She had hoped time with her family over the weekend would help her paranoia, but it hadn't. Her brother said he was fine but she couldn't believe him, especially since her parents acted like nothing had happened. They were more concerned about her than him, which made her afraid they were in on the plot. She was sick of it all. Every time her thoughts became clearer she felt a bit of hope, but then the paranoia returned and the hope would slip away. Today the delusions felt real and limitless. She knew she needed to report it to Dr. Linn, but it also seemed like Dr. Linn could be part of the plot against her. So could her driver, which is why she let him drone on about lake-effect clouds instead of telling him there were much bigger problems in town than gray skies.

As they exited the highway the sound of sirens triggered memories of her first psychosis. She could hear the voices of the demons that taunted her on the ambulance ride to the hospital and feel the eyes of the paramedics staring at her like she was crazy. She had to pull it together so her driver would not see her panic.

"Can I get you anything while you're in your session?" the driver asked. He had pulled into the Serenity lot without her realizing it.

She opened her eyes and tried to focus. *Just speak*, she thought, pushing the demonic voices away.

"No, I think I'm fine," she answered, unsure if her words made sense.

"I'd be happy to pick you up a coffee or some food."

She paused to think about her answer. *Is this a setup? Does he know about the demons?*

"Whatever you do is fine. Thanks for the ride." She opened the door and got out quickly. She did not want to bring attention to herself.

Unaware of her panic, her driver smiled as she closed the door. "See you in an hour. Maybe the sun will be out by then."

She stared at the entrance.

I can't go in, she thought as the voices swirled in her head.

"You have to go in," she said out loud.

God, what a nightmare, she thought. *Just open the door. You're OK.*

The lobby felt quieter than normal with only the sound machine to keep her company. She noticed Dr. Linn looked anxious when she walked out of the stairwell and across the lobby to get her.

It's not about you, she said to herself over and over as she followed her therapist into the office.

"How are you?" Dr. Linn asked as they settled into their seats.

"Fine," she said, still unsure if her words were real.

"I'm glad you're doing OK. I've just received some information and it's good timing for us to process it. I assume you haven't heard any news on your way here?"

"No." She picked up the pillow and hugged it tightly into her body.

"OK. First, I want you to know your brother is fine. I just talked to your parents."

The voices told her to run for the door. "OK . . . " she whispered.

"There was an incident at the high school. Another bomb threat. The good news is there's a suspect in custody." Dr. Linn appeared much too calm to be delivering such bad news.

"Who is it?" The need for information kept her in her seat, but the urge to run was still strong.

"It appears to be a student, but that's just speculation. The important thing for you to know right now is that your brother is safe and the police have a suspect."

"It's my fault." She felt her whole body begin to shake from the inside out like she was freezing and couldn't get warm.

"It is not your fault. Remember, you didn't do anything wrong. You couldn't have caused this to happen." Dr. Linn looked at her reassuringly.

"The guy at the hospital is after us. It's a conspiracy. I told you," she said, panic filling her body and her mind.

"Let's try to ground, OK?"

"OK."

"Let's take a deep breath together and then you can tell me about your weekend." She watched as Dr. Linn took a deep breath in and waited for her to respond.

"It was fine. I saw my family." *And I was paranoid about them*, she thought. *And if I tell you about the voices you might send me to the hospital, but if I don't I might lose touch with reality and end up there anyway.*

"How were your thoughts?"

"Fine," she lied.

Just pretend you're fine. Breathe when she says breathe and get out of this office before Dr. Linn realizes you know she's part of the plot to kill your brother. Just fake your way through the session.

It took all her strength, but she stayed calm enough to get herself out of Dr. Linn's office before she gave herself away. When she saw Dr. Linn's concern she knew she had to say as little as possible to try not to appear unbalanced.

So far so good. Now to get past the driver, she thought, running down the steps to the exit.

As soon as she got in the car she asked to be dropped at the school for her recovery meeting so she wouldn't have any further need to engage. The driver handed her a sandwich and she took it. Once he started to talk, she knew he'd entertain himself. She just had to survive until she could get out of her hometown and back to the safety of the city.

When they stopped in front of the school she was level enough to reengage. "Thanks for the ride and the sandwich," she said, waving goodbye. The sandwich had given her a perfect excuse not to talk. She knew her driver would never expect her to talk with her mouth full, so she'd made it last for the entire twenty-minute drive.

Now I can dance, she thought as she walked down the sidewalk. The janitor was out front and waved to her as she neared the building. *He might be my guardian angel. Yes, he's here to protect me so I can dance.*

She knew Dr. Linn was confused by their session but she did not want to think about it. *Ahhh, my ballet shoes, you're here*, she said, pulling them from her backpack. She had dug them out of a bin in the basement while she was at her parents' over the weekend and was excited to put them on. *You still fit perfectly*. She loved the feel of the leather on the wood floor. She just stood in the middle of the stage for a moment until the music in her mind propelled her across the floor and the voices quieted down for the show.

27

BETH

Beth saw the police officers enter the building as she rose to escort her last client out. She quickly closed her door and considered if it was possible to sprint down the stairs to her car in the time it would take them to get to the front desk. *Just be calm*, she thought, as she heard the sound of voices in the stairwell. *Maybe you can escape through the window*, her tiny fearful part said, looking out the window to see how far the drop was. A knock at the door startled her back to the moment.

"Dr. Linn, there are several police officers here who would like to speak with you," Dr. Meadows stated from the hallway.

Shit, shit, shit, she whispered. She had no way out.

"Hello, come in," she said, opening the door.

A female officer entered first. "We just have a few questions," she said. She appeared to be the senior officer, based on her colleagues' deferential treatment. "We understand you were at the high school on the day of the first bomb threat. Is that correct?"

"Yes." Beth motioned for them to take a seat but was ignored.

"Can you tell us what you saw?"

"I didn't see much. I had almost finished my talk when the fire alarm went off. I left with everyone else and was told it was just a drill."

"Did you see anything suspicious?"

Beth shook her head. "Not really. I had no idea there was a problem until after I left and made a call to my sister. She told me she'd gotten a text from the school's alert system about a threat."

The male officer held up a picture of Michael's client. "Did you see this young man there that day?" he asked.

"I did," Beth answered.

"Is he a client here?" the officer asked. He was exactly Beth's type. Fit, but not in a bulked-up way. Handsome without trying. Dark eyes. Dark hair. Nice smile. She wished she was meeting him anywhere else but here.

"As you know, I can't confirm or deny if he's a client here. Client information is confidential and can't be shared without a court order." She looked to Dr. Meadows for support but she remained silent.

"If he's your client and he's dangerous, you've got an obligation to the public to share that information," the officer said.

"I'm aware of my duty to warn. Is there anything else?" Beth wished there was a way to sound less mechanical, but client confidentiality had to be her priority.

The female officer continued. "If he is your client then you should know he's a suspect. Security cameras show him in both the area where the first bomb was detonated and also where the fire alarm was pulled on the day you were in the building. We'd hoped his therapist would want to help us to help him if he's in a psychological crisis. He could hurt himself and a lot of other people."

"I'm sure his therapist would appreciate your help. If he's involved then he's clearly in a crisis. You can be assured that if I have a dangerous client I'll follow the ethical guidelines and report it." Beth looked again to Dr. Meadows for guidance, but her face was like stone, with no expression and no recognition of Beth's appeal for help.

"Here's my card in case you have something to report," the female officer said, forcing her to make direct eye contact when she handed it to her.

"Got it." Beth took the card and walked toward her desk, hoping they'd take it as a cue to leave.

"Let me walk you out," Dr. Meadows said, leading them into the hallway.

Beth's stomach lurched as she listened to their banter as they descended the stairs. *What have I done?* she wondered. Her tiny fearful part stared at her from the top of her desk.

"Can I come in?" Michael asked, startling her.

"Of course. Close the door." She pulled herself together. Michael didn't need to see her fear.

"What was that about?" He took the seat in front of her desk and appeared as shaken up as she felt.

She took a minute to watch out the window for the officers to leave before she answered. "They want to know if one of our clients is the bomber."

"Fuck," he said.

Beth looked at him closely. "Do you know something you haven't told me?"

"No. You know everything I know."

"They showed me a photo of a kid they think is involved. It's your client," she told him. "I couldn't acknowledge that he's a client here and you can't confirm that either, unless you have cause."

Michael said nothing. He just stared at her.

"What? Do you know something?"

He closed his eyes and leaned back with his hands over his face. She waited in silence as her heart pounded and her tiny fearful part crawled under the desk and tried to disappear.

"Michael?"

"No. I don't *know* anything. I just know. He taunts me. He says he hates stupid Christians. Yesterday he made a comment about his Muslim teacher. He watches me for a reaction. It's bad."

Beth wished she could tell him what she saw in the park so they could sort this out together, but she couldn't expose her client. She was on her own, and she had to support Michael and his clients. "I'm glad they didn't question you. Your face and neck just turned bright red from talking to me. It makes you look like you have something to hide."

Michael sighed. "I've done nothing wrong, but I feel guilty. I can't sleep without dreaming of those reporters on my lawn, and I think my client is actually involved. I can't protect anyone. It just sucks."

"It does." She felt the heightened magnitude of the situation based on the events of the day, and knew she needed to be clear with Michael about the next steps.

"I'm sorry I didn't tell you about his comments last session. I didn't want to stir anything up," he said.

"You took a risk that was unwise to take. You have supervision to protect yourself and your clients."

"I know. I'm sorry."

"Anything else I need to know?"

"No. But if I notice anything I'll let you know."

"OK," she said. She wasn't sure if she believed him or not.

"I will. I promise," he said as he stood to leave. "I'll see you tomorrow."

"See you tomorrow," she said, and was left alone again with her own secrets.

28

CELESTE

Celeste tried to read Henry's mind as they sat together in the exam room. If his results were bad, they were out of options. Part of her felt compelled to give an optimistic pep talk, but the specter of death looming at the edge of her consciousness silenced her.

If the results were good, they'd be off on their trip to New York City the next day with an overnight stop in Pittsburgh to have dinner with some old friends. The suite she had booked in Midtown was at the hotel where they'd met. She needed to stand in that lobby and go to their favorite diner for breakfast. She wanted to be with him in the piano bar where they first danced.

A tap on the door startled her. "Ready?" the doctor asked.

"Always," Henry chuckled, masterfully hiding any anxiety he felt about the test results that were about to instruct his future.

"I have some good news," the doctor said.

"I like your opener," Henry said.

Celeste felt herself grow unexpectedly weightless. She watched the doctor's lips but struggled to comprehend his words, as if she was in a tunnel far away. She heard "no new growth" and "good markers," and then the doctor was gone.

Celeste was quiet as they walked to the car.

"Ready for a road trip?" Henry asked.

"I think I'm in shock. Did he say there's a chance for remission?"

"He said it was possible."

"Are you surprised?"

"I'm relieved," he said, opening his car door. "Relieved and surprised."

"Do you want to call the kids or do you want me to?" she asked.

"I think I'll just text them. I don't want to answer a bunch of questions unless you have a need to talk to them."

"Not really. If you text them, just let them know we leave in the morning and we can call on our drive."

"Perfect." He buckled his seat belt and pulled out his phone.

Celeste noticed Henry's profile as she turned to back out of her parking space. His face had captivated her since the day they first met. He appeared unbreakable. Strong and handsome. That chin. God, he messed with her head.

He laid down his phone and closed his eyes. "Sent."

His phone instantly pinged with questions and congratulations.

"Want to stop for dinner?" he asked. It was almost five o'clock, and she liked the idea of avoiding rush hour if he really felt well enough to go out.

"Are you up to it?" She watched his face for the truth.

"We're about to take a road trip. I'd better be up to it."

"It's been a long day. I can cook." Celeste wanted to be sure he wasn't just full of bravado.

"Exactly. It's been a long day. Let me take you out," he insisted. "We're five minutes from Mama Rosa's."

"OK," she said, turning toward Little Italy. She felt her body relax into the memories they had there. She remembered that her Jersey girl self hadn't believed good Italian food could exist in Ohio. Henry had loved it when he proved her wrong.

"*Buongiorno*, my friends," the owner cooed when they walked in. She greeted them with hugs. "It's been too long. Come, come. I have a good table for you. You look like you're starving!"

"Thank you, Bella," Henry said. Celeste helped him to navigate into his seat.

The staff pretended not to notice Henry's frailty as they filled the table with bread and wine. The restaurant hadn't changed in forty years. Red-checked tablecloths. Bottles of Chianti on every table. The staff impeccably dressed, ready to brush away crumbs between every course.

"I'd like to make a toast," Henry said, lifting his glass. "To your strength. To your courage. To your beauty. You keep our family together."

Celeste fought back tears. "To your test results!" she said.

"Oh yes, to my test results!" They both laughed at that and clinked their glasses together.

Celeste tried to enjoy the moment, but Ben's aura hung over her like a storm cloud. She knew she should bring him up but she didn't want to break the spell of the momentary return of Henry's old self. He was in his element. He even had the energy to flirt with the wait staff. They had to talk, but not tonight.

On the drive home he nodded off, and Celeste considered the problem of Ben while Henry snored beside her. From what she could determine, Ben had reached out to Beth for some reason and she must have learned something she wasn't sharing, because she'd been evasive since then any time Celeste asked about Ben.

What does she know? Celeste pondered, accelerating to pass a slow car. She couldn't help but be impressed when she thought about her youngest daughter. She'd always been a little sleuth. If Ben had shared something with her and she had questions, Celeste knew she was looking for answers.

Ben is my problem, she thought, as she slid back into the right lane and glanced at Henry beside her. Ben had been relentless with his phone calls, and Celeste finally relented and let him come over. He'd arrived on Monday with Henry's favorite Thai food and a bottle of Gewürztraminer. Henry, who never drank white wine, went on and on about how it paired perfectly. Celeste had listened as Ben encouraged Henry to tell him stories about the early days before his dad met his mom and before he was born. Henry happily regaled him with tales of the past as Ben eagerly probed for more information. She felt illogically angry with Ben, but her anger toward Henry was deserved.

"No wonder you're asleep—the 'Henry Show' takes a lot of energy," Celeste said quietly as she got him out of the car and guided him to bed. She made sure his breathing grew heavy before she went downstairs and poured herself a glass of wine. Alone with her thoughts, she curled up on the couch to think, but she still had no idea what to do. A part of her knew Greg would help, and she wanted that help desperately.

Not a good idea, she thought as she followed the movement of some deer in her backyard, the streetlight just bright enough to reveal their silhouettes.

But why not? she asked herself. She mulled it over. By the time she poured her second glass she'd written and deleted several emails and finally narrowed it down to one sentence: *I'm in town tomorrow if you're available for a late night catch-up.* She closed her eyes and hit send.

Before she had time to question herself, his response popped up on the screen.

Meet me at Sal's tomorrow at 11 p.m.?

Yes, she responded immediately.

Celeste felt a smile spread across her face. Tomorrow she'd tuck Henry in and then sneak out. She deserved it. She needed it. It would feel good to sit with Greg and feel him listen to her. Her. Not Henry's wife. Not someone's mom. Just her.

Greg saw most people clearly, Henry included, and he'd tried to warn her back then but she'd been charmed and before she knew it, she was trapped with Henry's secrets and a trail of lies to cover them.

Her therapist wanted her to share her story, but the tale was dark and she had only told it twice, once to Greg and once to the therapist. Her current homework was to tell the story out loud to someone, even if that person was gone.

She stared off into the night. *What the hell. If I have to tell my story out loud, it'll be to my mom. So Mom, if you're listening, my therapist thinks it might help. I wish I'd called you the day I found out, but I didn't. Tonight I need sleep, but I'll tell you soon. I promise.*

29

BETH

Beth paced the circumference of her office, thumb poised beside Nathan's name on her phone. The insecure part of her that poked at her fears wanted her to call him for reassurance that she had handled yesterday's events correctly. The business card the police officers had left her remained in her top desk drawer, an ominous reminder of what had transpired. She momentarily fantasized she could still move with Nathan and escape, but then a flurry of activity at the bell tower caught her attention. She saw Michael's client dart through the crowd and stop abruptly when the queen turned the corner, stepping back against the wall until she walked by without a flinch, as though the boy was invisible. No recognition. Or at least that's how it appeared to Beth.

With her phone still in her hand and Nathan's name still on the screen, she realized there were too many thoughts in her head to handle them alone. She texted *SOS* to her friend Renee. Renee worked in IT at the hospital and Beth had known her since they were roommates their freshman year in college. She'd been so preoccupied she hadn't called her in weeks, and she felt guilty when Renee responded by calling her immediately.

"Tell me everything," she said before Beth got out her hello.

"Everything's a lot." She started by describing the encounter with the police.

"Were either of the cops cute?" Renee asked.

Beth laughed. "One of them was, but that wasn't on my radar!"

"You noticed though, admit it. It's time. Nathan's been gone for months. You need to start dating." Beth appreciated Renee's ability to get her out of her head, even if it was just for a moment.

"I thought I might've been on a date a few weeks ago, but thankfully I didn't embarrass myself," she said, giving her friend the details of her meeting with Ben and everything that had transpired since.

"Oh shit. That's serious." Renee sounded shocked.

"Yeah, well, not too worried about dating right now." Beth sat down and watched the activity in the square.

"What're you going to do?" Renee asked.

"I need to talk to my mom, but she and my dad just left for a long weekend. He got positive test results and they decided to get away. I don't even know what I'd say to her anyway. 'Hey Mom, just wondering, were you having an affair with Dad's best friend when you got pregnant with Andrea? And me? And oh, by the way, is he Jonathan and Carrie's dad too?'" Beth felt the tightness in her chest that had become her norm when she thought about her parents.

"Hmmm," Renee said. "What if it's the other way around, and your dad was having an affair with Ben's mom? That seems more likely, doesn't it?" Her voice had a tone of curiosity.

"From Ben's research, it appears we have genetic relatives on his dad's side, so he's convinced his dad's our biological father. I made my account private and it makes me anxious when I make it public to dig around for relatives. I'm afraid someone will log in at the same time and see my profile. The only way to have proof is to get my dad's DNA, and there's no way I'm asking him." Beth wished she could lie down on her couch, cover her head with the pillows her clients hugged during session, and disappear.

"Seems like you've got to either talk to your mom, who clearly knows who your father is, or let it go. What other option do you have?"

"What if my dad did cheat on her, and he's Ben's dad and she doesn't know it?" Beth asked. "How could I do that to my mom with everything she's going through right now? I need to figure this out. I wish I could let it go but I can't, and even if I could, Ben isn't going to let me." Beth got up and started pacing again.

Renee asked, "Have you talked to the DNA testing company? They might help you with tracing things without having to involve your family." That was an option she hadn't considered, and she made a mental note to call on her next break.

"That's a thought. I'll do that today. Anything to keep Ben from blowing this up."

"I can't believe you used to have a crush on him." Renee had met Ben at a Linn Christmas party long before Nathan was in the picture.

Beth stood back up and resumed her pacing. "Delete that from your memory, please. Can you imagine if he knew? I was a little bit nervous when he asked to meet because I thought he might be interested. What if I'd flirted with him before he dropped the half-brother thing on me? I'd have died right there. It's bad enough without throwing incest in. God, it's like a reality show."

"I'm so sorry," Renee said. "I know how it's been for you lately. Look, I have to go but let's get dinner soon, OK?"

"Thanks, friend." Beth ended the call and went to the lobby to greet her whine and dine client.

As soon as they both sat down to begin the session, they heard sirens. Beth looked out the window to see a steady stream of emergency vehicles speeding through the square toward the south end of town.

"I wonder if it's another attack on the school? That's quite a procession," whine and dine said. He stood to get a better look.

Panic crept into Beth's consciousness, but she let her client continue.

"My nephew said he knows the guy who planted the first device but he won't tell anyone who it is. I'm glad my kids are in private school." He adjusted his tie that had slipped down from his collar.

Beth dug her nails into her chair to keep herself from asking the wrong questions. She had to stay focused.

"Your nephew is your godson, right?"

"Yes. I'm worried about him, but he says the guy doesn't intend to hurt anyone and I shouldn't worry. He asked me not to tell my brother because he thinks he'll overreact."

"Aren't you worried, though?"

"Sure, but what can I do?"

"You could do a lot. Your nephew is being influenced by someone who set off a bomb. It doesn't matter if the guy says he's not planning to hurt anyone. He's already hurt two people."

"I hear you. I'll think about it. I'm not exactly in the best spot to stir up trouble with my brother, but you've got a point, doc."

Beth knew she'd pushed as hard as she could and needed to redirect. "Have you and your brother talked about your issues with the estate, like we discussed last week?"

"He's not willing to budge, so I give up. I'm less anxious about it though since we met last week. I want to let it go."

Beth was able to contain her fear throughout his session, but when she walked him out she followed him down to the main lobby to see if there was anything happening. Before she got to the bottom of the steps she could hear the sound of breaking news on the lobby television. She stood in horror and listened to the reporter explain that a student had been injured when the explosives in his backpack detonated. No names were given, but the injured student was reportedly alive and en route to the hospital. The cameras showed a steady stream of students evacuating and police attempting to keep parents from rushing into the building.

Beth sat down on the couch beside the television. A feeling of paralysis began to move up from her feet through her body and into her throat. She knew she needed to talk to Michael, but she was transfixed by the television. *What is the queen doing there?* she wondered. The camera narrowed in and a reporter, who introduced her as the dean of the academy, proceeded to ask her opinion on school safety. Beth watched in horror as her client detailed the ineffectiveness of the public school system and praised her board for all the safety measures they had in place.

Beth's thoughts went to a very dark place as she walked back up the stairs to her office. *I've been played*, she thought as she tried to ignore her tiny fearful part who sat curled up in the lobby with her hands over her ears.

Michael was alone when she walked past his office, so she stepped inside. He was glued to his phone and didn't notice her until she said his name.

"Look at this." He held up his phone and showed her an amateur video taken at the scene.

"Is it him?" She watched as the injured student was lifted into the ambulance.

"I think so. I recognize the shoes, but I'm not positive. I just keep playing it over and over to see if I can figure it out. I don't know what else to do."

"Are you OK?" Beth felt powerless to help him.

He looked at her uncomfortably.

"Stupid question," Beth said. "At least we know he's alive and nobody else was hurt. That's something." She scrambled to find a lifeline for him.

He continued to stare at her, his despair palpable.

"I guess we wait to see what happens," Beth continued. "Have you reviewed your notes on him in case you get a call from the police?"

"Yes. There's nothing to tell them. He's evasive. I've got nothing." She could see his desperate need for reassurance, but she had nothing else in that moment to offer.

"If you hear anything let me know." She heard the emotion in her own voice as her throat began to close off. She walked back to her office and hoped Michael was too preoccupied to notice. If this kid died, she'd blame herself forever even though she knew she had no control of the situation.

Get it together, she said to herself, aware that her tiny fearful part was now curled up in the corner of the couch. She paced the length of her office to expend the energy from the adrenaline flooding her body and tried to make a plan. She needed to be confident when Dr. Meadows began asking questions. A knock on her partially opened door startled her. Michael peered around the corner.

"My client's mom just called," he said. "It was him. She wants to come in to talk to me tomorrow so she can review my case notes. She's angry I didn't see the signs and warn her."

"OK. Wow. I guess at least we know what's happening," Beth said. "How's he doing?"

"Unconscious. They're going to keep him in a medically induced coma until the swelling in his brain goes down."

"I'm a bit surprised his mom is going to leave him alone at the hospital to come here to talk to you," Beth said.

Michael shrugged. "She's out of her mind with anger. I'm not sure how to handle her request for my case notes. Her son has a right to his privacy."

"I think he's lost that right at this point. He's clearly a danger to himself and others."

"We don't really know what happened yet, so I'm not sure you're right," Michael said.

Beth tried to balance her response to avoid revealing her cascade of emotions. "Call our liability lawyer. My instinct is to give her complete access to the file, but I might be operating out of guilt. Get the facts."

"Guilt? Why?" He looked shocked by her response.

"I'm your supervisor. I dropped the ball."

"You can't drop a ball that doesn't exist," Michael said. "We had no way to stop this from happening."

Beth knew she couldn't tell Michael her guilt stemmed from what she had seen outside of the office, especially since the queen had a one o'clock appointment the next day when his client's mother would also be in the office.

"Let me know what you find out from the attorney," she said.

"Thanks for your help."

She walked to the door and closed it behind him, wondering if either one of them was truly doing the right thing.

30

THE DANCER

Where's my driver? she wondered as she stared out the window in the hope he would be early. It was Wednesday, and she had woken up without her usual sense of dread. Weirdly, she was actually looking forward to her session with Dr. Linn. The roller-coaster ride of her illness was hard to predict and harder to treat, but her psychiatrist had found a cocktail of medications to keep her mania in control. Unfortunately, her paranoia remained pervasive. Some days she could identify the delusional thoughts and talk herself back into reality, but other days it was impossible to do it on her own. Even Dr. Linn was powerless to deconstruct her delusions when the voices got too loud—but today, everything was quiet in her system.

I actually want to see Dr. Linn, she mused when she saw the car pull up. Her driver was an elderly gentleman she recognized from church, but he had no connection to her or her family. He was quiet throughout the drive, only asking her if the temperature was comfortable and if she was good with the radio station. The time passed quickly, her thoughts focused on what she wanted to discuss in her session. When her driver asked her if there was anything she needed him to pick up she was surprised they were already in the parking lot.

She rushed up the stairs, aware she was right on time, and was greeted by Dr. Linn, who had just come out of her office. She could barely contain her excitement about her idea.

"How've you been this week?" Dr. Linn asked.

"A lot better, and I have a plan. I want you to help my brother. Could you call and tell my parents about the EMDR and your light bar?"

"Why don't you tell them about it?" Dr. Linn looked confused.

"I don't like to talk about my therapy with my family. I know it reminds them of everything I put them through and that makes me sad." She felt a tightening in her chest.

"But you want me to?" A look of curiosity crossed Dr. Linn's face.

She paused to think. "I don't want you to talk about my therapy, just what you do."

"So you want me to randomly call your parents and tell them what I do?" Dr. Linn's tone was slightly playful.

She smiled. "Yes."

"Without talking about you?" Dr. Linn seemed to be contemplating how such a call might go without automatically shutting down the idea.

"Yes."

Dr. Linn smiled back, although she was clearly not sure how to proceed.

"I can't think of a way to do that without mentioning you. Maybe it would be good for you to talk to them and then they can call me."

"I'm going to see them this weekend, so I guess I could tell them about EMDR without making it about me. If they're interested, I'll give them your number. They're so consumed about my brother's safety they want to move him to the academy. I guess there's a huge wait list now, which I'm sure will get longer with what happened yesterday."

"Does your brother want to change schools?"

"No, he wants to stay with his friends. He's having trouble sleeping and stuff, but he told me that's from the explosion and not from being afraid of going to school. Especially now since the kid who did it is in the hospital."

"Does your brother believe he's the one who did it?"

"Yeah, why, don't you?" She felt confused and concerned by Dr. Linn's question, since she thought it was clear who was responsible for the violence.

"Sure, yeah, of course. I just want to make sure you and your brother are feeling OK." Dr. Linn's response reassured her.

"We're good. My parents probably need you more than my brother."

"They're in a tough spot," Dr. Linn said. "If you want me to do a family session with the four of you just let me know. You seem to be handling this all really well. Have you been sleeping OK?"

"My sleep's a lot better. I think my new medication is pretty good because I actually want to find a way to dance again. Not at the level I did in undergrad, but maybe somewhere like the studio I went to the summer before I started med school. Just take a modern class for fun." She waited for Dr. Linn's response.

Dr. Linn paused and smiled. "That's incredible. The last time I brought it up you shut the idea down before I could finish my sentence."

"I know, right? I guess maybe I feel a little bit more like myself. It's weird, but colors seem brighter. I noticed the smell of the rain last night when I was walking home from work, and I haven't noticed that forever. And the coffee smells so good to me when I get to work. It's amazing." She extended her arms like she had just woken up and was taking her first morning stretch.

"You've worked hard to get here." Dr. Linn looked genuinely happy.

"It's nice not to just see shades of gray all day. You know?" She tucked one leg under her and relaxed back into the couch.

"I can imagine."

"For sure. So are you ready to jump in?" Dr. Linn smiled at hearing her mimic the line she usually used.

After her session she floated down the steps and when she got outside she stopped to watch a hawk circle over her head. *I hope this lasts but even if it doesn't, I've had a good day today,* she thought. Acceptance of her diagnosis had been a struggle, but she could now see the value in it. The years of denial had led to a major crash she realized could have ended her life. In the dark days she sometimes wished it had, but today she was grateful it hadn't. For so long she had fixated on trying to outrun the darkness, only to find herself spiraling into more fear. Dr. Linn had helped her to turn on a light that dispersed some of the dark thoughts. At least the ones that were manageable. The rest were still a challenge, but a challenge she no longer faced alone. She had found a way to be more present, not stuck regretting the past or fearing the future, and she wanted to find a way to stay on this new path. Today she felt it might be possible if she stayed focused on one hour at a time.

31

THE COUPLE

"We don't want to give up on our marriage," the wife said before Dr. Linn could even close the door to her office.

"Great. Tell me what's happened." Dr. Linn turned around with a look of pleasant surprise.

"The violence at the high school has caused us both to take a step back," she said. "And we know the parents of the student who was injured," her husband said, scooting closer to his wife on the couch.

"I'm sorry to hear . . . "

"No, it's not about him," she said, cutting Dr. Linn off mid-sentence. "I mean it's bad that he's injured, but it's good it made us realize we have to stop wasting our lives fighting."

"We were up most of the night. She's decided to try to forgive me," he said, squeezing her hand.

"I've been angry long enough. I was afraid if I let go of the anger then he could hurt me again." She looked at him for support. She'd been angry for so long, and was amazed she was able to say this.

"I didn't understand that was why she was so upset," her husband said. "I just thought she hated me and wanted me to suffer. I didn't see *her*." He looked surprised and relieved by his own revelation.

"And I didn't believe he was sorry, so I used anger to protect myself, like you've said. It gave me a sense of control. Last night I realized none of us has control over anything. Horrible things happen and all we can do is try to live through them, and I don't want to do that alone."

He put his arm around her shoulder and pulled her closer. "I don't want you to either," he said. Dr. Linn looked from one to the other with a look of approval.

"All I could think about last night was that if we got divorced and something tragic happened then I'd be alone," she said.

"I'm glad this has given you both a new perspective on your relationship," she said. "Is your friend's son going to be OK?"

"From what I've heard he'll be fine. I'm just happy that it woke me up to the fact that my husband does love me." She squeezed his hand.

"And that it woke me up to the reality of how much my behavior devastated her. I'm grateful for the chance to make it up to her," he added.

Dr. Linn took a moment to affirm their commitment before she introduced a new exercise to help them build trust. At first it felt wrong to show any vulnerability, but something about her husband's tone invited her to try. It was a step she never thought she'd feel safe enough to take, but one she felt might have the power to lead them home.

32

BETH

Stay engaged. Do not ask anything about the boy, she commanded herself as she listened to the couple proclaim their newfound appreciation for their relationship. *I'm going to freak out. What if the queen put the bomb in his backpack? She's in the lobby waiting. I saw her walk across the street five minutes ago.* Beth was worried the queen would see the couple when they left their session. She was fairly certain the queen knew the husband. She tried to think. *I saw them make eye contact last week. Is he involved? Is this miraculous healing in their marriage all a huge lie? I can't breathe. I have to do my job. I have to stay focused and get them out of here without letting them know I know anything about anything.*

After they finished, she walked them to the door and said she hoped they had another good week. Then she closed the door behind them and leaned against it. She needed to regroup, but a knock on her door didn't allow her the time.

She opened it to find the queen standing there. "I don't mean to barge in, but I've got two hours' worth of material to update you on today and I saw your last clients leave," her client said, coming right in. "I've filed for divorce and he can't contest it, because I know he's responsible for that young man who was injured at the school. If I tell the police what he's done he'll go to jail." She sat in her regular spot on the couch.

Beth sat in the farthest chair from the couch, which was not her usual pattern. She felt desperate for space. She could barely breathe. "When did you file?" she asked.

"I had everything completed with the attorney last Friday, but I was too afraid to do it. Now that I have a way to threaten him, I told my attorney to go for it. He's scared enough to sign whatever we hand him. If he signs uncontested then I won't need you to be a witness anymore. I'm not too worried. I doubt he'll mess with me now that I have the upper hand." She looked smug sitting in her corner, hair and clothes perfect, a look of contentment on her face.

Keep the conversation going, Beth told herself. *Breathe*. "You have proof that he put the bomb in that boy's backpack?"

"What do you mean?" The queen looked at her incredulously.

"You said he's responsible, so I assumed you meant he planted the bomb," Beth said, holding eye contact longer than she felt comfortable doing. The queen's gaze was ice cold.

"I never said he put explosives in his backpack."

"OK." *What did the woman mean?*

"That's just strange that you thought I did."

"I misunderstood. What are you saying, then?" Beth asked.

"I'm saying I know he's involved. The kid's been at our house, and I have footage of it on our security video. And when I asked my husband about it he didn't have any answers."

"So you do know him?" *Be careful*, Beth thought as she shifted in her chair.

"It's a small town, Dr. Linn. I recognize him from the television coverage, which is why I checked our camera footage. My husband says he doesn't know him. He can say what he wants. I have witnesses who will testify that my husband has held anti-religion group meetings at our house when I'm not there. The police would love to have this information and the video footage. I have all the power I need to get out of this marriage."

"Do you believe your husband's a danger to anyone right now?" Beth tried to appear neutral while she watched her client for signs of deceit.

"No. He's a coward. He just incites other people to do what he's afraid to do. Now that I have evidence, I think he'll go into hiding."

"So you think your son's safe?"

"Yes. My husband's afraid of me now, so I think he'll tuck his tail and run." She looked pleased, like a cat who had just caught a mouse.

"That's a huge shift. Last week you were terrified of him."

The queen shrugged. It looked too casual to Beth. "I was but now I'm good," the queen said. "In fact, I think this will be one of our last sessions."

"I'm glad you're good. I have to admit I'm surprised you're not afraid anymore."

"I told you he's a coward. He wants this to go away. If he divorces me he can keep his secret."

"And continue hurting people?" Beth knew she'd lost her objectivity and taken on a judgmental posture, but it was too late to take it back.

"That's not my problem, but it's unlikely. I doubt he meant things to go this far." Beth did a double take. The queen had not lashed out at her and was almost defending her husband. She tried to adjust her mind to the change.

"What about the young man? Don't you think he'll testify against him?"

"I doubt he'll wake up." *What?* Beth thought. *Keep calm*, she told herself. *Keep asking questions.*

"Really? I heard he's expected to make a full recovery." She kept her features neutral.

"You can't believe everything you hear, Dr. Linn. I'm surprised you're so naive," the queen chided.

"If he does live, he'll probably out your husband. It's good you'll have filed for divorce. It gives you distance from it," Beth said.

She narrowed her eyes. "Why would you try to upset me?"

"What do you mean?" Beth asked.

"I'll be upset if he ruins my husband's reputation. Do you expect me to care about a kid who tried to bomb a school and kill a bunch of people?"

"I thought you believed your husband coerced him?"

"Look, the kid's capable of murder whether my husband coerced him or not. An eye for an eye. He got what he deserved."

"Well, if he wakes up and tells the media your husband orchestrated everything, it will create some issues for you," Beth said. She knew she was dangerously close to crossing a line that would reveal her suspicions.

Her client shrugged. "If he wakes up, I'll handle it," she said. "What I need from you right now is to go through my file to make sure you have sufficient documentation in case I still need you in court."

"OK," Beth said. She walked to her desk and opened her laptop to retrieve the file. It took all of her concentration to stop her hands from trembling when she picked up the documents from the printer and handed them over. She waited in silence while her client read through them.

"I'm impressed, Dr. Linn. You've captured my sessions well. Now it's time for me to celebrate. I'll see myself out," her client said, dismissive of any potential for closure protocol.

"OK. Best of luck," Beth said to her client's back, relieved not to have to walk her out but also frustrated with the lies hanging in the air that were impossible to clarify. What did she expect? The queen had taken control of their sessions from the beginning, so why would it change as they neared the end? *Who needs closure anyway?* she thought, aware of a voicemail notification on her phone that had come in during the session.

She checked her phone and saw it was from her mom, who never left voicemails. She pressed play and braced herself.

"Hi Beth. Please don't panic; just call me when you can. Dad's OK, but he's been admitted to the hospital. You can come see him tonight when you get off work. He's already giving the staff a hard time and keeping them on their toes. Breathe deeply, darling. I hated to call you during work but I didn't want one of your siblings to tell you. I promise he's OK. See you soon. Love you."

Beth collapsed into her chair, the air leaving her lungs and the energy draining from her body. It was 1:56 p.m. She didn't have time to call back before her next session. It felt like a blow had landed squarely in the center of her chest.

Be Dr. Linn again. She reminded herself that she'd done this numerous times, and she could do it again now.

Somehow, she managed to get through the rest of the afternoon. By the time she escorted her last client out she had regained focus for her meeting with Michael. She tapped on his partially opened door. *One crisis at a time,* she thought.

"How'd it go with your client's mom?" she asked him.

He glanced up. "She didn't fire me. Or sue me. So I guess it went OK."

"How's her son?"

"They think he's going to be OK. They've hired a private investigator to try to find out who else was involved. They believe he was set up, but the police don't buy it. She wanted to know my thoughts." He had dark circles under his eyes, but other than that he looked more put together than Beth expected.

Beth pulled a chair closer to his desk. "What do you mean?"

"I told her I don't know anything, so I definitely can't corroborate a setup."

"Why do they think he was set up?" Beth made sure her tone stayed neutral. Michael couldn't know her suspicions about the queen.

"They found a bunch of cash stashed in his room. They think someone paid him to carry the explosives into the school." *Do not show emotion*, she thought before she responded. *Stay neutral.*

"What do you think?"

He shrugged. "I have no idea. And that makes me very uncomfortable. It was my job to help him. I failed." He slumped back in his chair.

"We've been over this, Michael. What could you have done?"

"I don't know, but I should've done something."

"Go home and do what you'd tell your clients to do. Go for a run. Take a hot shower. Call a friend and go to dinner. Anything to stay busy. There's nothing you can do now, so you need to decompress." She listened to herself, thinking the least she could do was help him to disconnect. He'd done everything he could do.

She couldn't read Michael's expression. His office was dark, except for the light from his desk lamp illuminating his face.

"I'll try," he said with a weak smile.

Beth wanted to offer more, but she knew he needed to figure it out on his own.

"You've done your best, Michael, and you'll be here for him when he gets out of the hospital," she said on her way out the door.

"I hope you're right," he said.

The twenty-five-minute drive to the hospital gave Beth space to assimilate all she had witnessed that day. *She must be guilty. She has no empathy*, she thought, thinking of the queen. It was the only thing that made sense.

Could she be a sociopath? she wondered. She turned into the parking deck located between the Children's Hospital and City Hospital. As if she'd conjured her, after she made the turn, she saw the queen's familiar figure exit the front door of the Children's Hospital.

What if she sees me? Beth reflexively ducked, but the woman had walked past and disappeared. *Just park*, she told herself. *Breathe. It doesn't matter if she sees you. You're here for your dad. So just get out of the car and go see him. Don't let her intimidate you. Text your mom. Get the room number. Keep it together. Get on the elevator. Walk down the hall. Take a deep breath. You're fine.*

Her parents were what she needed to focus on now. They needed her. Whatever was happening with her client was out of her control, and it was time for her to follow the advice she'd given Michael and disconnect from work. Her calm demeanor back in place, she walked toward her father's room.

33

BETH

"Hi, pumpkin," her mom said when she walked into her father's room.

"How's the patient?" She gave her mom a hug.

"I'm right here. You don't have to refer to me in the third person," he responded.

"It looked like you were asleep, Dad." She leaned in to hug him. "How are you?"

"I'm fine. They overreact. I just had a little fall this morning. No big deal."

"He passed out and hit his head," Celeste said. "His doctor wants to run some tests to see what caused it." She sat back down in the chair beside his bed.

"Overkill," Henry insisted. "I'm fine. You look pale, though," he said to Beth. "What's happening? Are you worried about me or something?"

"Or something, for sure." Beth pulled a chair up to the other side of his bed and sat down near him.

"Andrea was here this afternoon and she looked just like you do," he said. "Pale and skittish. You kids have to stop worrying. I'm fine. In fact, why don't you get your mom out of this hospital and take her to dinner? She hasn't eaten all day."

Beth smiled at him fondly. "I just got here and you already want to get rid of me? Is there a game on or something?"

He looked up at the television, where a basketball game had just started. Beth rolled her eyes but smiled.

"I can watch the game with you, Dad. I promise to be quiet." She wanted to be strong for him.

He gave her a look that said he knew better.

Celeste intervened. "He's right. I could use some food and some air." She picked up her coat and motioned for Beth to join her. "We'll be back in an hour," she said as Henry waved them both away.

Beth followed her mom back down the long hallway to the elevators.

"What's really happening?" she asked her mother when they were out of his earshot.

"We're not sure. It could be anything from dehydration to new tumor growth. We'll have some results tomorrow. I don't want you to worry."

Beth pushed the elevator button. "I'll try, but it's not easy."

"Nothing is easy with him," Celeste said. "He was right about me being hungry, though. I'm glad he noticed." Beth felt her typical conflict with her dad. He really was charming—until he felt disrespected or unappreciated. She'd realized early in life that he could be quite cruel if provoked.

When the doors opened, they squeezed into the crowded elevator. A woman with a balloon bouquet scooted over to make space. Beth was reminded of the balloons that had been in her grandfather's hospital room during one of his many hospitalizations, and hoped the recipient of this bouquet would have a better outcome. Damn Pastor Dan for bringing him up and making her miss him again.

"What sounds good?" she asked her mom.

"How about sushi? There's a good place a block from here," Celeste said as they emerged onto the sidewalk.

"Sure," Beth said. "I'm glad to have some time with you." She hadn't realized how much she needed to see her mom until that moment.

"Me too. I've been wanting to talk to you about Ben. He stopped by yesterday to see your dad and he said you two have met up a few times. I told him you hadn't mentioned it."

Beth picked up her pace. "Didn't I? I thought I did."

"No. Anything you want to tell me?" Celeste asked.

"About Ben?"

"Yes. Can you slow down?"

"Sorry," Beth said. "I'm just thinking we're on a tight timetable here. Let's get inside." She opened the door and they squeezed in with a large group of people waiting for a table.

Beth skirted around them to approach the host and was able to secure a booth for two near the bar. She was grateful for the loud techno music and dim lighting. It created space for her to think. How should she answer her mother?

"This is nice," Celeste said.

Beth stared at her menu. She knew this was her chance to ask the questions she needed to ask. Her mom had set her up perfectly.

"What looks good?" Celeste asked.

"Everything," Beth replied, looking up to greet their server. She felt her mom analyzing her while she bantered and placed their orders. The minute he delivered their drinks her mom returned to her interrogation.

"So, what does Ben want from you?"

Beth took a sip of her cocktail before she responded. "What do you mean?"

"I'm not sure what I mean. I guess I'm just curious." Celeste appeared unaware of Beth's anxiety over the topic of Ben.

"About what?" *How long can I keep this up?* she thought. She wanted to give her mother the chance to tell her the truth first.

"Beth," Celeste said, looking at her levelly. "I think you need to tell me what's going on."

Beth sighed. "OK," she said. "Ben contacted me because his DNA matched with Andrea. She's a close relative. A cousin or a half-sibling. He met with me to see if I knew how this could be possible. When I didn't know anything, he asked me to take the same test so he could figure out what it meant. He wanted me to come to you but I told him it was a bad time because of Dad." *There.* That was the first step. Now what would her mom say?

"Did you take the test?" Celeste asked.

"I did. "

"And?"

"Do you feel up to this conversation?" She needed to make sure before saying more.

"I asked, didn't I?" Celeste appeared to be comfortable about continuing, even though Beth couldn't understand how that was possible given what she'd just told her.

"OK. I haven't talked to you because I didn't want to upset you. Are you really OK?"

"Yes, Beth. I'm fine. What did you find out?"

Beth paused to compose herself. Her mother looked a bit too calm, which made Beth feel both angry and sad.

"Apparently I'm his close relative too. We assume I'm his half sister, since Andrea definitely matched as my full sibling. From your expression it doesn't seem like any of this is a shock to you."

"It's not a shock," Celeste said.

"OK . . . did Dad have an affair with Ben's mom?"

"No."

"Did you have an affair with his dad?"

"No, Beth."

"Then how are we related? I don't understand," she said at the moment their server delivered vegetarian pot stickers. They both paused until he left. Celeste reached over and tried to put her hand over her daughter's hand.

"I'm sorry you found out this way. I'm so sorry."

Beth struggled to control her anger. "You need to tell me what happened."

"I promised your father I wouldn't tell you."

"Does Andrea know?"

"Of course not. Nobody knows."

"We need to know. It's our truth, Mom. I don't care what you promised Dad."

"I told you nobody cheated."

"Fine, nobody cheated. That doesn't answer my question." She all of a sudden felt betrayed by both her parents.

"If I tell you, then you'll have to carry the secret, and I'm not sure you understand how hard that can be."

"I already have a secret, Mom."

"OK. I'll tell you. I've always wanted you all to know, but your dad was against it and, in a way, I understood. He was afraid it would change your relationship with him."

"You think?" Beth couldn't hide her sarcasm.

"Please try not to judge the situation until you've had time to digest it."

"Fine. I'll try."

"First of all, I didn't know about Andrea's paternity until the day I got pregnant with you."

"What are you talking about? How could you not know?" Beth asked, staring at her mom in disbelief.

"I need to start at the beginning, so please be patient. When your dad and I got married he made it clear he wanted a large family, so we started trying right away. After two years we went to a fertility clinic for help and found out he was sterile. He was devastated. Eventually we decided to use a sperm donor."

"You used a sperm donor and didn't tell us? How could you not tell us?" Beth watched her mother's face for some clue of remorse.

"Your father didn't want you to know. He didn't want it to change the way you thought of him."

"I can't believe you would lie to us," Beth said. "Why?" She couldn't accept what her mother had done.

"I know. I'm sorry."

"So I assume you used the same donor for all of us?"

"Yes. We spent months looking through profiles until we came across the perfect person. Donor number 8746. He was healthy, intelligent, and athletic. All the traits we wanted for our children. When Andrea was little, I'd see a man who resembled her and wonder if he was the donor. After Carrie and Jonathan arrived—the three of them looked so much alike—I was sure I could recognize him on the street if I ever ran into him. I was always on the lookout for him."

"How does donor 8746 have anything to do with Ben?" Beth asked. "Did his parents use the same donor?"

"No. I've got a lot more to tell you."

"My god, Mom, what else can there be?" Beth asked, rubbing her temples.

"The day I had the procedure to get pregnant with you, I forgot to bring a book. The nurse had already left when I realized it. Things are different now, but when I was artificially inseminated, I couldn't get up for forty minutes. I was bored so I looked around for something to read. When I saw my file on the bedside table, I couldn't resist looking at it. I thought maybe the donor's picture would be in there, so I flipped through it. I was just curious. I never expected anything to be wrong." She stopped and took a drink of her wine. Beth's heart pounded in anticipation.

"Oh my god, was Ben's dad our sperm donor?" Beth asked at the same moment their server delivered their main courses.

Celeste seamlessly thanked him and took her first bite. Beth stared at her in disbelief.

"It's not how it looks," Celeste said calmly.

"Really, Mom? Because it looks like we spent our lives hanging out with our dad's best friend who was actually our father, but you all kept it a secret. That's how it looks."

"Let me finish the story, Beth. I started to read the file to learn about our anonymous donor, but the column for your donor information was blacked out. I thought it was strange so I went to Jonathan's page and his was also blacked out. I quickly flipped to Carrie's, afraid someone would walk in and I'd get caught before I figured out what was happening, and hers was blacked out too. When Andrea's was the same I got angry with the center. Why had they hidden our donor's number? We had worked so hard to find him. What if we needed to get in touch with him for a medical reason? The center had no idea that I had memorized it. I was ready to push the call button and demand to talk to the director but then I turned to the last page and saw a bright red CONFIDENTIAL notice stamped across the top. The notation below it said to direct any legal questions about the donor to Henry Linn. It took me a minute to grasp that your dad had done something without telling me, but once it hit me, I was frantic. I couldn't figure out why it would say to contact him about the donor we picked together. The confidential donor.

I combed every page searching for clues and finally saw the letters TK beside the date of initial sample." She took a bite of her California roll.

"TK. Tom Kelly. How can you say that this is not how it looks?" Beth asked. She wanted to scream at her mother.

"Just hang on," Celeste said. "I left the procedure and went straight to the office to confront your dad. I threatened to leave him if he didn't tell me the truth. I almost left him anyway once he told me what he'd done but clearly I didn't. The story gets worse."

"How can it get worse?" Beth asked.

"Tom didn't know. Your dad coerced him into donating sperm by saying there was a big need and that the two of them could help a lot of couples if they became donors. Your dad never told him we were having fertility issues, so Tom didn't suspect anything. He was a single guy at the time with no plans of getting married, so he probably just went along with your dad to be helpful."

"That's sick. I don't understand how he got away with it," Beth said, suddenly disgusted with her father on a level she hadn't imagined possible.

"He went with Tom and pretended he was making a donation too. He'd already paid off the clinical director, so he took care of the details. They went more than once. Your dad wanted to make sure there was ample sperm frozen so we could have as many children as we wanted to have. Tom never knew. If I hadn't opened the file I wouldn't have known either."

"Yeah, but you did know, Mom. You've known my whole life and you lied. How could you keep this from us? I could've dated Ben. It's insane." She pushed her plate away and sat back in her seat.

"I'm so sorry. I almost divorced your father over it, but he convinced me that what was done was done and a divorce wouldn't fix it. After Tom died it seemed like it would never come up until these damn DNA tests started to reveal everything about everyone's past. If I'd known, I would've told you sooner." She reached for Beth's hand with a look of contrition.

"Did you know Andrea took a DNA test?" Beth asked.

"Yes. She told me when she did it because she wanted to know about our family health history and thought it would be good to have any data she could because of your dad's diagnosis. When she got her results she called because she was surprised she had so much Scottish ancestry, but she didn't ask anything else. Her main interest was the genetic risk factors and they all came back fine, so I really don't think she'll give it any more thought."

"Did you freak out when she did it?" Beth demanded.

"Of course," Celeste replied. "Especially when Ben started to come around right after her results were back, but what could I do? Your father is stubborn. He doesn't want you to know and since he's dying, I don't feel like fighting with him."

"He's dying?" Beth felt the air go out of her lungs.

"Yes, he's dying. The cancer has metastasized to his brain in an inoperable place. It did not show up in his last scan. He might have six months. We'll know more when his tests come back tomorrow. I'm sorry, Beth, this is too much." Her mom looked exhausted but calm. Beth imagined it would be a relief for her mother to finally tell the truth, but Beth wished she had never lied at all. The weight of the betrayal was too much for her. She didn't trust herself to discuss what happened without saying something she would regret. She needed time alone to process before the conversation went any further.

"I don't know what to say right now, Mom. I know this has all been really hard on you and I don't want to add to your pain, but I'm kind of in shock. It's a lot to hear that Dad is dying and you've both been lying to us our entire lives. I need a minute to wrap my mind around it. I definitely can't face dad right now. I'm sorry. I think I just need to go home."

"Of course you're in shock. I am sorry, Beth." Celeste quickly handed the server her card when he brought the check and a box for leftovers.

"I really can't go up," Beth said. "He'll see it on my face."

"That's fine," Celeste said. "I'll go say goodnight. Just walk with me until we get to your car." She signed the check and put on her coat.

When Beth stood up she felt the earth under her sway. It felt surreal to walk beside her mother as though it were a normal day and hug her good-bye as though things would go back to normal. The numbness set in as she started her car and pulled out of the garage. It was 8:30 p.m., late enough to call Nate, and she decided that tonight she would use her lifeline.

34

CELESTE

Celeste felt a surge of anger as she pushed the elevator button. She'd been able to control it until Beth was out of range, but now it gripped her like a vice. She had to shove it back down before she walked into Henry's room or she might take it out on him, and that had never helped in the past. It would be misdirected anger anyway, and she knew it. She'd made the choice to lie, and she was living out the consequences.

"Hello, handsome," she said as she opened the door to Henry's room. "Did you miss me?" She wouldn't burden him with her emotions tonight.

"I had this fellow to entertain me," Henry said, motioning toward Ben, who sat in the chair next to him.

Celeste was caught off guard; she hadn't seen him. "Sorry. I didn't see you there," she said.

"I just got here a few minutes ago," Ben said. "I'm sorry I missed Beth." He was a picture of youth and health next to her dying husband, which made her even more annoyed that he was there. She was good at hiding feelings, but this was a lot in one night. After all, he was the reason Beth was driving home devastated, so the least he could do was give her some space.

"She had a situation at work and had to go." Celeste sat down beside Henry and tried to calm herself.

"I thought she looked bad," Henry said. "If she'd listened to me and become a chemical engineer, she wouldn't have to deal with those crazies."

"Henry, please, that's so inappropriate. Ben, how are you?"

"I'm fine. I just wanted to check in with this guy. Seems like he's doing OK. I'll leave you two alone. I'm sure it's been a long day. I'll stop by tomorrow," he said. He patted Celeste on the shoulder on his way to the door.

"Go find a nice girl and leave us old folks alone," Henry said as he waved him off. "That boy needs friends his age," he said to Celeste after Ben was gone.

"Maybe so," she said. "Is Ben what you really want to talk about, Henry? Don't you think we should talk about you?"

"We don't know anything until tomorrow, so what is there to say?" She saw his wall go up.

"I want to know what you're feeling. You can charm everyone else, but not me," she said, holding his gaze.

"You look awful, Celeste. Go home. Get some rest." His message was clear. He needed her to go.

"Are you sure?" She knew Henry Linn had no desire to appear weak, even to his wife.

"Yes, I'm sure," he said, smiling and reaching for her hand. "I want to catch up on email and watch the end of this game, and I don't need you here with that worried face. Go home."

"OK. I love you. I'll see you in the morning," she said, grateful to escape.

What do I do now? she thought as she walked to her car. Her first instinct was to call Beth, but she had nothing more to say to help her. Even if Henry were healthy he wouldn't have been helpful in smoothing over the repercussions of their secret. To this day, he continued to justify what he'd done, which would only have made things worse with Beth. *Call Greg. He's safe.* The second his number rang she hung up. *What are you doing? You'll just make it worse.* She put her car in reverse and inched out of her space. *You can figure this out alone. You're fine,* she said to herself as her phone rang and Greg's name popped up on her display.

"You must be in a crisis to call me," he said when she picked up. "You OK?"

"Beth knows everything," she said. A tight ball of anger mixed with grief swirled in her gut.

"How?"

"She asked me. I had to tell her."

"Are you in the car?"

"Yes."

"Pull over," he said. Celeste decided it was better to just keep driving.

"I just left the hospital," she said. "Henry was admitted today. I need to get home. I'm OK. I just needed a friend."

"Do you need me to come?" She could hear the concern in his voice.

"No, I don't think I can handle one more awkward explanation."

"How's Beth?"

"In shock. I can't believe I just dumped that on her. And now I have to tell them all the truth as soon as I can."

"You do. For them and for you. Henry's cost you a lot," Greg said.

"I know. I could've left. I could've told the truth. I could've done a lot of things instead of cover up his lie." Celeste knew she was complicit and hated herself for it.

"His lie. Not yours."

"And I went along with it." She and Greg never agreed on this point. She could hear him sigh.

"I give up. Does Beth know about me?" he asked.

"No. Why?"

"I'm coming to town tomorrow. You need a friend. You can figure out how to explain me or not; I don't care."

"Don't, Greg. I may not even have the time to see you." She wondered what it would be like to be a person who would let him rescue her.

"Celeste, you aren't superhuman," he said. "I'm coming there and I'm going to talk to Henry and tell him he's asked too much of you. It's time."

"You can't talk to Henry. He has no idea we're still in touch. Why would you even consider such a thing?"

"The last time I spoke to him, he asked me to trust him. He promised he'd take care of you. Beth had just been born and you felt like you had to leave him. You were so upset on the phone that I drove straight to your house. When I got there you were gone and he answered the door. He knew why I was there. He said you were his world and if I spirited you away, he couldn't go on. I believed him when he said he'd make it right so when you decided to stay with him, I respected it. I didn't want to rip your family to pieces. I think I have a right to ask him to honor his promise now."

Celeste was stunned. "Why didn't you tell me this when it happened?"

"What good would it have done?" Greg asked. "I needed to remove myself from the equation."

"You were with Elise then. Were you going to leave her for me?"

"You knew I would," he said.

"I didn't know."

"I begged you not to marry him, remember? And my feelings haven't changed."

"That's why you can't come here," Celeste said. "I don't need my kids thinking I've been having an affair their entire lives."

"Is that what we're having?"

"No. I don't know what this is, but it's not an affair." She refused to reduce what they had to something as common as an affair.

"So you're just my secret best friend, the person I want to tell every story to, and I just happen to find you breathtakingly beautiful. That's our story?"

"Can we *not* do this right now?" she pleaded.

"You want me to not tell the truth?"

"No, I want you to not talk about our relationship. I want you to not come to my rescue or insert yourself into my family crisis. You and Henry both want to take care of me, but I don't need taking care of."

He was quiet for longer than felt comfortable to Celeste before he spoke. "You realize you called me, right?" he said, a hint of sadness in his tone.

"Of course I do. I'm sorry, Greg. I know you're trying to help. I called because you're the only person who has been here since the beginning and really knows me. I just needed you to know about Beth. What you told me was a shock. I know Henry has done a lot of damage, but I still need to finish this with integrity. I don't want to make this any messier than it already is."

"I'm sorry, Celeste. I guess I still question leaving that day. Maybe that's why I never told you." She heard the regret in his voice.

"Hindsight, right?" she said as gently as she could.

"Right, it's always 20/20." He paused again long enough for her to almost change her mind. "Final offer. I can be on the road by six if you want me there."

Celeste knew what she had to do. "No, stay home tomorrow. I appreciate you, but I need to handle things myself."

"Fine," he said. "I won't come. You can be a superhero if you want to."

"I'm sorry if I was short with you. I just can't handle any more drama tonight. Thank you, Greg—truly. You know how much it means to me." She pulled into the driveway and saw Beth's car.

"I'm home," she told Greg. "And Beth's here, so I need to go in and see what's happening."

"OK. Call if you need me," Greg gently responded. Celeste felt his compassion surround her like a warm blanket.

"I will. Goodnight."

She turned off the car and sat for a moment in the silence before she walked in through the back door to the sound of Beth in an animated conversation. She closed the door hard so Beth would know she was there and immediately put on water for tea.

"He's dead," Beth said to her mom as she walked into the kitchen. "The student in the explosion is dead."

"Oh no, Beth. That's horrible," Celeste responded. She noticed her daughter's hands were shaking.

"I came over to apologize to you for my rudeness, but then I got this call from my office," she said in a ragged tone. Celeste put a hand on her shoulder to comfort her.

"Was he your client?"

"No. It's complicated, but I'd better go. I'm sorry about tonight." She gave Celeste a hug and slipped out the door.

Celeste stared out the window at Beth's headlights as she backed out of the driveway. *What have I done?* she asked herself again. Then she took a deep breath and decided it was time to tell her story; she hadn't told Beth the full truth.

"I guess it's time to tell you, Mom," she said out loud She poured herself a glass of wine and sat at the table, imagining her mother there to hear her.

"It should have been a celebration day. If things went as smoothly as they had with the first three pregnancies, we were on the path to having our fourth baby. We'd gotten away with it. Donor 8746 had provided us with three gorgeous kids, so we wanted to finish strong. 'It'll all be fine,' Henry kept telling me. When I found my file with the donor numbers blacked out and that CONFIDENTIAL stamp in bright red, it also said that only Henry Linn could have access to the donor information and that the donor had signed legal documents that were on file to agree to never reveal his involvement. I searched the file again. Nothing. Finally I looked closer and saw the initials TK. Who was TK? And then I knew. I saw the shape of the eyes. The dimple on the left cheek. Tom Kelly. Tom Kelly shared my children's DNA. My husband had gotten his best friend to father my children. And he lied to me and said it was random donor number 8746. He and his brilliant, handsome best friend had lied to me. Or so I thought. Are you ready for the next bit, Mom? Because it gets better. I lay there shivering in the hospital gown for forty more minutes until the attendant came in and told me I could go home. Forty minutes. Forty minutes to think about how I might kill your son-in-law, because that seemed like the right thing to do. But instead I decided to drive to the office. Our office. Our company. I walked straight into his office and shut the door. I asked him if we should invite Tom over to talk about shared custody, since he was the father of our children. I'm not sure if Henry was more shocked or impressed.

"'Very funny,' he said.

"I stayed silent.

"Then he said, 'Seriously, Celeste, what are you saying?'

"Again, I stayed silent. I knew how to get to him.

"'Do you want to call him or should I?' I asked him. Then he said—and he sounded so cold when he said this—he said Tom had no idea. That he could never know. He asked me why I would want to hurt Tom or our children. How I could be so selfish? He said he'd done it all for us. He wanted to make sure the donor was healthy and smart, so the donor couldn't be anonymous. He had to know who it was. So he fooled Tom into donating by telling him a sob story about couples who wanted to have children and the lack of quality sperm, and that they should both do it. That it was a noble thing to do, but not to tell me because I wouldn't understand. And now thirty plus years later I'm stuck with a monster of a secret, Mom."

She paused for a moment before continuing.

"I'm so sorry I didn't tell you then. And I'm sorry I didn't tell Tom before he died. He deserved to know. Do you remember when he married Shelly? It was a week after this happened. One week. I had to go to their wedding with the shame of knowing I was probably pregnant with his child. And Shelly got pregnant with Ben right away. Remember? You thought it was so nice that we could be pregnant together. The night of the wedding, I got nauseous watching my children with Tom on the dance floor. Our children. I was a wreck. I threatened to leave and to tell everyone the truth. To blow up our company. And somehow Henry convinced me to stay. Our relationship changed. I felt like it was too late to do anything else. My fourth child was on the way. I couldn't go back to the girl I'd been in college. You saw me, Mom. You knew. You knew I wasn't even sure I wanted children. I wanted to open a boutique hotel. I wanted to travel. I wanted . . ."

Celeste wrapped her arms around herself and cried tears that had been frozen in her heart for a very long time. After a while, she looked around and realized she was OK; the tears hadn't killed her. *The thaw feels good*, she thought, as the moon rose above the trees. She allowed herself to sit in silence as the moonlight created a dance of shadows across the room. She savored the beauty of the moment, appreciating the home she'd created.

35

BETH

On the drive to her office from her parents' house, Beth had too many thoughts from her bizarre night to contain any of them. Michael agreed to meet her there so they would have a private place to talk and now she needed to decide what was safe to say. Could she tell him she saw the queen leave the hospital one hour before his client died? Probably not. It would just put him in a compromised position with information he wasn't supposed to know, and it would solve nothing. Why cause him more distress? She tried to rein in her racing thoughts. Why had her client been there? She wanted more time to think, but Michael's car was in the parking lot when she arrived. He'd just unlocked the door and was outside waiting.

"I turned on the TV so we can watch the news," he said as he locked the door behind them.

Beth said, "I think we should go over all of your notes to make sure we have everything in order before tomorrow morning when we have to deal with the aftermath."

"Sure, but I'd like to watch this first if that's OK." He sat down on the couch directly in front of the television. Beth chose a chair and pulled it up close.

They sat together in silence as the newscaster began the broadcast with the announcement that the student had died unexpectedly that evening while in a chemically induced coma. The station ran clips from the scene of the explosion before a live feed took viewers to the sidewalk in front of the hospital, where a reporter asked a representative from the hospital to explain what had happened. The young doctor said a full investigation would be done based on the unusual turn in the patient's medical condition, but that at the moment there was no information to share. When asked if it was considered a crime scene, she said the police had not ruled anything out at that moment. The next sound bite was the one from the day of the accident, when the queen was interviewed about the higher level of security at her private school and the issues with public school funding.

Michael turned and looked at Beth. "I've seen her here. She's a client. Fuck, Beth, tell me she isn't your client?"

"I wish I could tell you that." Beth gave Michael a moment to pull himself together. There was nothing she could say.

"I'm sorry," he said. "I'm just freaked out right now. I knew I'd seen her here but I had no idea she was the dean at the academy. It's just eerie seeing her on the news talking about this on the same night we found out my client died. Then to find out you're her therapist. It's just a lot to absorb. Please tell me this is just an ironic coincidence." Beth weighed her words before she responded,

"It's a small town, Michael. You're going to have this happen a lot. Clients will tell you different versions of a similar story, and suddenly you'll realize it's the same story, and your clients know each other. I know it's a lot right now, but I want you to know my role is to help you navigate it, OK? I'm here to help." She watched his face for a response.

"Yeah, I get it," he said. "I guess it just took me by surprise to see her on TV talking about this when you and I have talked about nothing else for weeks. I'm OK."

"OK. Let's just focus on what you'll say to Dr. Meadows tomorrow," Beth said. "She'll need a statement from you in case there are inquiries. Hopefully you won't be subpoenaed, but we need a statement ready to go in case that happens." She could at least work with him on that. She knew he'd need an immense amount of support once the shock of the situation wore off and he began to feel the weight of what happened.

At home later that night, the memory of seeing her client with the boy at the park continued to invade her thoughts. *What am I going to do?* she wondered as the events rolled through her mind like a slideshow. The day in the gym. The park. The day of the explosion when the boy brushed by her client. The sirens. The news reports. The sessions. The smirks. The strange lack of emotion. Over and over the scenes repeated in a continual loop.

At 3:13 a.m. a noise on the deck woke her up. She was amazed she'd fallen asleep at all. When she heard the sound again, she crawled out of bed with her phone and inched across the floor on her hands and knees to the window. For a crazy moment she was afraid it was her client, but she shook that thought away. *Of course not*, she told herself. *Get a grip.* She summoned her courage and pulled the blind away just enough to peek out the window. The clear skies let the moonlight shine down on two raccoons working to open the lid to her grill. She laughed in relief as she remembered how the raccoons at Girl Scout camp would hurl themselves at the door of the lodge to try to get inside and raid the food stocks in the staff kitchen. She pounded on the window and they skittered away.

· · ·

The next morning, Dr. Meadows had coffee and pastries ready when Michael and Beth came to her office for their meeting. Beth tried to eat a pastry but her stomach was in knots. While Michael gave his update, she nervously anticipated what Dr. Meadows might ask. But she didn't ask him anything. In ten minutes his update was done, and Dr. Meadows cheerily dismissed them.

"That was weird," Michael said when they reached Beth's office and she closed the door.

"He wasn't her client. She didn't know him."

"I thought she'd care." He shook his head in disbelief.

"You don't know if she cares. She's been a therapist for thirty years. Maybe she just hides her feelings." Beth wasn't sure she even believed that herself, but right now she couldn't allow herself to think about what Dr. Meadows's seeming indifference meant.

"She offered us a Danish," Michael said. "She didn't even ask me how I'm feeling, and he *was* my client."

"Maybe it's her emotional wall," Beth said as she sat down at her desk and took a sip of the coffee she brought from the meeting.

"He was a kid and a client of this office. How cold does she have to be not to care?"

"Let's focus on you. You lost a client. Talk to me about how you're feeling?" She wanted to spew every negative thought she had about Dr. Meadows and spend the hour complaining about her with him, but she knew that wasn't what Michael needed.

"Not great. Last night I dreamed he was drowning and he screamed for me to help him. I couldn't move. I just watched him drown." Beth understood his pain and searched for words to help.

"You know it's normal to have bad dreams after something like this happens. Do you have a therapist you see regularly?" She hoped he was working with someone good.

"I don't, but I know I need to find one." He ran his fingers through his hair and let his head fall into his hands.

"Let's talk again at the end of the day," Beth said. "If you need to take some time off nobody will judge you. The front desk can reschedule your clients."

Michael shook his head. "I think I'd rather be here right now. I'll talk to you later." He closed the door behind him as he left.

Beth dreaded what waited for her on the other side of the door. Her anxiety rose as she looked out the window and recognized the queen's quick, deliberate steps as she crossed the street. She remembered the odd thought that had jumped into her mind the night before when the raccoons had startled her. Her tiny fearful part stared at her from behind her coffee mug. *She won't kill us,* Beth told her before she walked to the lobby.

"Good morning," Beth said with a forced smile when she saw her client waiting.

"It is a good morning," the queen replied as she walked past Beth into her office. "I think our time together is done." She relaxed into the couch and placed her phone beside her.

"That seems positive," Beth responded as she tried to see if her client had hit record on her phone.

"It is. I'm much better now that the divorce is in process. My anxiety is basically gone. Work is great and it appears the psychopath that tried to blow up the high school won't be able to cause any more problems. Things are getting back to normal." She was still perplexed by the queen's aloof attitude, even though she had been witnessing it for months.

"What do you mean he won't be able to cause any more problems?"

"Didn't you hear? He died in the hospital last night. It's probably for the best. I've heard he was quite the head case. Lots of anger. Somebody told me he saw a counselor here but I knew it couldn't be you or you would've told me."

"I couldn't have told you if he was my client," Beth said, feeling her anger rise. "But to answer your question, no, he wasn't. You said he'd been at your house and your husband knew him, so aren't you concerned that if he was part of that group there's still a threat to the community?"

"I'm not worried at all," the queen said smoothly. "My husband's terrified. I doubt he or his group will cause any issues for anyone at this point. I just want him to leave so I can move on with my life. My son's decided to stay with me, so I won't have to worry about him either. Everything's good."

A child was dead, his parents had lost a son, and her client saw it as a win. The queen's cold demeanor was chilling.

"I need one more thing from you before we wrap up today," she said briskly. "I need you to destroy my file. I don't want anyone to know I ever saw you."

"Our files are secure and your privacy is protected," Beth said.

"Can a judge subpoena records?"

"Possibly, but why would that happen?" She couldn't resist baiting her. She knew it was unprofessional, but what did it matter now?

"Dr. Linn, I want my records destroyed. I didn't use insurance, so there's no trail except your notes. I want our relationship erased from the computer system at this office. Am I clear?"

"Yes. You're completely clear. May I ask why you need this to happen?" She felt nothing but contempt for this client. No compassion. No empathy.

She felt used and played for a fool, and a lot of other things that didn't match up with a therapeutic alliance.

Beth felt heat rise in her face. Her feelings were dangerously close to the surface. If her client could read her mind things would go very dark, very quickly.

The queen sighed condescendingly. "Isn't it obvious? I'm a prominent person in this town. I don't need someone to accidentally run across my name in your system someday down the road and get curious. Anyone could get a job in this office and they'd have access to client names. I came here to get help with an issue that no longer exists. I don't want it to look like I required therapy."

"I'll have to talk to Dr. Meadows about our office policies, because we are required to retain records for seven years. I'll ask if I can store a paper record in my file cabinet and remove it from the computer storage."

"I don't want it to exist electronically. I guess you can keep a paper record if it's the law, but I want the electronic version erased."

"I'll talk to her as soon as I can and let you know." Beth watched the queen for any sign of humanity but saw nothing warm or kind.

"I can always bring my lawyer into it," the queen said. "Make Dr. Meadows aware that the only satisfactory answer is yes."

"I'll let her know. Is there anything else you want to discuss before we close out your relationship here?" Beth kept her tone all business.

"Not really. I've accomplished what I came here to do. I appreciate the extra time you gave me when things were so bad with my son. I'm sure we'll cross paths in town. In fact, I think I saw you out on a run one morning a few weeks ago. Do you run the lake trail?"

Beth felt an electrical current between them suddenly. She watched the queen's face, but the woman was giving nothing away.

"I do when I can," she responded. "I didn't realize you were a runner. Did we pass?" *Does she know it was me?* she wondered. She didn't want to confirm anything.

The queen gazed at her. "I guess not," she said after a moment. "It must have been someone who looked like you."

Beth used her cool, professional smile. "I'm sure we'll run into each other in public, but as I explained at our first session, I won't speak to you unless you speak to me first. Nobody will know we're acquainted, so in that way you're completely erased."

"Good. We have fifteen minutes left on the clock. Would you go and ask Dr. Meadows about my records now?"

"I'll see if she's available." Beth was grateful to be able to leave the room. She worried about how to explain the awkward request, and was surprised when Dr. Meadows brushed it off as no big deal.

"It's done," Beth told the queen when she returned to her office. "As soon as I compile your case summary and print it, I'll be able to delete your electronic records."

"Can't you just print them now and delete them? I want to watch you do it."

"I'll have to wait for you to pay for this session first," Beth said, stalling. "But I'll delete all the files tonight before I leave."

The queen didn't look pleased. "Fine," she said crisply. "But call me this evening to confirm it's done." Beth nodded in response and her client left.

She stood at the window and watched the queen walk across the street, past the spot where Beth had seen Michael's client right before the explosion. She still didn't know what to make of her client being at the hospital right before the boy's death.

She wanted to believe he had just died from his injuries, but what if her client had killed him? How could she prove it? She couldn't call the police without revealing more than she should. *The cameras*, she thought suddenly. She needed to see the security cameras at the hospital.

When she was a child, Beth's therapist, Miss Rachel, had taught her to use art during their therapy to release her pain. Maybe the touch of pencil to paper would help now. She pulled a sketch pad from her desk drawer. The reality that she was alone with information that could implicate her client in a murder was in direct opposition to the possibility that she might just be paranoid about things that appeared more ominous than they were. Maybe the boy was just a disturbed kid who brought bombs to school and got injured by one of them and died from his injuries. Maybe, but there was still the question of why her client was at the hospital. And why did she want her records destroyed? And why did she ask about the park? There had to have been a reason she asked about the park.

I need to know, she said to her fearful part who had crossed her arms and did not want to let her make a call to her friend who worked at the hospital. *I promise it will be OK,* she reassured that part of her after she hung up with her friend. She really couldn't be sure it would be OK, but she needed access to those security cameras to find out.

36

BETH

When she arrived at work the next morning, Beth wasn't surprised to see an emergency session with the dancer added to the beginning of her day. Even though she'd been doing much better at her last session, Beth worried she might feel triggered by the bomber's death. She was glad to see her name on the schedule. She focused on grounding herself before she started the emergency session.

The look of panic in her client's eyes was evident from across the lobby. When she saw Beth she popped up out of her chair and rushed into the office and directly to the couch.

"I'm not OK. I'm seriously not OK." She hugged her favorite pillow tightly to her like a stuffed animal.

"Tell me what's happening," Beth said, closing her office door.

"The kid from the bombing is dead. He never woke up and nobody knows what happened. He never got to tell his story. My brother doesn't believe he caused the two explosions. He says a lot of the kids at school think he was setup. I'm worried about my brother. What if somebody killed that kid on purpose? What if they try to kill my brother?" Her voice was elevated and her eyes were wide. Beth knew it was critical to help her get back into reality.

"Those are all normal questions after a tragedy. Let's get a little bit calmer and then we can talk through them together. Would that be OK?" She spoke quietly, making it clear through her facial expressions that she acknowledged her client's distress.

"OK."

"Let's do some diaphragmatic breathing to bring you into the present moment. Remember, in this moment you're safe and so is your brother. He's safe at home, right?"

"Yes."

"Good. Focus on that for a minute. Picture your brother at home safe."

"OK. I can see him at the house eating breakfast with my parents. It feels good to see him there." Beth waited to be sure her client was able to take deep breaths and access a calm state.

"Good. Now look around the room. Notice where you are. Notice the colors and feel the fabric of the pillow you're holding. Notice that you're safe here." She spoke quietly and slowly, to help her client's nervous system mirror her calming cadence.

"OK. I feel safe here. I think I can try to access my safe place now."

"That's really good. Let's go there now. As you breathe deeply close your eyes and visualize your safe place beside the waterfall and all the brilliant colors of flowers and birds surrounding you. Can you feel yourself there?"

"Yes, I'm there."

"Great. Just allow yourself to breathe and release everything on your mind. Give your body the opportunity to relax so it can slow down the flood of adrenaline and cortisol. When you need them they'll be there for you, but right now you don't need them. You're safe right now."

Beth accessed her own safe place as she watched her client begin to relax. She could not let her sense her own fears about the boy's death or sense her tiny fearful part, who had her arms crossed waiting for answers just like her client was.

"OK, now that you're calm let's consider where your thoughts have taken you. The police will investigate this young man's death and they'll find out what happened. The gossip from the kids at the school is just gossip. They don't actually know anything."

"I guess you're right."

"Do you still think your brother is safe right now?"

"Yes. My parents did end up getting him into the academy and the security is better there, but what if they still find him?" Panic started to show in her eyes.

"Tell me why someone would want to find him."

"If they think he knows about them and their plot, they'd have to do something. If they think he's on to them they could kill him too."

"Let's keep your nervous system relaxed, OK? Continue to breathe deeply and let's unpack what you just said. The idea that there's a 'they' out there with a plot and that 'they' set up the explosions is unlikely if you consider that the boy who died was at the school during the first scare and the explosion that hurt your brother. Witnesses have said he acted strangely around both of the first two events. It makes sense he'd have an explosive in his bag, right? Isn't it possible he was just disturbed and acted alone and that's the end of it?" *I'm asking for myself as well as for her*, Beth thought. *Because I just don't know.*

"Maybe, but I don't believe it. Things feel off to me and it's not just my paranoia. I'm taking my meds and I'm doing fine. I know you think I'm delusional, but I'm not paranoid. I think it's my fault this time," the dancer said, arms crossed.

"I don't think you're delusional," Beth reassured her. "I just want to help you break down the facts of what we know so that your fears don't hijack your rational thoughts. Did your brother tell you anything specific about what his classmates suspect?"

Her client shifted in her seat. "Yeah. I guess my brother saw this lady from the academy with him a few times. He said she's high up there. Anyway, some of his friends saw her by the bell tower with him the day it happened and then one of the same kids saw her leave his hospital room the night he died. Maybe it's a coincidence, but I think it's creepy. My brother heard that her son and the kid were friends from preschool so maybe it's nothing, but it could be something. And now he goes there. What if she's behind it all? Maybe she has other people ready to follow her orders."

"All we can do right now is make sure that you and your brother are safe,"

Beth said. "If you're worried, you could tell the police what you heard. Any leads could help them."

"Would they think I'm crazy?"

"It's not crazy to give the police information."

"It would feel good to actually do something." Beth saw a look of clarity on her face and wondered if her client could feel the strength that she had just witnessed.

"I can help you write up what you want to say if that would help," Beth said, aware she was in a precarious position.

"Do you think I should go to our police department, or the one close to the hospital?"

"I'd go to the precinct where he died if you suspect a crime happened there. The department here will conduct the investigation, but this is a separate issue. Also, if the person you suspect works at the academy, then most likely the police in town will know her and they may not take you seriously."

The client turned to look out the window at the square below her. "Could you go with me? Never mind. I know you can't. I shouldn't ask. I'm just scared."

"I wish I could go, but that's not possible," Beth said. "I'm sorry. Maybe your driver will take you when you leave today and he can go in with you."

"I'm sure he'll take me if I ask. He's super flexible. I don't want him to go in with me though. Do you think it's possible I'm right?" She looked at Beth directly, questioning but also with a level of confidence that she knew she was right.

"I think anything is possible. The important thing is for you to follow your intuition and do what you think is right. That's your work. The last few years you've felt disempowered and lost. I think this will help you feel like you can trust yourself again."

"What if I'm wrong?"

"You're going to tell them what you heard and what people saw. That's it. You don't need to tell them your theory. They can take the information and follow the leads from there."

Her client paused for a moment, considering. "I think my brother wants me to do something, and that's why he told me," she said after a minute. "So I'm going to do it." She looked back at the square with a look of resolve.

"That's a great plan," Beth said. "You've been stable and independent for almost a year. You're doing amazing."

For the first time in a long time, her client smiled. "Would it be OK if I hugged you?" she asked as she stood to leave.

"Of course," Beth said. She hoped she hadn't just put her client in danger, but she was proud of her, too.

The irony of her final task of the day did not escape Beth as she sat down to delete the queen's electronic file. The veil that separated these two clients was much too thin for comfort. Beth felt her anger grow as she read through the printed copy she'd have to keep locked in her file for the next seven years. She wasn't sure if it was her client's lack of empathy or the chill in her voice that infuriated her most. Maybe it was her lack of respect or how she had manipulated her, session after session, to try to get her to report her husband. Beth wondered if any of the stories were true. She'd written her notes carefully, so that an outsider wouldn't notice the clues she'd left to help her recall every moment of doubt.

File it and let it go, she told herself, but she couldn't stop reading. In the note dated the day after the first bomb scare under the area for "mood," she'd written her client had a "sense of detachment"—which had been her clue that her client seemed to no longer care about the anti-religion group, an organization she had raged about for weeks. She remembered when she walked her client out that day she had seen her lock eyes with the boy who was about to be buried.

Each note brought Beth more clarity, until she solidified her resolve to see the video footage from the hospital. Her friend planned to meet her at 8 p.m., which gave her ten more minutes to read the notes before she deleted the electronic master copy. On the day after the first explosion, she'd noted her client seemed "edgy and distracted by the news," which she attributed to the possible connection to her husband. Beth scribbled some notes for herself just in case she needed to remember her impression of her client that day. She knew it was risky, but who would know what her messy notes meant?

The gravity of her client's possible involvement sent a chill down her spine. She glanced over her shoulder, suddenly aware that if her client was involved, she could be in danger. Her dad's voice promptly chided her that this was one more of her overreactions. *Why are you so difficult?* She heard him ask as clearly as if he were in the room. "Something is off, Dad," she said out loud to calm her own nerves as she dialed the queen's number.

"I finished deleting your electronic notes," she said when she had the queen on the line. "The hard copy will be filed in my office for seven years and then that will be destroyed too."

"Good. I appreciate the call. Don't forget. We never met." She hung up without a goodbye.

Beth slammed down the office phone and let out a stream of expletives for the first time since the nightmare began. Dropping onto the couch, she punched wildly into the pillow for relief. *I wish I could slap the smirk off her face.* She felt powerless, and wasn't sure what to so.

The cameras, she reminded herself, grabbing her things and leaving the building. That's what she needed to see.

37

BETH

When she arrived at the pub, she checked her makeup in her rearview mirror to make sure she looked composed. Her anger had gotten to her. She felt used. Unseen. It had felt good to scream as loud as she could on the drive. She couldn't get the boy's face out of her mind or the concern that she and Michael had missed something that could have saved him. Had they been blinded by their assumptions?

Maybe Dad's right. Maybe I'm in the wrong job, she thought as she spotted Renee and walked toward her.

"Hey, lady," Renee said. She gave Beth a hug and kissed her on the cheek.

"Thanks for coming." Beth squeezed her back. It was good to see her friend.

"You look like shit," Renee said. "What's going on?"

"Thanks," Beth laughed as she took a seat at a high-top table. "I need your help, so I'll just get straight to it. Can you access the security cameras at the hospital?"

Renee looked at her wide-eyed. "Damn. Can we get a drink first?"

"Yes, of course, sorry. You asked and I'm just so messed up right now I have no filter. What sucks is that I can't even tell you why I need your help."

"You need food. Can we have two merlots and a margherita pizza?" Renee said to the young server who approached their table.

"Right away," he said and walked briskly away.

"OK, why do you need to see the security cameras?" Renee leaned in close and Beth knew she was there for her, but she also needed the truth.

"I need information."

"It's that kid, isn't it? The one who died yesterday who was involved in the school bombing."

"I just need to see the security cameras around his room," Beth said. "Who came in and out. Is that possible?"

"I can get the footage, but I'd imagine the police already have it if there's an investigation."

"I don't know if there is, and I can't ask." Beth said.

"So is this kid your client?" Renee asked.

"No."

"But you're involved."

"Yep."

"Shit," Renee said, shaking her head.

"Yep."

Renee stepped outside to make a call to a friend in the security department while Beth stared at her phone. There were three calls from her mom, a call from Nate, and an unread text from Ben. She had to focus on this right now, although she had no idea what she might see or what she would do once she saw it. Who could she tell? And now she had involved Renee.

"OK, I've gotten permission to go to the security office," Renee said. "It's a stretch, but I told them you're a possible job candidate for the hospital and you want to understand how our security is set up. I told them I'd bring you over as soon as we finish dinner."

"Are you always such a good liar?" Beth asked, laughing.

"Always," Renee smiled as she took a bite of pizza with a grin from ear to ear.

• • •

After dinner, they went to the security office at the hospital and Renee introduced her. "Sully, this is my friend Beth. She's the one I just called you about.

I appreciate you taking the time for us." She stepped over so Beth could shake his hand.

"Hi, Beth. Renee tells me you want to see my security system." He reminded her of a saintly WWE wrestler.

"I'd just like to know whether I'd feel safe here at night. You understand, I'm sure, given your position." She hoped he was really buying this cover story.

"We have monitored cameras twenty-four hours a day throughout the campus. Renee can walk you through it on this backup computer, since she helped install it," he responded, directing them into a small room at the back of the office.

"Thank you," Beth answered. Renee was already sitting at the computer and logged in.

"What's the date and time you need?" she asked. Beth handed her a note with the date, time, and wing of the hospital.

"What if we see something we have to report?" Beth asked.

"The cameras are in the hallways, so they don't show anything in the patient rooms. All you'll see is who went in and out of the rooms and who entered and left the hospital. What exactly would you report? People are allowed to be in the hospital." Renee looked at her with concern.

"You're right. Oh my gosh, there she is. Can you pause?"

"The red coat at the entrance?"

"That's her. Let me write down the exact time."

"OK. Let's see what else we have here," Renee said.

Beth watched multiple screens of the queen as she went into the hospital and entered the elevator, and then reappeared on a different screen when she came out of the elevator on the ICU floor. She peered around the corner and slid out of the camera's view for six minutes before she reappeared and got back on the elevator. Renee replayed the footage for Beth three times before they thanked Sully and left the office. They walked out of the hospital together and back to the pub parking lot.

"Thanks for your help," Beth said. "I needed proof she was there. The question is what do I do with this information now?"

Renee raised her eyebrows. "You can't tell me anything about it, right?"

"Right. And keep this to yourself. It'll be bad if anyone hears I have questions."

Renee stopped beside her car and looked at Beth directly. "Of course. Not a word. I'm worried about you, though. Are you sure you're OK?"

"I'm OK. I just need to sort some things out. Thanks again, Renee. Let's do something fun soon. Maybe we can hike the gorge when things calm down?"

"I'd love to go for a hike. Text me some dates and we'll make a plan." She hugged her goodbye.

Beth didn't want to leave her friend's embrace to get into her car. The original ripples of fear now felt like a cresting wave of panic about to crash down on her the minute she was left alone with her thoughts.

She killed him! her tiny self yelled from her perch on the dashboard. *And she'll kill you too if she knows you're on to her.*

Beth considered that possibility as she backed out of her parking space. She was tempted to call Nate back, but decided to turn up the radio to drown out the noise of her tiny fearful part who continued to rant about everything wrong in Beth's world.

38

THE DANCER

"'d like to stop at the downtown police department on my way home if you don't mind," she said to her driver when she got into the car after her session.

"Everything OK?" he asked, glancing back at her.

She nodded. "I just want to talk to them. I might have information that could keep people safe."

"Does this have to do with your little brother?"

"No, it's about the lady who runs the academy," she said. "One of my brother's friends saw her in the injured kid's room right before he died. His friends think she had something to do with it and that he was set up."

The driver frowned. "She seems like the last person who'd be involved with those anti-religion group nut jobs. She teaches my daughter's Sunday school class. I can't imagine she was at the hospital for any reason other than to pray for that boy. Are you sure you want to go to the police with information from a bunch of high school students?"

"I have to, even if it doesn't make sense to you." She watched his face in the rearview mirror, ready to call 911 if she felt afraid. She acknowledged her fear could be paranoia, but she wanted to be safe in case it wasn't.

"Pastor is not going to be happy about this at all. If you bring negative attention to the church the media will be all over it." She tried to ignore his irritation in order to speak up for herself.

"I won't involve the media, but I do need to tell the police. She's proba-bly innocent, but what if she's not and I didn't tell anyone?" No change in his facial expression; she wasn't sure if that was good or bad.

"You do what you need to do. The station's right off this exit, so I can take you if you really need to go."

"I do," she said, aware her request had caused him to accelerate. She decided to stay quiet to pull her thoughts together about what she was going to say. They reached the station sooner than she anticipated and she was star-tled by her driver's abrupt stop.

"Go on in then. I'll wait here," he said.

"Thank you." She didn't see him pick up his phone as she left.

A voice in her head told her to go back or something bad would happen. Would they know about her hospitalization and think she was crazy? *This is not a delusion,* she told herself as she approached the desk. Somehow it was easier than she'd imagined: she felt empowered to tell the officer the truth of what she knew, so there was no possibility her silence would cause anyone else to be unprotected.

Afterward, the officer reassured her she had done the right thing. He walked her to the door and back to the parking lot. *It took less than fifteen minutes and I'm fine,* she thought. Then she heard the loud voice of her driver. He was clearly upset and his voice carried across the parking lot, which made her pause behind a truck to listen.

"What do you want me to do now?" he was saying into the phone. "She's already been in there long enough to talk to someone."

The silence while the other person spoke kept her frozen in place.

"I couldn't stop her. What'd you want me to say? Look, she could come out any minute. I'll find out what happened and call you back when I drop her off."

What should she do? She considered going back into the station and asking for help, but she felt like she had no choice but to walk to the car. She won-dered if she was delusional again and had heard something that was not real.

"How'd it go?" her driver asked when she opened the door.

"Fine," she said. "They probably just think I'm crazy. I doubt they'll even look into it. I feel kind of upset. Could you take me to my parents'?" she asked.

"Sure, if that's what you want to do. What did you tell the cops?" She saw his look of disdain in the mirror and tailored her answer to divert that hate away from her.

"I just told them that some of the students in the school had said some things and I knew it was important to say something if you see something. Or hear something, I guess. I'm sure they think I'm crazy," she repeated. She tried to breathe like Dr. Linn had taught her. *Focus on calm*, she said to herself. She didn't like the sound of his call and she had no idea what to do. She tried to hold onto Dr. Linn's words so she could breathe and stay calm. *Nothing bad is happening now*, she repeated over and over in her mind until her parents' house was in sight.

"Tell your parents I said hello," her least favorite driver said when he pulled into their driveway.

"I will. Thanks for your help today." She grabbed her things and bolted from the car.

39

BEN

Ben took the front steps two at time in the hope the empty driveway meant Henry was home alone and he'd have privacy to talk to him. Beth had avoided his calls all week and his patience was wearing thin. He knocked on the door, trying to push aside his guilt. No one answered, so he turned the knob and cracked it open to announce his presence since he knew Henry may not be able to come to the door.

"Anybody home?" he called, entering the foyer.

"Back here," Henry responded.

"Thanks for letting me come over," Ben said. "I really need to talk to you about something and it would be uncomfortable with anyone else here." He stood in the doorway, hesitant to enter any further without invitation.

"Come in and sit. What's happening? How's your mom doing?" Henry looked even more frail than he had in the hospital.

Ben walked over to the chair closest to Henry. "My mom's OK. This is about my dad. You were his best friend and I need to ask you something I wish I could've asked him."

Henry nodded. "I'll answer the best that I can."

"I don't know how to ease into this, so I'll just ask you straight up." Ben took a deep breath. "I did a DNA test and two of your children are my half siblings. Can you explain that to me?"

"That's quite a question, Ben." Henry appeared more calm than Ben had expected.

"Do you have an answer?"

"I have an answer, but it's a very long story that my children don't know and I have no intention of ever telling them." Henry's strong response was expected, but Ben was determined to get to the truth.

"Did my dad have an affair with Celeste?" Ben decided the direct route was his only option.

"Oh, god no," Henry said with a laugh. "Your parents were crazy about each other from the day they met. Your dad was the best."

"So you had an affair with my mom?"

"Of course not. I just told you your parents were madly in love. Why would your mom have an affair with me?"

"Nothing else makes sense."

"Nobody had an affair. Can you trust me and just let it go?"

"Seriously? Could you let it go?"

Henry stared at Ben for a long moment without replying.

"If you don't tell me then I'll have to ask my mom," Ben said. "But I don't want to upset her. If he cheated on her I don't want her to know, but if you won't tell me I'll have to ask her."

"It won't help to ask her," Henry said. "She doesn't know a thing."

"Then please tell me. I deserve to know."

"It has nothing to do with you."

"You've got to be kidding me. I have half siblings, Henry. It has everything to do with me."

"Your dad didn't know, so I don't see why you need to know."

"This makes no sense at all. Just tell me if you're my father."

"No, I'm not. Your dad is your dad and I'm the father of my children. Does biology really matter?"

"Yes! It matters. I deserve the truth, so if you refuse to tell me then I'll ask Celeste," Ben said as he rose to leave.

"Wait," Henry said. He seemed willing to continue to lie to protect himself, but not at the expense of Celeste. Ben hoped he had found Henry's Achilles' heel. "If I tell you, then you have to keep it to yourself."

"Is that your bargain? You tell the truth and then I have to lie?" Ben knew he would agree to anything to know the truth.

"I've been a difficult man, Ben. I've hurt a lot of people. Your father was one of those people but he never even knew what I did. I hope you'll be able to understand that I was desperate." He paused and closed his eyes.

"Go on," Ben responded.

Henry explained the fertility issues he and Celeste had gone through. "We needed a sperm donor," he said. "We were already upset enough that we couldn't get pregnant naturally, and it felt like too much to roll the dice and say 'OK, who's your daddy?' So I took control of the situation. I decided your dad would be the sperm donor. The hard part was I had to convince him without telling him that it was for us. So I told him I'd read an article about infertility and that we could help a lot of people if we donated sperm together. He was happy to do it. I paid off the director of the sperm bank and they froze his donation for me and we used it for all four of our artificial inseminations."

"You've got to be kidding me."

"Your dad was my answer," Henry said. "He would've done it for me if I asked, but I didn't want to make it strange for him to be around us."

Ben shook his head in disbelief. "That's so dark."

"That's one perspective." Henry appeared comfortable with his choice.

"I can't believe Celeste agreed to this," Ben said.

"She didn't," Henry told him. "She thought our donor was some anonymous guy we picked together. But then she found her file and read it and learned the truth. She almost left me over it."

"I can't believe she didn't," Ben said with disgust.

Henry shrugged. "If it makes you feel any better, she's never totally forgiven me."

"I can't believe you did this to my dad. He loved Andrea and Carrie and Jonathan and Beth and he never knew they were his. That's cruel, Henry. He was your best friend."

"Your dad donated to a sperm bank. He knew he could have children out there if someone chose his profile. He wasn't concerned. You're his son. The child he raised. He wasn't worried about biological children that might possibly be out there. He made that choice."

"But we spent holidays together. He coached them. He would've wanted to know he was their father. You're unbelievable." Ben kept waiting for a sign of remorse, but Henry maintained his stance.

"What do you want me to say?" Henry asked. "What's done is done. They're amazing people. I think he'd be proud of them."

"I think he would've hated you for lying to him." Still no remorse.

"Maybe. Or maybe he'd understand that I gave him the highest compliment a friend could give another friend. I thought so highly of him that I wanted my children to be like him."

Ben shook his head. "I almost asked Beth to the prom!" he said. "How would you have handled that?"

"I would have stopped it."

"With more lies?"

"Probably. You're not a father, Ben. You're not a husband. You have no idea what you might do if you were me, so you can drop the judgmental bullshit."

Ben sat back in his chair and stared at Henry incredulously. "I know I'd never lie for my own selfish reasons and hurt everyone I love. There's no justification for what you did."

"I had no idea your dad would ever get married. He was a committed bachelor at the time this started. If I knew he'd meet your mom and have you, I might've made a different choice."

"They were engaged before Beth was conceived, and that didn't stop you."

"The trajectory was set. Should I have changed donors for my last child?"

Ben didn't know what to say to that.

"I regret what I did, Ben, but it's too late now."

"You regret which part of it? Using his sperm? Lying? What?"

"I regret that I didn't tell him. I almost did when he found out he had cancer, but I was afraid it would distract him from the last few months he had with you and your mom. Plus I was afraid he'd say something to the kids."

"You stole that from him. He would've been happy. He always wanted more kids," Ben said, angry tears forming in his eyes.

"I'm truly sorry, but I can't change anything now," Henry said. "I wouldn't change what I did, but I do regret the deception." Ben was incredulous. How could it be so cut-and-dried for him?

"What happens now?" he asked Henry. "They're my half-siblings. I want to tell them, but I'm not going to force you to do it when you're this sick."

Henry surprised him by saying, "I'll tell them."

"You will?" Ben didn't know if he could trust Henry. After all this secrecy, why was he agreeing now?

"I just need to think about how to do it," Henry said, nodding. "Will you give me some time?"

Ben wanted to push him for a timeline, but the shock of the revelation had left him a bit unstable. And he knew how stubborn Henry was.

"Fine. OK. Just make sure you do it soon," he said. He stood up to leave. "I'm contacting you again in a few weeks if I haven't heard from you."

"Fair enough." They heard the back door open and close, and Celeste's voice calling out. "You need to go," Henry said.

Ben grabbed his coat and headed for the front door, slipping through the hallway to avoid her. He'd gotten what he wanted, but never in his most out-rageous fantasies could he have predicted what he got.

40

CELESTE

"Where's Ben?" she asked when she walked into Henry's room. She was relieved he was gone. She didn't have to deal with him.

"He just left," Henry said.

"I saw his car in the driveway. What did he want?" She hoped he hadn't been interrogating Henry.

"The truth."

"Did you tell him?"

"I had no choice."

Celeste sat down and stared at Henry, unable to believe his words. She had waited for this moment for a lifetime, and now Ben had managed to accomplish what she hadn't been able to. She was unsure if she was grateful or angry.

"What now?"

"He wants me to tell the kids. Actually, he insists. If I don't tell them he will."

"Are you going to?" she asked. He nodded.

"When?"

Henry looked calmer than she had expected. He shrugged. "As soon as I see them, I guess. I suppose I should do it when they're all together, or the first one I tell will blow up everyone else's phones and spoil the surprise," he said, trying to joke. But Celeste could see his distress.

"What can I do?" Now that it was finally going to happen, she felt too many things at once. She was angry at Henry for ignoring her all these years but responding to Ben's request in minutes. How insulting. Her needs had always come second to his. Always been less than his ego. She wanted to break every plate in the house, scream in the street, or set something on fire, but instead she had just asked him what she could do. She almost laughed out loud.

"Can you call them and get them here tonight? I'd like to get this over with before Ben does something stupid." He looked tired suddenly, and Celeste felt her compassionate side pushing down all her hateful thoughts.

"I can. Why don't you try to nap?" she said. She laid a blanket across his lap and wondered if he actually had the strength to do what he needed to do.

41

BETH

A knock at the front door of her condo sent Beth to her window to peek out undetected. She was in no mood for a religious debate or a sales pitch. It was Friday, and she desperately needed her afternoon off.

Her heart dropped at the sight of a police car in her driveway. She decided she'd better open the door after the second round of knocks.

"Can I help you?" There were two officers standing there, but unfortunately neither of them looked familiar. If she had to deal with police, she wished it could have at least been the attractive one who had been in her office.

"Beth Linn?" the first officer asked. He held up his badge.

"Yes," she answered.

"I'm Sergeant Andrews and this is Officer Myer. We need you to answer some questions for us." He stood closer to her than was comfortable.

"May I ask what this is about?" It felt ridiculous to ask a question that all three of them clearly knew the answer to, but how else was she supposed to proceed? This was new to her.

"We're investigating the explosion at the high school. We think you might have information that'll help us," Sergeant Andrews said.

Here it was, the ethical code that she had grown tired of repeating but had no option to ignore. "I have an ethical code of confidentiality in regard to clients," she replied. She felt her grip tighten on the door.

"One of your clients told us you suggested she file a report with us." This information took her by surprise.

"I can't confirm or deny what I've said to my clients or who my clients are. You know I'm bound by my professional license not to speak to you without a release." She hated the disdainful looks on their faces, but she also understood them. She was as frustrated by the code as they were.

"Ms. Linn, we're in search of a perpetrator that targeted the school. Are you refusing to help us find that person because you're afraid to lose your license?"

"If you get a release, I'll tell you anything you want to know. I just can't talk to you without one." She had to maintain confidentiality for her client's protection, no matter how uncomfortable it became. She reminded herself that the code existed for a reason. Confidentiality was the foundation of the client–therapist relationship. If she shared private information about any of her clients it could harm them, but it was especially true for this one because she struggled with paranoia. If Beth had known she would give her name at the police station, she would have gotten a release from her before she left her office.

"Then we'll be back with a release," Officer Myers said. Before Beth could respond, he abruptly turned around and started walking back to the squad car. Sergeant Andrews handed her his card and walked away just as her phone rang. She answered it immediately when she saw it was from Serenity.

"You need to get to the office," Eleanor said. "One of your clients is flipping out and says she needs to see you immediately. I can't find her file, even though I know she was just here. She's on her way. How fast can you get here?"

The queen, Beth thought. "I'll be there in ten," Beth said. She grabbed her coat and dashed to her car, trying to avoid eye contact with the officers as she backed out of her driveway. She hoped they wouldn't be curious enough to follow her.

When she arrived at Serenity she waved at Eleanor, who gestured up the stairs. Beth heard her client on her cell phone in the lobby.

"We need to talk," she said the moment Beth hit the top step.

"Give me a minute to open my door." She fumbled for her office key and tried to focus on the fact that she wasn't alone in the building, so there was no reason for her to be afraid.

"What did you tell the police?" her client hissed as she closed the door behind them.

"I didn't tell the police anything." Beth sat at her desk to put a barrier between them.

"Really? Because I was taken in this morning and they told me that one of the kids who was injured at the high school has accused me of collusion with the suspect. They said you told your client, his sister, to report it to them so they came to question me. Is that true?" The queen sat down in the chair facing the desk. Her expression was menacing, her arms crossed, her eyes piercingly direct.

Cold chills crawled up Beth's spine and creeped over her scalp. She had to be cautious.

"You know I can't talk about my clients," she said.

"You keep saying that," the queen said.

Beth tried another tactic. "Did the police accuse you of something?"

"No, but apparently someone thinks I'm involved. You know I'd never hurt anyone, right?"

"If the police didn't accuse you of anything, why are you so upset?"

"I'm terrified they'll tie this to me because of my husband. You've got to believe I had nothing to do with it." She pushed her hair behind her ear and stared directly into Beth's eyes. *Is she worried?* Beth wondered. She couldn't decipher the woman's expression.

"Did they mention your husband?" Beth felt off-balance with this unexpected shift from anger to vulnerability.

"No, but they've taken him in for questioning. I sent our son to stay with his grandparents up on the lake. I need you to promise me you'll be my witness if I need you to go to court."

Beth waited. Maybe it would make the queen tell her more.

"I made a mistake. I'm sorry. I got scared. I need you to believe me that I had nothing to do with any of the violence." Her voice broke off as though she had more to say.

"Are you worried about what your husband's done? Do you think he's at fault?" Beth watched the queen for any sign of deception.

"I don't know and I don't care. I just need to know that you believe me."

Beth had to take advantage of this opportunity for information even if she crossed a line. Too much was at stake. "Did you know the boy who died?"

"Yes. I know I told you he'd been at our house and that I saw him on the security camera, but I didn't tell you he was blackmailing me."

"Blackmailing you for what?" Beth asked. She fought down her panic.

"When he realized where I worked, he decided he could extort money from me because he knew it would look bad for me to be married to a radical atheist trying to get rid of all forms of religion. He took a photo of me when I walked through the kitchen one night during a meeting. The propaganda posters were everywhere. He threatened to send it to the board members at the academy. I paid him off, but he asked for more. After the first bomb scare he said he'd pin it on me if I didn't come up with $5,000."

"When was the last time you saw him?" Beth asked.

"The day he was injured," the queen replied. "We were supposed to meet in the square, but he ducked out when he saw a cop. The explosion happened an hour later. I went to the hospital to talk to him but he never came out of the coma. I wanted to find out what happened. I'm sure he had no intention of bombing the school, but I have no proof. He had no reason to because I had what he wanted."

"Cash?"

"Yes. He needed money to go see his brother, who's a missionary in some third world country. He thought his brother had been brainwashed or some nonsense and that if he went he could get him to come back." She spoke in her usual condescending tone, which somehow made Beth feel calmer.

"The explosives were in his backpack," Beth said. "Why do you doubt that he intended to use them?"

"I think he was set up. I don't even think that was his backpack. I think there's a bigger conspiracy and he was just a pawn."

Beth paused, unsure of what to do. She had been so caught up in the fear that her client was behind it all that she had not considered any other alternative.

"Who would benefit so much from your fall that they'd commit a murder?" she asked.

"I don't know," the queen said, holding eye contact long enough to make Beth squirm.

"So you want me to believe this whole conspiracy without any idea who's behind it?"

"Yes."

"I guess it doesn't matter what I believe. All I can do is try to support you as this investigation unfolds. I'm not sure what else there is to do. Do you feel safe to go home?"

"Definitely not. I'm going to a friend's house. I feel safe there. Can I get a message to you if I need something?"

Beth nodded. "You can send an email to the office marked urgent and I'll get an alert to call you as soon as possible."

"OK." The queen looked back at Beth with a mixture of relief and gratitude. "Thank you for seeing me. I really thought that you'd talked to the police. I'm sorry I was short with you in our last session. It's just been a lot."

"Just take care of yourself," Beth said.

"I'll try," the queen said as she rose from the chair.

Beth sat in her office for a long time after the queen left, afraid to let her mind drift too far into the possibilities that now bubbled to the surface. *I really need to schedule a session for myself,* she thought. *I need a safe place to talk.* When she pulled out her phone she saw a bunch of new messages on her family text and several from Ben. Her mom had sent a group text to invite her and her siblings to the house for pizza and a family meeting at 7 that night. She was the only one who hadn't responded. She sent a quick yes and tried to ignore the fear that it was going to be bad news about her dad. Ben's text said that he needed to meet with her as soon as possible, so she texted back to see if he could meet an hour earlier, at 6. He promptly agreed.

So much for my afternoon off, she said to her fearful part who was seated beside her laptop, clearly afraid to go home. *I might as well stay here and do paperwork until I meet Ben.* She heard Michael in his office so she checked on him. By the time she returned to her desk, the busy hum of normal office activity helped to calm her nervous system so she could focus on documentation.

A sharp ding alerted Beth that she had an urgent email from the queen. *Don't call. Just meet me at the Community Church.*

Why? Beth texted back. She couldn't imagine what this meant.

One of the pastors wants to talk. Not in your office. You promised to help.

Beth weighed everything the queen had just told her and felt an immense amount of guilt for judging her client. Everything added up. Blackmail would account for the meetings between the boy and her client that she had witnessed and also for the money in the boy's room. She regretted allowing her fearful part to influence her attitude toward her client. She'd lost sight of one of her core values, unconditional positive regard for every client, and now she needed to get it back. Here was her chance. She had promised to help.

Be there right away, she responded, bolting out of the office. If she hurried, she could get there and still meet Ben on time.

Driving the short distance to the megachurch, she wondered if she would cross paths with Pastor Dan. *I'll know in a minute,* she thought. She had been raised Catholic so she'd never been inside the walls of the massive building that housed the popular evangelical church, but she had heard many stories about it from her clients.

Beth parked her car in the deserted lot and walked up to the giant front doors. The banner hanging above the entryway depicted a cross with two large Cs intersecting in the center to showcase the bright red Community Church logo.

She was greeted by the eerie silence of a deserted building on a quiet weekday. She looked around in the hope the queen would be there waiting for her, but all she saw were dark hallways. She followed the signs to the pastoral offices until she saw lights under a door of an inner office. She heard voices inside so she knocked loudly and then stepped away to avoid the perception she was eavesdropping. When there was no response, she pulled up the email on her phone and typed, *I'm here.* A second later, the door opened.

"Dr. Linn, so glad you could join us," Pastor Dan said, meeting her surprised gaze. "I hope it wasn't an inconvenience."

Beth looked past him to acknowledge her client, who appeared very upset.

"It's not a problem. How can I help?" She walked into the office, taking surprised note of an overturned chair and papers scattered on the floor.

"Apparently your little investigative work has gotten our mutual friend here into quite a pickle, and you're the key to help her get out of it," Pastor Dan answered. He closed and locked the door.

"What do you mean?" she asked. She sensed an authentic level of fear from her client, though she hadn't spoken. Something was seriously wrong.

"You couldn't leave the explosion alone, could you? You had to get the police involved. It's unfortunate, but now you'll have to help me make this all go away." His face was threatening, his eyes accusatory.

"I'm not going to help you do anything," she said, turning toward the door.

He blocked her. "You aren't going anywhere."

"You can't keep me here." She knew in that moment her life was at risk and she had to get out.

"Oh . . . but I can and I will," Pastor Dan said. "I'm afraid the church is locked for the evening, and you can't leave without setting off the security system, which would bring the police in less than three minutes. I don't think you want to do that. If you do, I have video footage that I'll give them to prove your client planted the bombs. I'm pretty sure the footage will destroy her, and I don't think you want her life destroyed."

Beth looked at her client for a response but she just stared back, wide-eyed.

Pastor Dan walked behind the desk and sat down in a leather chair. "I think it would be good for you to sit down, Dr. Linn, and listen to what I have to say. You've caused me major problems and now you need to fix them."

"I'm listening," Beth said, aware of her silent client. She could see the pastor was unstable, and rational conversation wasn't going to work.

He pulled a handgun from the drawer. "Good, I didn't want to have to threaten you."

"I said I'm listening," Beth said sharply. "Now what do you want from me?" She looked from the pastor to her client, who was startled enough to finally speak.

"Why do you have a gun? We agreed no guns," the queen said.

"I have to clean up your mess, so I'm doing it my way," he responded.

"How does threatening Dr. Linn clean up my mess?"

Beth saw a glimmer of her client's usual strength.

"She's going to be an innocent victim caught in the cross fire when your terrorist husband shows up in a rage because he found out you set him up," he answered smoothly.

"I didn't set him up; you did. Why are you lying?"

For a moment, Beth fantasized that the queen's ability to win at verbal sparring would get them both out of there.

"Of course you set him up. You needed to scare people into sending their kids to the academy, so you created a threat to the school. His group was the perfect scapegoat." He laughed in her face as though she were a ridiculous child.

"What are you saying? You know you set him up to help me get free so we could be together. The rest was an accidental benefit. Why would you make her think I did it to get students? That's horrible," the queen said, her voice escalating. Beth tried to make sense of what was happening. She never would have guessed the queen was having an affair with Pastor Dan, but now it all made sense. Her need to get out of her marriage with no damage to her husband's reputation was really because he hadn't done anything, but she wanted Beth to think he had so she could threaten him in court. Or did he really pose a threat, and maybe that was why the queen had started a relationship with the pastor in the first place?

"So blackmailing your husband to get a divorce isn't horrible? You're so hypocritical, my dear," he smirked.

"I don't understand what you're doing. I finally got your idiot wife to leave and your plan worked to get me a lucrative divorce. Dr. Linn's ready to help us so we can move forward with our lives together, and you're acting crazy," she said.

"Shut up," he growled. "Did you really think this was about you? When the media gets through with this I'll be Pastor Dan, the savior who rid our town of the deceitful administrator who tried to control the minds of our young people by targeting the faithful with violent threats so parents would have no choice but the academy. It'll be clear your husband's goal was to spread his poisonous anti-religion agenda, but you threw him under the bus for your own benefit. I'll show great remorse that I arrived moments too late to save you from your violent husband's attack caused by his rage over your framing him. While I tried to save your life, he fled the office. Once all of the evidence is collected they'll know about the plot and unfortunately, as I said, Dr. Linn, you'll be collateral damage. But don't worry. You'll be remembered as the brave counselor who figured out the mystery and tried to save the day." He grinned and twirled the gun on his finger.

Beth stared back at the pastor with a look of defiance. She would not let him win without a fight.

42

BEN

At 6:05 p.m. Ben started to wonder where Beth was. He texted to check on her and she didn't respond. He waited a few minutes and then called, but the call went right to voicemail. Maybe she was still with a client. He could picture her as she tapped the face of her watch as she often did when they were together. He tried again at 6:15, but there was still no answer.

Everything OK? he texted.

N, came an immediate response.

She must be upset with him. Maybe she'd gone straight to her parents'. He called Celeste, but she hadn't heard from Beth since she'd responded to her mom's request to be there at 7.

Now he was alarmed. *What does N mean?* he wondered as he got in his car to try to find her. *N* seemed like a no, but if she wasn't with her parents then Ben wondered if a client was the problem. He drove to her office but there were no cars in the parking lot or lights on in the building. He tried to call again as he drove to her condo, which was also dark. And her car wasn't there. He jumped out of his car and peered into the window, but saw no movement. No car in the garage either. Every few minutes he tried to call, but it kept going straight to voicemail, so he drove to her parents' house to make sure she hadn't arrived there. Now it was 6:40, and he saw Andrea pulling into the driveway. He drove past and pulled over several houses away to figure out what to do.

Then a text came through from her: *H.* That was it. He pictured her watch. He knew she could draw on the face of the watch without detection. An *H* could mean help.

Do you need help? He got back an instant *Y.*

Where are you? His mind began to race as the realization hit him that she was in trouble.

CC.

CC? What was CC? He frantically searched his mind for anything that made sense and then the logo of the church came into his mind. Community Church. But why would she be there? And why would she need help?

Another text came through from her: *911.* Now he knew for certain something was wrong. He needed to help and to get there as soon as possible. This was his half sister—his sister. And she needed him.

OK, he texted back. And then he called 911, whipping his car around in the direction of the church, afraid of what he might find.

43

CELESTE

"It's 7:15. Where the heck is Beth? She lives the closest," Andrea said, opening a box of pizza. "I need to eat, so I say we start without her."

Celeste looked at Henry and wondered if she should tell him that Ben had called looking for Beth. She didn't want to bring up Ben's name until all the kids had gathered, so she decided to stay quiet. This evening was going to be hard enough. Celeste had also decided not to tell Henry that Beth already knew. What was the point? She'd allow Beth to share her journey in whatever way she wanted to share it. Tonight the other three would have to deal with the news that would shake their sense of identity.

"Can somebody call her?" Jonathan asked. "I need to leave by 8:30 to pick up Raya from dance. I can't be late." He had his normal look of annoyance when anyone caused him inconvenience.

"Can't Melinda do it?" Andrea asked.

"Just call her," he responded.

"It went to voicemail after one ring," Carrie said. "Maybe she's running over with a client." She looked around the room for someone to confirm the possibility.

"She had the afternoon off," Henry replied.

Celeste didn't know what was going on, so she left the room and called Ben.

"Something's wrong," he said. "I'm on the way to help and I've called the police." Celeste could hear the sound of traffic in the background.

"What do you mean?" she whispered. She looked quickly back to the kitchen; she didn't want to draw attention to herself.

"I don't know," Ben said. "She's at the Community Church. She's been sending one-letter texts but I know she's in trouble. I've called the police."

"The police—" Celeste caught her breath. Why would Beth be at the Community Church?

"I'm almost there," Ben said. "I see the police pulling in."

"Tell me what's happening," Celeste said anxiously.

She heard a car door slam. "I'll call you when I know something," Ben said.

"Be careful," she said. Before Ben even hung up she realized she couldn't sit and wait for him to call her back. Whatever was happening, she needed to be there for Beth and for herself. She hoped he would call her when she was en route and tell her it was a false alarm, but something about Beth's texts made her know he wouldn't.

Celeste grabbed her keys and told her family she would be right back without giving them time to ask a question. She ran to her car and headed straight to the church.

44

BETH

Pastor Dan kept his gun in his hand. He took Beth's purse and her phone and put them on the floor out of her reach. The queen had no bag or phone in her hands either, so Beth assumed the pastor had taken those too.

The pastor's phone pinged.

While he was occupied with his messages, Beth surreptitiously typed her one-letter texts to Ben. Fortunately her phone was in silent mode, so no sound could alert the pastor to her communications. She carefully covered her watch after every response because she was terrified the pastor would figure out she was texting from it.

Please let Ben know what this means. Please let him send help. Beth was counting on Ben to understand and know what to do.

The pastor looked up at them for a moment and then checked his phone again. He frowned, apparently frustrated by something, and put his phone down. She hoped whatever he was waiting for would take longer than he expected.

"Your husband is taking his time at the precinct." The pastor looked at the queen with contempt.

She stared back at him, appearing to measure her words before she spoke. "How do you know my husband's still at the precinct?"

"Don't act so naive. You know I have people everywhere feeding me

information. You've benefited from it many times." He clearly enjoyed taunting her. Beth hoped he would continue to direct his vitriol toward the queen
instead of focusing on her.

Keep calm, she told herself. *Breathe.* She could sense her tiny self crouching under the chair she was sitting on, so she tried to reassure her she'd find
a way out. She just needed to stay calm.

Was that a car? She heard something outside, but she couldn't be sure.
The pastor was occupied with another text and didn't seem to notice, but the
queen looked at Beth like she'd heard it too. Beth wanted to let the queen
know she'd made contact with the outside world and that the car they heard
might be the police, but she couldn't risk it. Their only chance was to work
together against the pastor, and Beth knew she could count on the queen to
act if they had a plan.

She decided to distract the pastor to give them time to do something.

"I need to use the bathroom," she said, standing up from the chair.

"You're not leaving my sight," Pastor Dan said. He towered over her, gun
at the ready.

"Fine," Beth replied, meeting his gaze. "We can all three go. Unless you
want me to have an accident here? Wouldn't that mess up your perfect crime
scene?"

He looked at the queen and back at Beth dismissively, as though they
were a waste of his time. "Just remember I have a gun aimed at your head,
so don't think about doing anything stupid," he said. He waved her and the
queen out the door and followed them down the hall to the restroom.

There were two stalls in the bathroom, and one small window, locked and
too high to get to. The queen went directly into the first stall, shaking her
head no when Beth opened her mouth to speak to her. Beth took a moment
to quickly peek out the window to see if the police had arrived, but from the
angle of the window all she saw was a sliver of the dark parking lot.

Inside the stall, she quickly texted Ben. *Pastor office gun.* There was no
time to do more.

"Hurry up," the pastor yelled through the door.

"I'm washing my hands," Beth replied. She turned on the water and gave herself a minute to breathe. *Stay calm. Don't show fear. You can do this if you stay calm.*

The queen joined her at the sink and a look passed between them that Beth received as a sign of solidarity. No words were spoken, but the intention was clear.

"I said hurry up," the pastor yelled as he jerked the door open. "Just get out here." He shoved both of them back out into the hallway. "Don't say another word."

Do something, she urged herself. Anything to not be trapped back in that office. Anything that might buy some time while Ben or the police came to find them. She pretended to trip and landed hard on her face.

"What are you trying to pull?" The pastor glared down at her.

She shoved herself up on her elbow. "My legs are shaking. You have a gun. I'm scared. What do you think I'm trying to do?"

He grabbed her arm and lifted her up. "Just shut up and get back into the office," he said, shoving her inside. He locked the door behind them, eyes back on his phone as it pinged again.

Beth tried to re-establish eye contact with her client, but she wouldn't look up. Her posture looked defeated.

A sound from outside caught their attention, but miraculously the pastor was glued to his phone, frantically typing a message. It appeared something was going wrong. He was growing more and more agitated. Beth looked at her client and tilted her head toward the door, hoping to indicate that she knew someone was out there. Her client gave her a brief nod, barely perceptible, but it was clear she understood.

Beth felt her watch vibrate but was afraid to look. The pastor was scowling at his phone, but she knew that at any moment his attention could be back on her and she couldn't risk getting caught.

"You think you're really smart, don't you?" Beth was shocked to hear the queen speak.

The pastor looked up but didn't respond. He acted as though she wasn't there.

"Look at me," she demanded.

He stopped mid-text and picked up his gun, daring here to continue.

"I'm not afraid of you, Dan. I know how weak you are. You disgust me," the queen went on. With the pastor momentarily distracted, Beth shifted her sleeve to see her watch face, where the words *Help is here* jumped off the screen. She remained expressionless, but her heart leapt in her chest. She just had to keep the pastor engaged until the police could get inside the building.

45

CELESTE

Celeste pulled into the church parking lot minutes behind the police and immediately turned off her engine and her lights. She saw Beth's car, and Ben's, and another one she didn't recognize. Ben wasn't in his car, so she texted him to let him know she was there. He immediately responded that he was at the far side of the building. In moments they were together at a barrier the police had formed nearby.

"I'm so glad you're here," Ben said, giving her a hug, the relief on his face obvious.

"Oh my god, Ben, tell me what happened." She kept her hand on his arm for reassurance.

"I don't really know anything more than I told you. I got these cryptic one-letter texts from Beth and I figured out she was in danger, and that she was here. I called the police and I've heard nothing from her since they arrived."

"Have you spoken with the police?"

"Yes. They told me to stay behind the barrier and to let them know if I got any more messages from her. The SWAT team will try to get inside while a hostage negotiator attempts to make contact with whoever is holding her in the building. Hopefully that's happening now."

"I can't believe she's in there—being held hostage. Do you have any idea what brought her here?"

"No clue. She was supposed to meet me at 6, which is why I texted to see where she was."

Celeste turned to look directly at Ben. "Why were you meeting her at 6?"

"I wanted to talk to her before she went to the meeting at your house. I wanted her to know what I knew."

"I'm sure your meeting with Henry has you asking a lot of questions, Ben. I want you to know I'm sorry about my part in hiding this from all of you." She looked at him with regret.

"Does anyone else know?" he asked, avoiding her eyes.

"Just you. We were going to tell everyone tonight." She paused, unsure of what else to say.

"Look, Celeste, I know you didn't cause this or want it to happen, OK? We can talk more once Beth is safe."

"I appreciate that, Ben."

They stood in silence until Celeste's phone rang. It was Henry.

"I better take this," she said as she answered the call. Ben nodded. Celeste was grateful to have him there as support.

"Where are you?" Henry asked, sounding confused.

"I'm at the Community Church," Celeste told him. "Beth's in trouble. It seems that she's being held hostage, but I don't really know anything else."

"Beth's what? You're not making sense, Celeste. Did you say she's being held hostage?" Henry shouted. Celeste could hear the rest of the family reacting in the background.

"Put me on speaker, Henry. I'll try to explain," she responded as calmly as she could. She looked at Ben, who placed his hand on her shoulder, and took a deep breath before she proceeded.

"Mom, what's happening?" Andrea was the first to speak.

"Beth is apparently being held hostage at the Community Church. I'm here with Ben. He got some texts from her and figured out she was in trouble. He called the police and they're here. We're pretty far away—they set up a barrier to keep people away from the building—but it looks like they may have gotten inside now. That's all we know." Celeste paused and Ben nodded his head.

"How do you know she's there?" Jonathan asked.

"She texted Ben that she was here and her car is here." She heard one of her daughters gasp in response.

"I'll be there in a minute," Henry yelled, apparently from the other side of the room.

Celeste hoped one of her children would stop Henry from getting in the car. As much as she wanted her family there, she knew he was too fragile to be in the middle of whatever was about to happen.

Ben took the phone and said, "Hey Henry, it's Ben. I know you want to come down here but maybe hold off for a minute. It seems like the police want us to stay back so they can do their jobs. We can keep you on the phone so you know what's happening and that way we won't get in the way." Celeste gave Ben a thumbs-up while they waited for Henry's response.

"We'll try to keep him here," Jonathan responded. "Can you just stay on the call so we can hear what's going on?"

"Of course. I'm right here," Celeste said, taking the phone back from Ben. The horror of the situation landed squarely on her. She couldn't let her mind go to what might happen, so she stood beside Ben and prayed for a miracle.

46

BETH

Back in the office, Pastor Dan motioned for Beth and the queen to sit. He kept the gun trained on them while holding his phone in the other hand. *He must be waiting for some news*, Beth guessed. She didn't want him to hear any noises from the parking lot, so she decided to get him talking.

"So, does your whole congregation know what kind of man you are, or do you just save your cruel side for people you use to get what you want?" she asked.

"I lead my flock to righteousness any way I can. The scourge in this town had to be cleaned up. They'll flee now and we'll have a pure Christian community again. Your kind will never understand. Your judgment of me is meaningless," he responded.

"My kind?"

"You liberals who don't respect the Word of God. You think you can include everyone into the fold, but that's blasphemy. The Bible's clear on what's pure. You defile God's Word."

"How do you think I personally defile God's Word?" She was grasping at whatever she could to keep him talking.

"Everything you do defiles God's Word." He looked at her as though she should know he was stating the obvious.

"Name one thing I do," she challenged. *Keep him talking*, she told herself.

"You counsel gays and act like they're fine like they are! You support marriage between Christ's chosen and pagans! You support divorce! You think women are equal to their husbands! You're pro-abortion!" he snarled, his voice rising with each statement. He stood over her with his finger pointed in anger.

"Do you think everyone is pro-abortion?" Beth asked, searching for a way to engage him in a debate.

"You're all pro-abortion. You don't care about the sanctity of life. You're all selfish." He walked over to the queen and lifted her chin with his hand. "Especially you," he said. The queen pulled her chin away and looked at Beth.

"Nobody wakes up one day and says 'I want to get pregnant so I can go have an abortion,'" Beth said angrily. "Nobody wakes up and says 'I want to go out in the street and convince pregnant women to terminate their pregnancies.' Nobody is pro-abortion." She couldn't believe she was having this conversation with someone who was planning to kill her. It was surreal.

"Murderer," he said, taunting her. "You're either pro-life or pro-abortion. Clearly, you're a pro-abortion murderer."

"Said by the man who's about to kill me," she said.

He sneered. "You think you're clever, but your death is a sacrifice for God. Your death will save countless people who are influenced by the liberal bias you propagate in this town. I'm not a murderer. I'm an agent of God and just like Abraham knew he'd have to sacrifice Isaac, I know I have to sacrifice you."

"Didn't God provide a lamb at the last minute to save Isaac?" Beth asked. *Hurry,* she thought. What was happening out there? Was a rescue plan in place? How much time did they have?

"Isaac was a chosen child of God. You're a pagan," Pastor Dan said.

"I was baptized at St. Andrews. I'm in good standing with the Catholic church."

"Exactly—a heathen! You worship false idols. You elevate Mary. You corrupt the young people who come to your office. Don't you see? You poison their thoughts."

"You sent a client to me and you pay for her therapy," Beth said, referring to the dancer. "Why would you send her to me if I'm so bad?"

"She's expendable," the pastor replied with a shrug. "She was the perfect way for me to keep an eye on you. I knew you couldn't do any more damage to her because she's already lost."

"You set that young woman up so you could spy on me? Why?" Beth was stunned.

"Why you?" he laughed. "The daughter of Henry Linn, my biggest critic. Why wouldn't I want to manipulate you?"

"What are you talking about?"

"Don't act so naive. You know your grandfather left us a lot of money and your father was angry so he created unnecessary problems for me. Clearly your grandfather cared more about the church than his son and it pissed your dad off."

"So you're telling me that in the middle of your scheme to trick the town into believing you saved them, you also wanted to get revenge on my dad by using me as a pawn?"

"It was an added bonus for my personal enjoyment," he smirked.

Beth took her time before she responded, aware that every minute she could distract him was crucial. "Wow. I'm amazed you spent this much time on insignificant details."

"It must be humiliating to see how you were played, Dr. Linn. Let me tell you more. Your client here started therapy to get you to help her nail her husband when she went to court. I needed to make sure you were personally involved so that I could control you. Your client's little brother was targeted so I could suck you in, and the bomber was chosen because he was your supervisee's client. I found out the kid needed money, so he was easy to persuade to join our cause."

Beth looked at the queen in disbelief, but she couldn't read her face. Was it contrition she saw there?

"How could you be so ruthless? Both of you." She felt dizzy, but she knew she had to keep the pastor talking and diverted. *I can't let him win,* she thought as she stared back at his smirking face.

Simultaneously, the office phone rang and the pastor's phone pinged with a message. He didn't answer the phone but scowled at the text.

"You think you're smart, don't you?" he said, pointing his gun at Beth.

"What do you mean?"

"You got the cops here. My contact just let me know the place is surrounded." He rushed toward her, pulling her against him with the gun against her head.

"How could I do that when I've been with you the whole time?" Beth responded. *Don't panic. Stay calm. You can do this. Help is right outside.*

"Witchcraft." He looked at her and Beth looked back into the eyes of a crazed believer.

"Of course I didn't summon the police through witchcraft," Beth said. "But they're here. I don't think it's in your best interest to kill me and have them walk in right now—do you?"

The phone rang again and this time he picked it up, dragging her with him to the desk.

"Pastor Dan, this is Officer Smith here. Everything OK?" Beth could hear him clearly. Where was he? Were they right outside? Would they get there in time?

"No," the pastor said. "Two women are holding me at gunpoint. They're the ringleaders of the anti-religion group that killed that young man at the school."

"OK, don't fight them," Beth heard the officer say. "We'll come into the building now and get you out of there. Tell them we'll provide them with whatever they want if they'll let you go free." *Please, trust him*, Beth thought fervently.

"You're going to have to call maintenance to get into the building," Pastor Dan said. "Right now I have a gun aimed at my head." He pushed the gun harder into Beth's temple.

Breathe, she told herself.

"Can you put your captors on the phone?" the officer asked. *Good.* Beth thought. He's stalling for time too while they make their way inside.

"Let me ask them," Pastor Dan said. "Ladies, will one of you talk to the hostage negotiator? No?" He shook his head vigorously. Beth watched the queen silently acknowledge his words. "Sorry chief, they shook their heads no. They seem to enjoy my pain. You know they hate Christians, sir, and they don't respect the Lord."

The officer replied soothingly. "OK, Pastor. Just do what they ask you to do and we'll do our best to get in there. We'll let you know when we're able to get inside the building."

Before the pastor could hang up, there was a noise in the hall. Beth saw a look of betrayal cross his face. He dragged her across the room toward the door, one arm around her neck and the other holding the gun to her head.

"You little bitch," he snarled. "You thought you could beat me."

"I'm not trying to do anything," she said. "You don't have to do this. You can end this right now and take a plea deal." The noises outside the office were getting closer.

"That's never going to happen," he whispered, tightening his arm around her neck and pushing the gun into her temple.

She heard a gunshot and felt pain rip across her shoulder as the pastor fell backward, dragging her with him. Disoriented, she tried to get up but her vision was blurry and her shoulder hurt. Reaching up, she felt blood, and then she realized the pastor was not moving.

For a moment, everything stopped. She was aware when the police came through the door, but her mind and body were frozen. She looked up and saw her client across the room, pistol in hand, motionless. The queen had saved her.

47

BETH

"Can I come in?" Ben asked. He stood at the entrance of Beth's hospital room with flowers in hand.

"The genius who figured out where I was and called the police? I guess so." She smiled. It was the next afternoon, and Beth had managed to get some sleep overnight. Her left shoulder throbbed and it was hard to move her arm.

"How are you feeling?"

"OK. It's just a surface wound. The bullet grazed my shoulder before it went through his heart, but it caused a lot of bruising." She shifted her hospital gown to show him her bruise and he winced as though he could feel it.

"Do you think they'll let you go today?"

"Probably," Beth said. "They think I'm stable now. And the police came to get my statement this morning. Did you see my mom? I just sent her down to get some food."

Ben smiled. "No, but I'll stay until she comes back up. Last night I was worried I'd put her in danger. I didn't know she was going to show up at the church." He put the flowers on the window ledge and pulled a chair up beside her bed.

"You did the right thing," Beth reassured him. "If you hadn't told her the truth then she might have kept calling my phone. You know her." They both smiled. "That could have alerted the pastor that I could use my watch to communicate. He might have shot me right then." She still felt a bit numb thinking about it.

"Did you have any idea you were in danger?" Ben asked.

"I should have," she said, though she wondered if that was really true. *Should I have known?* "I think I was distracted by this whole family thing and I kept second-guessing myself about my client. But no, I did not see this coming."

"I'm just so glad you're OK," he said.

"Thanks to you," Beth said. Then she asked, "Why did you want to meet last night, by the way?"

"Your mom didn't tell you?"

"No."

He held her gaze. "I wanted to see you before your family meeting to tell you about my visit with your dad. He told me everything. So I didn't want you to be taken off guard. And I wanted to make sure you knew you could come and talk to me after."

"Wow, big night," she said, smiling. "I bet you regret digging into the mystery of your DNA now."

He looked at her with a serious expression that surprised her. "Just the opposite. I'm really glad I dug in and found all of this out. I'm really glad you're my sister."

"You have no idea what you've gotten yourself into," she said with a laugh.

"I can't wait for you to tell me all about it. Seriously, Beth, I want to get to know all of you better. It's crazy to go from being an only child to having four siblings. It's kind of awesome."

"It is." She could see how much this meant to him, but she was still in too much shock from the shooting to tune into his feelings. She knew she'd be able to soon, and she looked forward to the years ahead when he would settle in as one of the family.

"Once your parents tell everyone, I plan to be around to support all of you and help with your dad," he said. She squeezed his hand.

Beth sat in silence for a moment, unsure how to proceed.

"Would it be OK if we wait to talk about this later?" she asked.

Ben smiled at her. "Are you kidding? Of course."

Her mother walked into the room with smoothies in each hand. "Hi Ben," she said, handing Beth a bright green drink. She looked at the flowers. "Did you bring these? They're beautiful."

"I did," he said and leaned down to give Beth a kiss on the top of the head. "I'm gonna go and let you rest. Let me know when you feel like company and I'll pick up dinner." He hugged Celeste on the way out the door.

"I will," Beth said. "See you soon."

Celeste sat down on the edge of the bed. "Did he tell you that he spoke to your father?" she asked.

Beth nodded. "He did. I can't believe that less than twenty-four hours ago I thought *that* would be the big drama last night." She shook her head in disbelief.

The shift nurse popped her head in the door. "Beth, we're keeping you until later night," she said. "Just to be sure you're rested and fit to go. OK?"

"That's fine," Beth said. "I think I'm ready for a nap now anyway." She reached out her hand for her mom to come closer.

Celeste got up off the edge of the bed and leaned down to hug her.

"I'm really proud of you Beth," she said.

"Thanks, Mom," she said, closing her eyes.

• • •

The worst is over, the queen's in custody, and the police will handle the rest, Beth told her tiny fearful part who peeked out from behind Ben's flowers. *It's all OK, I promise,* she said, and her tiny part smiled back at her. In that moment, she felt a profound sense of calm even though the events of the last week had shaken her at her core. She knew in time she would need to engage with her family about their unexpected origin story, and eventually she would have to face her father's prognosis, but not today. Right now, she just wanted to tune into the strange feeling she was having. Was it peace? Maybe. All she knew was that for the first time she could remember, she didn't feel afraid that she was going to make a huge mistake or disappoint someone. It was obvious and a cliché—so absurd she smiled—but maybe the truth she had been so afraid of had actually set her free. In time she would put the puzzle together—how the incongruence had affected her over her lifetime. But for now, she would rest and enjoy the fact that her younger part no longer felt afraid.

ACKNOWLEDGMENTS

My first thank you is to my nephew, Jerry Wong, who gave me the idea for this book one evening at a family gathering. As an accomplished piano professor, he often traveled internationally for performances, which I found fascinating. He said that what happens behind the closed door of my office is equally fascinating and that's how this idea began. As we talked, I thought about how humbling it is to be a therapist and to hold such sacred space for people. To hear their stories and to help them to heal and make meaning from those stories is the greatest honor I could have.

Although these characters are fictional, they evolved from the thousands of clients who have trusted me to be part of their sacred journeys. I want to thank each of my clients for that trust. Your resilience and strength inspire me.

My deep gratitude also goes out to my family and friends who have encouraged me to write. I'm touched by the gifts of love and connection you each extend to me. Thank you for believing in this book.

Thank you to Michelle Richmond, my first reader for the novel. Meeting you at the Sanibel Island Writers Conference, and taking your novel writing course, has made this process exciting and fun. And Beth appreciates that your notes gave her so much more dimension!

Finally, I have nothing but praise for the amazing team at Greenleaf Book Group. Thank you Steve Elizalde, Benito Salazar, Sally Garland, Jen Glynn, Anne Sanow, Stephanie Bouchard, and Cameron Stein for the creativity and care you've provided throughout this process. Your guidance and support mean more than I can express.

ABOUT THE AUTHOR

KIM ST. CLAIR is a trauma-informed psychotherapist certified in Internal Family Systems (IFS) and Eye Movement Desensitization and Reprocessing (EMDR) currently working in private practice. She was born in Northeast Ohio and spent most of her life there but has enjoyed moving around the country for the last thirteen years, and currently lives near Austin, Texas. When not seeing clients or writing, she is happiest outside practicing yoga, biking, or sitting beside water enjoying the view.

Made in the USA
Monee, IL
10 September 2024

65460170R00152